GUNFIGHT AT COLD DEVIL

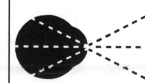

This Large Print Book carries the
Seal of Approval of N.A.V.H.

GUNFIGHT AT COLD DEVIL

RALPH COTTON

THORNDIKE PRESS

An imprint of Thomson Gale, a part of The Thomson Corporation

Detroit • New York • San Francisco • New Haven, Conn. • Waterville, Maine • London

Thorndike Press® Large Print Western.

The text of this Large Print edition is unabridged.

Other aspects of the book may vary from the original edition.

Set in 16 pt. Plantin.

LIBRARY OF CONGRESS CATALOGING-IN-PUBLICATION DATA

Cotton, Ralph W.
  Gunfight at Cold Devil / by Ralph Cotton.
    p. cm.
  ISBN-13: 978-0-7862-9351-3 (lg. print : alk. paper)
  ISBN-10: 0-7862-9351-9 (lg. print : alk. paper)
  1. Large type books. I. Title.
PS3553.O766G85 2007
813'.6—dc22   2006037578

Published in 2007 by arrangement with NAL Signet,
a member of Penguin Group (USA) Inc.

Printed in the United States of America on permanent paper
10 9 8 7 6 5 4 3 2 1

For Mary Lynn . . . *of course*

PART 1

CHAPTER 1

Ranger Sam Burrack stepped back from the crowded bar and left as quietly as he'd entered, through the rear door of Texas Jack Spain's Gay Lady Saloon. A cold gust of air swirled in and dissipated behind him. Save for the bartender, Ned Rose, who'd poured him a shot of whiskey, and one of the old miners standing beside him, who had picked up the half-full shot glass and drained it when he'd left, no one had noticed the ranger among the early drinking and gambling crowd.

"Didn't say much, did he?" the old miner, Scratch Ebbons, commented to the bartender, wiping the back of his hand across his wiry gray mustache. Five feet away a potbellied stove glowed and crackled in the dim smoky light.

"No, he didn't," said the bartender, having noted the sizable amount of whiskey the stranger had left, here in this cold land where whiskey and gold were held in equal reverence. Staring warily toward the rear door, he also noted to himself the way the pearl gray sombrero had remained tipped a bit more forward than was customary. *Hiding his face . . . ?* Ned asked himself. "Who was he? Did you know him, Scratch?" he asked the miner.

Scratch gave a crafty grin and said, "It might be I could come up with his name, over a drink or two."

"I see, then," said Ned, returning the grin good-naturedly. His hand closed around a bottle of rye as if ready to pour. Yet, instead of holding the bottle toward the old man's glass, he drew it back slightly and said in a quickly changing tone, "What say instead of me pouring you a drink, I knock what few teeth you've got out the side of your gawddamn head?"

Before old Scratch could duck away, Ned Rose's free hand reached out and grabbed him by his shirt, not letting him move. "Pl-please, Ned!" Scratch whimpered. "I was only funning! I meant no harm! If I knew who that feller was, I would've told you, *for free!* No drink needed!"

"Yeah, I figured you didn't know his name, you worthless old son of a bitch," Ned growled, turning Scratch loose. "Get out of my sight!"

As the old miner scurried away, Ned straightened his short black necktie and straightened the garters on his white shirtsleeves. He gave the drinkers across the bar from him a hard stare. "Any of you other old dolts ever seen that man before?"

"The sombrero?" said an older miner called Rags Stiles.

"Yeah, the sombrero, gawddamn it," said Ned, sounding impatient. "Who the hell do you think we're talking about here?"

"Easy, Mr. Ned," said Rags, not caring about Ned Rose's growing reputation for having a white-hot temper and a fast gun hand. "You draw more flies with sugar than you can with . . ." He stalled for a second as if to recall what else drew flies. "Well, more than you can with . . . stuff not as sweet . . . as sugar that is," he said weakly.

"Jesus," Ned muttered, shaking his head. "No wonder I'd like to strangle all you old bastards to death!"

"As *gray sombreros* go," said Rags, unmoved by Ned Rose's attitude and insults, "there's two from these parts I can think of. One is Whitey Stone, runs a big herd for some Englishmen north of the territory. The other is a ranger named Sam something or other. But this is too far up country for the ranger. He'd be way off his graze."

"Whitey Stone died of snake bite, is what I heard," said one of the old men.

"Me too," another replied.

"Sam Burrack!" said Ned Rose, ignoring the others' comments, his senses seeming to pique suddenly. His right hand instinctively slipped behind the bib of his bartender's apron and touched the bone handle of his Remington .45 caliber revolver. His voice lowered to a whisper to himself. "Christ, that's him."

The old men looked back and forth at one another as the bartender walked away along the bar, not in a big hurry, yet not taking his time either. "After a *drink or two?*" Rags said, mocking Scratch with a critical look. "What the hell was you thinking?"

"Me?" said Scratch. "What the hell about *you?* Something *not as sweet as sugar . . .*" he said with equal contempt, all of them watching Ned Rose flip up a hinged flap at the far end of the bar.

Rose walked across the hard-packed dirt floor and pushed his way through a collection of men gathered beneath a halo of cigar smoke. "I think you're bluffing, mister," he heard a voice say from amid the onlookers. "I think you've been bluffing all night and all day."

At the edge of a battered, round-topped gaming table, Texas Jack Spain looked up and saw Rose step into sight as he dropped stack after stack of twenty-dollar gold pieces into the center of the table. "It'll only cost you another two thousand to find out, my friend," he replied, speaking above the ring and jingle of newly minted gold. A cigar stood loosely cocked in the corner of his mouth.

"That's what I figured," the cattleman sitting across the table from him said in a bitter tone. Inches from his right hand a LeMat horse pistol lay, its big bore agape, like some sleeping demon.

Paying the cattleman little regard, Jack Spain motioned impatiently for Ned Rose to step over to him. "What is it, bartender?" he asked, sounding just a bit annoyed by Ned's presence. "You know I don't like being disturbed in a poker game."

"You told me to keep you informed of all strangers coming in," said Ned, bending slightly and speaking up close, to keep the conversation between the two of them.

Jack Spain pulled his face away from the persistent bartender. "Yeah, but use some good judgment, Rose!" he said. "This whole mountain range is made up of *strangers*. I don't need to hear about one in the midst of a card game, do I?" He gave an annoyed smile and pulled back farther, as Rose tried leaning in closer.

"This one I thought you *might* need to," said the bartender, getting irritated himself. "He wore a gray sombrero —"

"Jesus, Rose, back off!" said Spain, pulling his face farther away, this time with a wince, fanning a hand in front of his face. "Your breath smells like you've been chewing rabbit guts."

Rose's face reddened; a chuckle arose among the bystanders. The cattleman gave a short grin beneath a thick mustache and commented idly, "I call you, Spain." Adding his bid to the already large pile of chips, cash and gold coin lying in the middle of the table, he said, "That is, if it's all right with your bartender here."

Before Jack Spain could answer, Ned Rose cut the cattleman a sharp stare. "Did anybody say a gawddamn word to you, Whitfield?"

"Hey," the cattleman replied, the grin gone from his face, his right hand tensing a bit, "there was no harm intended in my remark . . . nothing to get nervous about."

Rose took a step back and replied, "*Nervous,* am I?" His hand raised an inch, then streaked to the handle of the revolver beneath the bib of his apron. "Here's *nervous* for you, you cow-sucking son of a bitch!"

Leonard Whitfield saw the bartender's move, but was too late to make a play of his own. Before he could even start to reach toward his big LeMat, Rose's Remington came out, cocked and pointed, only inches from his face. "Who's nervous now?" Rose shouted. The onlookers around the table stepped back warily.

"Looks like you got the drop on me, bartender," said Leonard Whitfield, no longer attempting to grab his gun, his hand slumping. Yet defiance shined in his narrowed eyes. "Now either *pull* that trigger or else stop wasting my time."

Rose's gun hand stiffended. "My pleasur—"

"Whoa, whoa, *whoa!*" shouted Jack Spain, cutting Ned Rose off. Half rising from his chair, he said, "Put that gun away, Rose! Jesus! This is nothing worth killing over! You know Whitfield! He's never showed you anything but respect! Ain't that right, Leonard?" he asked Whitfield, hoping for support.

"I'm still sitting here," the cattleman commented, staring straight into Rose's eyes. "Where's all your guts, bartender?"

"Well, hell, then." Spain shrugged. He stood the rest of the way up and took a step back from the table. "Let 'er fly, if you two can't stand living!" He stared at Whitfield. "But he'll kill you, deader than hell, Leonard." He turned his stare to the angry bartender, adding, "And they'll *hang* you for murder before Leonard's washed and stuck underground."

Rose considered something for a second, something that didn't appear to be a fear of hanging. At the end of his thought, he let out a breath, tipped the gun barrel up quickly and let the hammer down with a flick of his thumb and trigger finger. All the while his eyes never left Whitfield's. In a lowered voice, he said to the unshaken cattleman, "You ever need to talk more about *nervous,* come let me know."

The whole barroom crowd watched in silence as Rose turned and walked away, showing his back to Leonard Whitfield. Only when he'd walked back behind the bar and lowered the flap on the bar top did the silence lift slowly like some unseen vapor. Then, in an even tone, as if nothing had happened, Whitfield said to Jack Spain, "Well, are you going to show me them cards? I damn sure paid enough to see them."

Spain took the cigar from between his teeth and shook his head. "Ned's got a temper a mile wide but only a hair thick. I ought to fire his ass for pulling that kind of shenanigan." As he spoke, he snapped his cards onto the green felt and spread them, a diamond ring glittering on his hand. "Two pair, aces over sevens."

"Damn it to hell," Whitfield growled, flipping his cards away. "I wish he *had* shot me."

As he stood back behind the bar waiting on the drinkers, Ned Rose's temper simmered, under control. But he had not forgotten Spain's remark about his breath. When Spain had gathered all of his winnings and stopped long enough to take his big wool greatcoat from a peg on the wall on his way to the side door, he gave Rose a flat, smug grin and said, "Now, then, Rose, what was it you wanted to tell me about a stranger wearing a derby?" He threw the big coat around him and pointed toward the door. "Make it quick, I'm headed for the jake."

"It wasn't a derby," Rose said in a tight voice, gazing toward the door.

"Well, whatever it was, you need to calm down, not to let things rile you so easily," said Spain. He spread his arms in a grand manner, stopping long enough at the door to turn and say to the bartender, "Enjoy life. Learn not to take everything so serious!"

Rose grumbled under his breath, watching Spain throw open the door and stride through it with a bounce in his step. No sooner than Spain walked out, Rose heard the deep thump of a metal gun barrel hitting human skull bone. Then, as quickly as Spain had left, he came staggering backward in three loose-legged steps, sinking lower with each step until he collapsed flat on his back and lay staring at the ceiling, knocked senseless. A blast of cold swirled in the open doorway.

"Sombrero, is what I said," Rose murmured to himself, a look of satisfaction on his face.

The ranger stepped inside the door, his big Colt in hand, his eyes making a quick sweep across the room. "I'm acting Federal Marshal Sam Burrack," he said, loud enough to be heard, but in a calm even voice. "I'm arresting Jack Spain for participating in a stagecoach robbery in Arizona Territory last fall." He paused, his thumb across the hammer of his Colt, ready to cock it.

"And I'm U.S. Marshal Pete Summers," said a voice. From against the bar, a young man stepped back to the middle of the floor, swinging a sawed-off shotgun up from under his long riding duster. Looking straight at Ned Rose, Summers asked, "Does everybody understand us?"

Rose shrugged. "I just tend bar here, fellows. I've got no fight with you two . . . unless *you* pick it."

"That's a good attitude," said the ranger, even though he noted a harsh tone in the bartender's voice. Stepping in closer, stooping down over Spain as Spain moaned and tried to rise up onto his haunches, the ranger pulled out a pair of handcuffs, flipped Spain over his belly and pulled his arms behind his back. Marshal Summers held the crowd covered with the cocked shotgun.

"Jesus!" said Spain, shaking his head in attempt to clear it. "What the hell is this?" His voice sounded thick. "You can't just crack a man's head with no word of warning!"

"I decided it was better than having to kill you," Sam said, clicking the cuffs snug around Spain's wrists and dragging him to his feet.

Staggering on wobbly legs, Spain tried to focus his swimming eyes on his bartender. "Damn it, Rose, are you just going to *stand* there?" he shouted in a strained and groggy voice. "Grab up that scattergun and let him have both barrels! These men are Arizona Rangers! They've got no jurisdiction here!"

"I've never been a ranger in my life," Summers called out, still keeping an eye on the crowd. "But I am a United Sates marshal — you can count on it."

"See? That's good enough for me." Rose raised his hands chest high, showing the two lawmen that he had no intention of trying any such thing. "No trouble out of me," he said, stepping backward away from the bar.

"You damn coward!" Spain said. "Don't let them take me out of here! I can't go to prison! I've got responsibilities! I won't last a week in prison!"

"You'll do just fine, Texas Jack," said Rose, concealing a smile. "Learn not to take it all so serious."

Spain stared coldly at him, his eyes starting to settle down and focus. "I'll get a lawyer and I'll beat this charge. I'm coming back, and I better find everything here just the way I left it, Rose. Or you'll wish to God you was never born."

"I don't want you to worry about a thing," Rose said, grinning, ignoring Spain's threat. He picked up a shot glass, inspected it and poured himself a drink. "Here's to *breaking rocks with hammers,* Spain," he said, raising the glass. "Don't you worry about a thing. I'll keep a close watch on the Gay Lady."

"You better, gawddamn it!" Spain bellowed as the ranger pulled him to the side door, opening it with his free hand. Toward the crowd that had left the gaming table and ventured closer for a better look, Spain shouted, "Ten thousand dollars, boys! Hard cash to whoever kills these lawdogs and sets me free!"

"That's enough of that," the ranger said, shaking Spain by his handcuffs and pulling him toward the open door. To the crowd, he called out, "Put it out of your minds. We're both lawmen in the pursuit of our duty. Don't try to stop us. Don't get yourself killed for Texas Jack Spain."

Stepping forward from the crowd with his hands chest high in a show of peace, Leonard Whitfield said, "Ranger, not to butt into your business, but you're not going to get much support from our *part-time* sheriff, especially when it comes to this man." He pointed a rough crooked finger toward Spain.

"Shut your mouth, Whitfield, you sore loser son of a bitch!" shouted Spain, trying to lean back inside the door. The ranger had to give him a strong shove. Summers stepped out behind him and closed the door.

"There was no reason for you to pull a stunt like that, Spain," Sam said to Spain, his breath steaming in the cold. He shoved him along the boardwalk in the direction of a small cabin and stone framed building with a sign reading SHERIFF'S OFFICE above the door. "This is no hanging offense we're taking you in for."

"What do you know about anything, Ranger!" Spain bellowed at him. "I've spent the whole past year and every dollar to my name getting this business up and running! Now I'll lose it all before I get back to look after things! Ned Rose is in there right now, stealing from me with both hands!"

"You built this business with the money you made robbing the Cottonwood stage," Sam replied. "So don't look to me for sympathy." He ushered Spain on, taking a firm grip on his upper arm.

"Then to hell with *sympathy*," Spain said in a lowered voice, sounding desperate. "Let's talk about some hard cash!" He stumbled along the boardwalk, half-turned toward the ranger and the marshal, his hands cuffed behind his back. A thin trickle of blood ran down from the swollen welt at his hairline. "I'm on the spot, fellows! What will it cost to get these cuffs off me?"

"Save your breath, Spain," Sam said, starting straight ahead.

"All right then, you hardheaded, stiff-necked lawdog son of a —"

"Easy, Spain," Summers cautioned him. "Don't think I won't knock you cold and carry you over my shoulder."

Spain settled himself and walked along, still a bit blurry from the blow to his forehead. At the door to the sheriff's office, he tried one more play, saying, "You two best consider taking my offer. You're going to find Whitfield is right. This sheriff and me are friends. He won't stand for you dragging me out of here. . . ."

Spain's voice trailed away as Sam shoved the wooden door open. On the other side of the office, inside a single cell, Sheriff Max Denton stood facing them with a stoic look on his face. A welt on his forehead matched the one on Spain's.

"I'll be damned," said Spain. "You've arrested the sheriff too?"

"Yep," said the ranger. "Max here had a pretty long run at robbing and killing before he ever pinned on a badge. The federal judge figured we might as well gather you both up since I was coming this way."

"Federal judge?" Spain asked. "What's a

federal judge got to do with this? You're a territory ranger."

On the way across the floor to the cell, Sam took a U.S. marshal's badge from his vest pocket and said, "I'm working with Marshal Summers for a while. I have an appointment as a U.S. marshal for as long as I need it."

"Jesus," Spain moaned. "This country is going straight to hell. It's getting to where a man don't stand a chance."

Chapter 2

Within a minute after the ranger had closed the side door behind him at the Gay Lady, Ned Rose poured himself a shot of whiskey and downed it in one gulp, as the customers milled and drank and talked among themselves about what they had just witnessed. All right, here was just the chance he'd always dreamed of, he told himself. It was time to make himself some real money and get out of Cold Devil. No good gunman could make a reputation for himself in a place like this.

Across the bar top from Rose stood a short, powerfully built teamster named James Earl Coots. Water dripped from the lower edge of his ragged buffalo fur greatcoat, where a thin layer of ice had melted from the heat inside the warm building. "I don't know what just went on here," he said to Rose, holding a delivery order in a thick glove. "But I've got seven barrels of beer out back that's going to be seven chunks of ice if we don't get them inside before long."

"So? Get them on in here, James Earl, gawddamn it," said Rose, snapping out of his deep thoughts.

"Mr. Rudiheil says no more beer unless I collect for *this* load *this* trip," said the teamster. "I don't unload till I collect forty-eight dollars for this trip and at least ten dollars on the balance that Mr. Spain already owes on his account."

"Spain owes money for beer?" said Rose. "How much?"

"Close to two hundred, according to the old German," said the teamster, "and he says he's tired of waiting on it."

"Two hundred gawddamn dollars," Rose growled to himself, "Spain, you cheap turd." He turned to the metal cash box just beneath the bar and flipped it open. "Just one minute. Let me see what I've got here."

Walking up beside the waiting teamster and leaning on the bar, Stanley Woods, who worked as a pimp for the Gay Lady's two prostitutes, stood watching Rose in silence.

"Damn it to hell!" Rose cursed after a moment of counting money from one hand to the other. Snapping the metal lid shut, he turned, took off his bartender's apron, wadded it up and tossed it under the bar. He raised the Remington from his waist, checked it and shoved it back down behind his red waist sash.

"I know what you're thinking. You're thinking about collecting that ten thousand dollars, ain't you?" Stanley Woods asked, staring at Rose from beneath the brim of a frayed bowler hat drawn low on his forehead.

"Not me. But point out one other sumbitch here who's not," Rose said, a serious look in his eyes. "Ten thousand dollars is a hell of lot of money."

"Yeah, all these mules thought about it as soon as Spain said it," said Woods, sliding an uninterested glance over his shoulder, then back to Ned Rose. "But thinking about it's one thing. Acting on it is another." He picked up the bottle sitting on the bar and poured himself a drink as he spoke. "You're about on the verge of acting on it. I see it in your eyes."

"Yeah?" said Rose, staring at him. "Do you see anything in my eyes that tells you I give a damn what you think about *anything* . . . anything at all?"

Paying little attention to their conversation as he looked all about the saloon, the teamster finally said, "What about that beer, Rose?"

"Yeah, just a minute," said Rose, raising a finger toward him to keep him waiting.

"It'll freeze sure as hell," the teamster said in a lowered tone.

"I'm getting your money, James Earl," said Rose, sounding irritated.

"I'm trying to talk business with you, Ned," said Woods, returning Rose's hard stare. "I know you and me ain't been on friendly terms ever since I started running whores for Spain. But we don't have to like one another in order to team up and make ourselves a fast five thousand each." He shrugged a shoulder. "What's your problem with that?"

"My problem? Well, let me see. . . ." Snatching the whiskey bottle from the bar top, Rose appeared to give the matter serious thought while he jammed a cork into the bottle and set it out of arm's reach. "If I *was* interested, which I'm not, my *problem* is, as soon as you opened your mouth, *ten* thousand dollars dropped to *five* thousand dollars."

"But your risk of getting killed by that ranger dropped in half *too*," Woods said in defense of the two forming an alliance. "Sam Burrack is not a light piece of work, in case you haven't heard."

"Neither am I, in case *you* haven't noticed." Rose rapped his knuckle on the bar and added, "That'll be two bits for the whiskey. You just stick with the whores. It better suits your nature."

Woods' face reddened in anger and embarrassment. "You've got no reason to insult me like that, Rose," he said. "I came to you in an offer of partnership for both our own good."

"I told you I'm not interested. But if you demand satisfaction for anything I've said, I'll gladly oblige you, Woods," Rose replied with a smug grin. "You're packing a gun. We can go settle up in the street right now."

"I don't want a gunfight with you, Rose," said Woods, feeling things start to get out of hand.

"You're damn right, you don't," Rose said with all the confidence in the world, "because we both know I could nail your shirt buttons into your belly before you could get a hand wrapped around your Colt. Now does that give you any idea why I don't *need you* as a partner?"

Humiliated, Woods said, "I shouldn't have brought it up. I'll collect that money without you. Me and Carney will take care of the ranger."

"Carney Blake? Don't make me laugh." Rose chuckled, his hand still extended for payment. "He's been down drunk all summer. He'll be lucky if he doesn't shoot *himself*."

"He used to be a hell of a gunman," said Woods, trying to save face. "All he needs is a —"

"Yeah, yeah, whatever you say," Rose said, cutting him off. "Now pay me two bits for the drink. Don't make me tell you again."

"Two bits?" Woods gave him a skeptical look. "Since when did a shot of rye cost two bits here?"

"The rye only costs a dime," Rose said, motioning with a finger for Woods to hand over the money. "The other fifteen cents is for me having to listen to your mouth. Now come up with it."

"Here's your two bits," said Woods, giving Rose a disgruntled look. He pulled a silver dollar from his pocket and laid it on the bar. "I said my piece. Now I'm going on with my plans. If you don't want to join me, that's your choice. Me and Carney Blake will do just fine without you."

"That's good to hear," Rose said sarcastically. "Don't try sobering ole Carney up too fast, or he'll start seeing lights flying around in the sky again."

"There were other people up around Benton who claim they saw the same damn thing," said Woods in Carney Blake's defense. "Some of them were sober as a judge."

"Then they must've been standing too close to Carney and it rubbed off them," Rose said. "Stick around that drunken old gunslinger long enough, he'll have you seeing angels riding alligators."

"I'll take my chances with him," said Woods.

"Good for you." Rose made change from his pocket and dropped the silver dollar into his trousers instead of placing it in the big metal cash box lying just below the bar top. Seeing the curious look on Woods' face, he said bluntly, "As long as I'm having to run this joint by myself, I'm paying myself top wages."

At the top of a steep stairs, a young woman stepped out of a room, straightening her dress. Right behind her a young man named Riley Padgett swaggered along, buttoning his shirt, a drunken glow on his face. Rose raised a hand and motioned the woman down to him as he said to Woods, "You keep on running these whores. Only now you're answering to me instead of Spain. It's that simple. Any questions?"

"Spain didn't put you in charge," Woods ventured. "Until I hear from him, I'm going to —"

"Do as you're gawddamn told," Rose interrupted, finishing Woods' words for him. "I don't have to be put in charge. I took charge." He thumbed himself on the chest. "You'll either do like you're told, or else get the hell out of here."

He stared hard at Woods as the young woman came down the stairs and over to the bar. Behind her Riley Padgett smoothed back his hair, placed his hat down atop his head and drifted away toward a gaming table. "Any *other* questions?" Rose asked.

"Whoa!" said the young woman, hearing Rose's harsh tone of voice. "What's got your bowels in an uproar?" She reached out to Woods and put three folded dollars into his hand. Woods took the money and put it away.

Without answering her, Rose said bluntly, "Trixie, you're going to tend bar for me."

"Tend bar?" Trixie Minton gave Woods a startled look, then looked quickly back at Rose. "I don't know nothing about tending bar!" She looked all around. "Where's Jack?"

"Forget Spain. He's gotten his sorry ass arrested," said Rose. "Can you count — at least enough to *look like* you know what you're doing?"

"I can count some, sure," said Trixie, giving a slight shrug. "But not real good. Hell, not enough to make change . . . without getting us all in trouble."

"Then don't *make change* unless they ask for it," said Rose, dismissing the matter. "Keep them drunk and staring at your teats. I've got some business to take care of. Get on back here." He nodded toward the wooden flap at the far end of the bar.

"Is he serious?" Trixie asked Woods. "Margo has two miners waiting up in her room. She needs me to help her. Two miners at once is more than just a handful."

"Hey, whore!" Rose shouted, slapping a loud palm down on the bar top before Woods could answer. "Am I going to have to slap you cross-eyed before you start doing like I tell you?"

"Yeah, he's serious, Trixie," Woods said quietly. "You go on, do what he says. Margo can handle both miners on her own just this once."

Trixie walked to the far end of the bar, cursing under her breath as she lifted the hinged wooden flap. Rose swung himself up over the bar and landed beside Woods. Trixie picked up the wadded apron, put it on and tied the string behind her. On the other side of the bar, Rose straightened his vest and his tie and held out a hand to Woods.

"What now?" Woods asked.

"The whore's money, that's what," said Rose, snapping his fingers to hurry Woods. "She just gave it you. Don't start acting dumb on me."

"Spain always let me hold on to the money and turn it in twice a day."

"That was his way of making you feel important, going around with a roll of cash in your pocket," said Rose. "But not me. I don't give a damn how little you think of yourself — you deserve it. Now give me the damn money before I lose my temper with you."

"All right." Woods handed him the money Trixie had just given him, along with another thicker roll of bills and a leather bag of coins he'd collected from the two women since the night before. "Does this mean I'm supposed to hand the money over as soon as the girls earn it?"

"No, but be prepared to hand it over anytime I ask for it," said Rose, offering a slight grin. "It'll keep you paying attention." He quickly counted the bills from one hand to another.

Seeing the money caused the teamster to say, "I need to get moving. I need some money here."

"I hear you, James Earl." Rose shot him a sharp dark glance, nodded and finished counting.

"Divide what you've got there by two, and you'll know how many customers they've taken upstairs this morning," said Woods.

Rose cut Woods the same sharp glance. "I know how to count money, Woods," he said. "From now on make sure these whores turn in any extra money the men give them. I want a full count on every dollar coming through the doors."

"Damn, that's their money, Rose," said Woods. "How will I even know they're getting any extra? They'll just lie about it. They'll be hard to handle if we start messing with their tips."

"Search them for it, gawddamn it!" said Rose. "If you can't search whores and keep them under control, what do I need you for? I can have them turn money in to me, if that's all *you're* doing."

"There's lots more to running whores than that," said Woods. "You have to —"

"I don't want to hear it," said Rose. "Just do like I'm telling you." He reached over the bar, pulled up a heavy wool coat and put it on. "Search them for money each time as soon as they're finished, while they're still naked, before they hide it," he said, buttoning the coat. "Another thing. I want them telling us about anybody who's carrying lots of money."

"You mean . . . ?" Woods let his words trail.

"Yeah, I want it," said Rose. "There's too much money getting through this place without us getting it." He paused for a moment, then said, "If you can sober Carney Blake up, and you really want to make some money, you ought to both be out there every night, knocking these old goats in the head and robbing them when they leave here."

"That's quick money, but it's bad for business in the long run," said Woods. "We'll get a bad reputation for people getting robbed here, and you'll see business go to hell. Spain would never stood for nothing like that."

"I know you're stupid, Woods, so let me make sure you understand what's going on," Rose said, getting impatient with him. "Texas Jack Spain is gone! The ranger has him. I don't know how long I'll get the chance to make myself some money here, but for as long as I can, I'm going to squeeze the settlement of Cold Devil for every dollar I can get my hand around. Is that clear enough for you?"

"I need to get paid here," said the teamster. "The beer's freezing."

Rose snapped round toward him. "Mention that gawddamn beer freezing one more gawddamn time, James Earl," he said in a tense but even tone, "and I will shoot you dead on the very spot where you're now standing!"

The teamster snarled, but backed away a step and fell silent.

"Yeah, you've made yourself clear enough," Woods said grudgingly, ignoring what had happened with the teamster.

"If you had any sense, you'd do the same," said Rose. Backing away to turn and leave, Rose pointed a finger at Woods and added, "But don't let me catch you stealing from me. This is my game now."

"Stealing from *him*, is it?" Trixie Minton said to Woods when Rose was safely across the floor and out of hearing range. "Since when did Jack Spain let this gunslinging bully start running the Gay Lady?"

"Have you not heard a damn thing that's been said here, Trixie?" Woods asked, getting cross and impatient himself now that Rose had walked out the front door.

"Yeah, I heard that Spain is in jail," said Trixie. "That's about as much as I could make out of it. What's he in jail for?"

"Jesus." Woods sighed, not wanting to

have to repeat the story. From one of the rooms on the upstairs landing came a hard rapid thumping sound. Dismissing her question, he nodded toward the room and said, "Go on up there and help Margo. I've got the bar covered."

"But he told me to tend bar," Trixie offered.

"And now *I'm* telling you to do otherwise," Woods said in a stronger tone.

"If he gets mad . . ." Trixie said, hesitating.

"Don't worry. I'll take care of it," said Woods. "I'm as much a part of this place as he is."

Trixie Minton shook her head. "I hate thinking what's going to happen to the Gay Lady with Spain gone." She picked up a damp rag and began idly wiping the bar top.

"Me too," Woods said to himself, tapping his fingers on a Colt he carried holstered on his hip. "But I'm starting to get some ideas of my own."

"If you're thinking about that ten thousand Spain promised, it'll only get you killed. I've heard of that ranger. He's a tough one."

Looking all around the large saloon, Woods said almost to himself, "Forget the ten thousand. Maybe there's bigger money right here just waiting for the taking."

CHAPTER 3

Inside the single cell, Jack Spain sat on the side of a cot with a damp cloth pressed to his forehead. He cut a sidelong glance to Max Denton, who slouched on the far end of the cot, and said, "You told me nobody was looking for you when I offered to make you sheriff."

"Far as I knew they *wasn't*," Denton replied, holding a wet cloth to his own head. "The law seldom comes this far north. They must figure if a man makes it up this high into the mountain range, he'd most likely go on over into the Canadians."

"The law has gone crazy," Spain offered. "You can't put nothing past them anymore. I always figured one really big haul from a robbery and I could go legitimate the rest of my life. But *no-ooo*," he growled. "These sonsabitches won't leave you alone. Whatever happened to forgive and *forget* — to live and *let* live?"

The two leered with hatred toward the lawmen, who stood putting Spain's personal property into a canvas bag for safekeeping. He watched Sam drop his pocket watch, a large brass key, a roll of bills and a leather pouch full of gold coins into a canvas bag. "I offered ten thousand dollars to anybody who will kill these two bastards and set me free," Spain whispered to Denton.

"Was any of Morgan Waite's boys there when you made the offer?" Denton asked, watching the ranger fold the canvas bag and place it into an open saddlebag hanging over a chair back. "If they were, Waite is one son of a bitch who'll take you up on the offer."

"Riley Padgett might have still been there," Spain whispered. "He'd been there all morning, bucking back and forth between Trixie's and Margo's rooms like a stag elk. I hope to God he'll tell Waite."

"Me too. Waite hates lawmen as bad as we do," said Denton. "There's times I felt a little tense being around him *myself,* that tin star pinned on my chest. I never knew when he might get drunk, start recalling some bitter memories and shoot the hell out of me."

"I hope he hears about it," Spain whispered. "Raymond Curly and his boys are coming any day. I've got to be here when they arrive. I expect you realize that I *don't* want to disappoint Raymond Curly."

Denton shook his head slowly with a troubled look and said, "Not if you want to go on living, you don't."

The two sat in silent contemplation for a moment. Then Spain said, "That same offer goes out to you, Max. If you see a chance for us to kill these two and make a break, I'll pay you the same as I would anybody else." He reconsidered and said, "Well, not ten thousand, not with you needing to get away as bad as I do. But you'll be well paid — you can count on that."

"How much then?" Denton asked in a hushed tone of voice.

"Enough," said Spain.

"How much is that?" Denton persisted.

Before Spain could reply, Sam called out to them from the battered sheriff's desk, "Where's the best place in Cold Devil to order in some hot food? This might be our last hot meal for a week, so pick wisely."

"Bracket's," Denton and Spain both said without hesitation. "Look for the sign at the north end of town, if the whole place hasn't fallen over the edge of the cliffs," Denton added. "The Brackets was among the first to come up here, followed the miners. George Bracket fell over the cliffs building their place. Widow Claire Bracket stayed on, cooking and darning for the miners."

Gigging Denton in his ribs, Spain said, "Don't tell these sonsabitches all that. To hell with them."

Denton fell silent.

"I'll go find the place while you fix us a pot of coffee," Pete Summers offered.

"All right," Sam replied. "I'll watch your back from the boardwalk, in case anybody from the saloon decides to take up Spain's offer."

From the cell, Spain called out, "You said *last hot meal for a week*. Does that mean we're leaving here soon?"

"You'll know when we're leaving, Spain," the ranger said flatly. "You'll see the town start getting smaller behind you."

Spain gritted his teeth. "There's no call for being rude, lawman. A man has a right to know where he's being taken and when he's being taken there."

"Any right you think you had went out the window the minute you made an offer to have us killed, Spain," Sam said, turning toward the cell. "The smartest thing you can do for yourself is try to keep your mouth shut as much as possible this whole trip."

Before Spain could offer a reply, the sound

of boots walking up onto the boardwalk caused both lawmen to turn quickly toward the front door. Their guns came up from their holsters, cocked and ready. Upon hearing a knock, Sam gave Summers a calm look, both men knowing that, when trouble came, it seldom knocked.

"Who's there?" Summers asked, as Sam and he both listened for the sound of any more boots, either near the front door or around the side of the building.

"It's Ned Rose, bartender from the Gay Lady," the voice said through the rough pine door. "Can I come in?"

"Yes, come on in, but make it slow and easy," Sam called out.

The door creaked open slowly and Rose stepped cautiously inside. Seeing the two big revolvers pointed at him, he raised his hands chest high in a show of peace and said with a cordial smile, "Damn, I'm glad I showed good manners instead of just barging on in."

Without returning his smile, Sam stepped forward, his and Summers' Colts still pointed, and flipped the front of Rose's coat open. He saw the Remington standing behind the waist sash, but didn't reach out for it. Knowing its whereabouts was good enough.

"I always wear it, Ranger, even to church," Rose said in explanation. "No offense."

"It's all right with me if it's all right with your preacher," Sam said. "What can we do for you?"

"I'm hoping you'll allow me to speak to Jack Spain. I'm running the Gay Lady. I need him to tell me how to get some cash for operating expenses and whatnot."

"And *whatnot?*" Summers asked warily. "You mean like the ten thousand dollars he's offering to pay somebody to kill us?"

Behind them, Spain and Denton stood up from the edge of the cot, taking interest in Ned Rose being there.

"No, you've got me pegged all wrong, Marshal," said Rose. "I've got nothing to do with that. And I don't condone hired killing." He gave a narrowed gaze past the two lawmen to Jack Spain. "Far as I'm concerned, a man with big nuts ought to be able to defend himself, or else keep his mouth shut and take what's handed him."

"Damn you, Rose," Spain growled, gripping the bars tightly with both hands.

Ignoring Spain, Rose continued. "The fact is, I need operating cash, if I'm to keep his business from going bust."

The two lawmen looked at each other for a moment. Finally Sam said, "You can talk to him from here, bartender, but don't try going near the cell."

"Obliged, lawman," said Rose. Turning to face Spain across the room, he said, "Seven barrels of beer is sitting out in the alley freezing. Rudiheil gave Earl strict orders not to unload it until he's paid fifty-six dollars for the load and a hundred dollars on the account you've been shirking on," he lied.

"Fifty-six dollars!" Spain turned red. "For seven barrels of *beer?* That's eight dollars a barrel! It's more than I've ever paid!"

"Then I'll tell him to take them back because we've quit selling beer at the Gay Lady." Rose said, unconcerned, as if dismissing the matter. He started to turn toward the door.

"Wait!" said Spain, stopping him from leaving. He stood staring at Rose with a smoldering look of hatred on his face. "Ranger, can I give this man some money out of my personal roll?" he asked Sam.

Rose held back a smile of satisfaction.

Sam looked Rose up and down and said, "I don't see why not, do you, Marshal Summers, to keep a saloon from running out of beer?"

"Sure. Why not?" said Summers.

As Sam reached down inside his saddlebags and pulled up the canvas bag containing Spain's personal items, Rose said to Spain and the lawmen, "What I really need is the key to the office safe." His words turned toward Spain. "I'll need operating cash to keep the saloon afloat."

"Like hell," said Spain. "Nobody gets the key to my safe, or to my office!"

"You forgot to lock your office door," said Rose, "so that's not a problem."

"I never forget to lock my office door!" said Spain, but he gave a puzzled look as he questioned himself. "You broke in!"

"It wasn't locked, Spain," Rose said firmly. He paused for a moment, then said, "Look, you could be gone a long time even if you get a lawyer and beat this thing. How long do you think that safe will sit there once the Gay Lady goes broke and the building is standing there empty? I'll run the saloon for you, but I'll need money to do it."

Spain knew Rose was right, but he couldn't make himself turn everything he owned over to a man he was convinced was out to rob him. Swallowing a hard knot in his throat, Spain said, "All right. The truth is, I lost the key to that safe a long time ago. There's no money in it anyway — maybe a few dollars is all."

"Then you won't mind if I go through your personal stuff, make sure it's not there.

Maybe you overlooked it somehow?" said Rose.

Before Spain could answer, Sam cut in, saying, "Nobody can go through a prisoner's personal items without the prisoner's permission."

Rose turned to Spain. "Are you going to tell him it's okay to let me search your stuff?"

"Hell, no," said Spain. "It's the same as you calling me a liar, Rose."

"Is there a key there?" Rose turned and asked the ranger. He studied Sam's eyes closely, seeing if he could detect anything.

"I won't talk about a prisoner's personal items," Sam said, eyes giving up nothing.

Rose looked back at Spain. "All right, then, the key is lost," he said. "I'll have to make do on what cash there is in the till, and what the whores bring in." He paused as if considering everything, then said to Spain, "I'm only running this place for your benefit, Spain, thinking maybe you *will* get off easy and get back here real quick. If you want somebody else to run things, you say the word right now before I even take the hundred and fifty-six dollars for the beer."

Spain gritted his teeth and gripped the bars even tighter. "Take the money, Rose, gawddamn you!"

Rose ignored the cursing and asked, "Then you *do* want me to run the Gay Lady until you come back?"

"I said take the money, didn't I?" Spain rasped, barely holding on to his temper.

"Because if you'd rather get Woods, or Trixie, or Margo to run things, I'll gladly step aside —"

"Ranger!" Spain shouted. "*Please* give him the gawddamn beer money!"

Rose relaxed and watched the ranger turn away from him and began to count money from Spain's roll of cash.

"I'm warning you, Rose," Spain called, sticking his arm out through the bars and pointing a stiffened finger at his bartender, "I better not come back here and find you've been stealing from the saloon! I won't stand for it! Do you hear me? I won't stand for it!"

"Neither will I, Spain," said Rose, a slight smile on his face. "Anybody stealing from the Gay Lady will answer to me, as long as I'm running things. I already told Woods as much, in case he decides to try something. The main thing is, you get yourself a good lawyer and get on back to us." His smile widened. "That's what *I'll* be praying for."

"Son of a bitch," Spain growled under his breath.

Sam placed the roll of cash back into the canvas bag, and placed the canvas bag in his saddlebags. Turning to Rose, he counted the money aloud into his palm, making sure Spain saw and heard him do it. When he'd finished, he said to Rose, "I expect this will be the last we see of you while we're in Cold Devil?"

"That would suit me, Ranger," said Rose, seeming less cordial now that he'd gotten what he came for. He folded the bills and put them away inside his coat. But before he could turn to leave, a shot rang out in the street and splinters exploded from the pine door. "Jesus!" Rose shouted, ducking away and reaching instinctively for the Remington in his sash. In the cell, Spain and Denton both dropped to the floor for cover.

Sam and Summers both jumped a step away from the splintered door; but even as they did so, Sam's cocked Colt leveled toward Rose, causing the bartender to jerk his hand away from his gun. "It's not my doing, Ranger!" Rose said quickly. "I came here alone. I swear it."

"Then you won't mind giving this up," said Summers, reaching in and snatching Rose's gun from his waist.

Before Rose could respond, a drunken voice called out from the street, "Lawdogs!

Get out here and face me! I come to set Texas Jack Spain free as the wind! Hear me, Jack? I'm here to free ya! Get my money ready!"

"Damn it," said Rose, "that's Riley Padgett. He's been drunk and randy as hell the past three days."

"Jesus!" Spain cried out from the cell. "I'm bleeding! I'm shot here!"

"How bad?" Summers asked, Sam and him both wary of a trick.

"A graze above my ear," said Spain, "but damn it, I'm hit!"

"Hang on, Spain," said Sam. While Marshal Summers kept watch on Ned Rose, Sam stepped to the front wall and peeped out from the edge of a window. Giving the staggering gunman only a once-over glance, Sam searched the roof lines, doorways and alleyways along the street. "Who's been drinking with him?" he asked Rose over his shoulder.

"Nobody in particular," said Rose. "He's spent most of his time with the whores, Margo and Trixie." Giving Spain a quick disdainful glance, he added, "I guess he heard about the ten thousand dollars and couldn't pass it up."

"Don't give me that look, Rose!" Spain shouted. "I'm the one bleeding here!"

"You're lucky to be alive," Rose called out. "Only a fool would offer that kind of money. You'll draw every drunk and lunatic west of the Mississippi. They'll all be shooting in *your* direction."

"I was desperate," Spain shouted. "I wasn't thinking straight! Look at me! I'm shot!"

"And you deserve it," Rose shouted back at him.

"Rose, listen to me," Spain pleaded. "Tell everybody I didn't mean it! Tell them the deal is off, will you? Will you, please? Just tell Waite to come get me out. Just him, nobody else!"

"Shut up over there," said Summers, hearing Spain's message.

"Yeah, sure thing," Rose replied to Spain, sounding skeptical of the idea. "Why don't I put a sign up over the bar, saying, 'Spain didn't mean it'? Would that do it for you?"

"Both of you shut up," said Summers. He took a threatening step closer to Rose.

The bartender stopped talking to Spain. But he said to Summers and the ranger, "What about you two? Want me to put up a sign saying no reward for killing yas?"

From the street, the drunken gunman called out, "Are you coming out, or am I coming in blazing?"

Sam let out a breath. He gave Summers a nod and walked to the front door. "Keep an eye on my back," the ranger said over his shoulder. "When I give a signal open the window and let Spain talk some sense to his man."

"You're covered, Sam," said Summers, seeing Sam reach for the door handle. Then to Rose, he said, "Do what suits you after you leave here. But right now, keep still and keep your hands up. We don't know where you stand in this."

"I understand," said Rose, hiking his hands a little higher and away from his coat. "I came here for the beer money. I've got it. That's all I wanted. Let me know when I can leave." He tossed Spain a glance and said, "I left a *whore* tending bar. She says she can't count worth a damn."

"Jesus!" Spain moaned, blood running beneath the hand he held to his grazed head.

CHAPTER 4

The ranger stepped out on the boardwalk with his big Colt hanging loosely, yet poised, in his right hand, his thumb over the hammer. "Go home, *Riley Padgett,* and sober up, before you get yourself into something you can't get out of," he said, hoping that hearing his name might make the man think twice before taking things any further.

But the young gunman would have none of it. "Huh-uh," he said, shaking his head drunkenly. "I'm taking Spain out of that jail. You can hand him over or go down where you stand. It makes no difference to me. You won't be the first man I killed."

"Listen up, Padgett," said Sam, "before this gets out of hand." He motioned toward the front window, where Summers stood watching. Summers saw Sam give him a slight nod, and he raised the window quietly. "Jack Spain wants to tell you something. Pay attention."

"This has all been a mistake, Riley!" Spain called out all the way from his cell. "There's no reward money on these lawmen's heads. Go sober up. I've called off the reward! Please go away! You've already wounded me!"

Padgett gave the ranger a drunken scowl. "I never wounded him," he said. "What have you lawdogs done to him?"

"Nothing yet." Sam took a step down off the boardwalk, then another step closer to where the young gunman stood swaying, blurry-eyed on rye. "But if shooting starts, I can't say what will happen to him or to anybody else, for that matter." As he spoke, he moved ever closer until he stopped no more than six feet from the drunken gunman.

"So you're saying there's no ten-thousand-dollar reward in this for me? Not for killing you and the other lawdog?" Padgett asked, sounding more and more on the verge of passing out on the cold dirt street.

Sam shook his head slowly as he ventured another step forward. "If you were to do that and not get yourself killed, all you'd have to look forward to is dying at the end of a hemp rope. Men like you and me know a losing proposition when we see one, don't we?"

"Men like you and me? *Ha!*" said Padgett. "I can take you, Ranger! Don't ever think I can't!"

"You look capable enough," Sam said, seeing the young man struggle to keep his eyes focused. "But is this Texas Jack Spain worth the trouble?"

Padgett started to reply, but suddenly the ranger was upon him. He felt his gun snatched from his hand. At the same time, he felt the solid thud of a gun barrel along his jaw line and felt himself hit the ground. He seemed to slip down a dark narrow hole in the street. The last thing he felt before he lost consciousness was his limp body being dragged across the cold, hard dirt toward the sheriff's office.

Inside the cell, Denton and Spain stood watching while the ranger dragged the knocked-out gunman across the rough plank floor. "You can go now," Summers said to Rose, handing him his Remington butt first.

"Obliged." Rose took the pistol, shoved it behind his sash and looked down smiling, shaking his head at the limp boot toes scraping through the dust on the floor. "This has to be one of the most stupid sonsabitches I ever met," he remarked. He walked out the door, closed it behind himself, stepped off the boardwalk and headed toward the Gay Lady Saloon.

Summers stepped over and latched the front door. He moved ahead of the ranger, unlocked the barred cell door and swung it open. He kept watch on the two prisoners until Sam dragged Padgett into the cell, raised him and dropped him onto the cot.

"Lay a wet cloth on his jaw," Sam said, turning and walking out of the cell.

Spain and Denton looked at each other, then at the only cot in the cell, where Padgett now lay. "We're all out of cloths," Denton said cynically. "I wasn't expecting a rash of my *citizens* getting pistol-whipped."

"Tear your wet cloth in half and share it," said the ranger, "since it's for one of your *citizens.*" With the cell door closed and locked, Sam asked Spain through the bars, "Who is Waite?"

"Huh? Who?" Spain looked caught off-guard.

"The man you just told your bartender to come get you out," said Sam. "We both heard you. So come on, out with it."

"I — I didn't mean anything by it, Ranger," said Spain, holding a bloody cloth to his grazed head. "Look at me. I could have been killed!"

"Who is Waite?" Sam asked Denton.

Denton gave the ranger a tight-jawed look. But then, as if having reconsidered, he sighed and said, "All right, what the hell? Waite is a fellow who sort of looks out for everybody's interests up here."

"Keep your mouth shut, Denton," said Spain. "I'll tell Waite every word you've said about him."

"I'm not saying nothing against him," said Denton. "Far as I know, he's got nothing to hide. He's sort of the law in places up here where there is no law."

"He's a regulator," Sam said flatly.

"I'd say it's accurate to call him and his men regulators," said Denton.

Sam turned his gaze to Spain. "And you'll sic him and his men on us?"

Spain collected himself for a moment, then said, "I didn't ask to be beaten and dragged off to jail, Ranger. If my good friend Morgan Waite comes with an offer of help for me, I sure as hell won't turn it down."

"Morgan Waite," said Marshal Summers, recognizing the name. "The same Morgan Waite who rode for the stars and bars, did all the killing along the Kansas border?"

"I believe my friend Morgan *is* a veteran at that," said Spain with an arrogant expression, watching the lawmen's eyes, seeing if any of this strengthened his position. "But whatever killing he and his men might have done, they was pardoned for at the end of the war. He's a force to be reckoned with here in the high country."

Summers looked at Sam and motioned toward the front door. Inside the cell, Spain gave Denton a sly smile and gestured a sidelong glance toward the two lawmen as they stepped out onto the boardwalk. "I think I might have just done myself some good. These lawmen don't want to mess with a bunch like Waite and his men."

"So there still *is* a reward for Waite and his men getting you out of here?" Denton asked.

"Oh, hell, yes," said Spain. "That little episode with this idiot doesn't change anything. I still want out of here, bullet graze or not." He gestured toward Riley Padgett, who had begun to moan faintly and roll his head back and forth. His jaw had already swollen twice its size. A long red-blue welt ran the length from his chin to his earlobe. "It was just my bad luck that he showed up drunk."

"So, if I get us out of here, the ten thousand dollars is still mine?" Denton asked.

"I told you, Denton," said Spain, "you *will* get a fair share for helping me break loose."

"But you never did say just how much that *fair share* is," Denton said.

Spain gave him a sour look. "This is not the time to quibble over money, Sheriff. You want to get out of here just as bad as I do, don't you?"

"That's no answer," said Denton, pondering, realizing that no answer was coming.

"Hey, sleeping angel!" Spain said to the knocked-out gunman, who'd begun to awaken, but still lay sprawled on the narrow cot. "Drag up from there and let us sit down." As he spoke, he reached out and shook the toe of Riley Padgett's boot.

"Take your hand off me, Spain, if you plan on ever using it again," Padgett said in a low growl through his swollen jaw. "Which one of you hit me?"

Spain and Denton looked at each other. "Jesus, Riley, you're in jail," said Spain.

"Where?" Padgett asked, a foggy swirling look in his bloodshot eyes.

"Don't you remember anything, Riley?" Denton asked, as Spain and he leaned over the cot.

Padgett thought things over, his head pounding hard with each beat of his heart. He groaned in realization and said, "Damn, did I kill anybody?" His hand went instinctively to his right hip, finding only his empty holster.

"No, but you intended to," said Spain, "and don't think I don't appreciate it." He reached down, took Padgett's hand and help him sit up on the edge of the cot. As soon as space became available, he and Denton slid in on either side of the swaying gunman and claimed themselves a seat.

"The ranger did this to me, didn't he?" Padgett asked cupping his half of the damp cloth gently to his throbbing jaw.

"Yes, he did," said Spain. "You stood up to him, but damn it, man, you were too drunk to do any good. What got into you anyway, trying something like that?"

"'Ten thousand dollars is what got into him," Denton cut in.

Padgett gave the sheriff a puzzled look. "What are you doing this side of the bars?"

"That's a long story," Denton said, brushing the question off. "The thing is, we're all in this fix together."

"Yeah," said Spain. "Where are Morgan Waite and the rest of your pals?"

"*Pals?*" Padgett said with a look of offense. "What do you think we are, some sort of circus riders?"

"Sorry," said Spain. "I'm not myself in this miserable jail cell."

Padgett said, "Don't concern yourself with

where Waite and the boys are, Spain. They'll be coming here, once I tell them what happened to me."

"That's what I'm wanting to hear," said Spain.

"He could have killed you out there, you know," Denton cut in.

"Whose side are you on, Sheriff?" Spain said in sharp tone. "I think we need to see where everybody stands here before we go any further."

"Hell, look where I am, Spain," said Denton, spreading his hands. "I'm in a worse fix than you are. I've done things I could hang for!" As soon as he spoke, he ducked his head and looked around to see if the lawmen might have heard him. "*Allegedly*, I've done things, that is. But I deny them as rumors and nothing more. All I'm saying is that Waite might not figure a crack in the jaw ain't worth riding in here and killing two lawmen over."

"If it's not, then ten thousand dollars is," said Padgett.

Spain squirmed on the edge of the cot. "Is money all anybody ever thinks about?"

Out front on the boardwalk, Sam and Marshal Summers looked back and forth along the almost empty street, keeping watch for anybody who might appear interested in Spain's reward offer. "Sam, we could have our hands full if Morgan Waite and his men come riding in and take Spain's side in this," said Summers.

"I understand," said Sam. "I've heard of Morgan Waite myself. I can't imagine him and his men backing a four-flusher like Spain."

"Ten thousand dollars is a lot of money, Sam," said Summers. "It buys loyalty, for a while anyway."

"That's if Spain really has ten thousand dollars," said Sam. "This whole thing could be a mouthful of desperate talk."

"It could be," said Summers. "But we could both end up dead before anybody realizes he's blowing hot air."

The two stood looking along the cold dirt street for a moment in contemplation. "How well do you know the high passes north of here?" Sam asked.

Nodding, already getting an idea of what Sam had in mind, Summers said, "Well enough that we can give most anybody the slip if we get out of here with a few hours' head start." He considered, then added, "It'll be hard on the prisoners, riding handcuffed, at night, through rocky country."

"Spain asked for it," said Sam, "setting a

reward on our heads. Denton caught a bad hand, but he's stuck with it."

"What about the drunk, Padgett?" Summers asked.

"We've got to let him go," Sam said.

"He meant to kill you, Sam," said Summers. "Drunk or sober, that's a hard charge for me to turn loose of."

"He's not the first drunk to get his head cracked trying to shoot a lawman," Sam replied. "Besides, we don't need another prisoner with us, not if there's a possibility we could end up with Waite and his men dogging our trail down out of these mountains."

"That's true, but once we turn him loose, he's going straight to Waite. We can count on it."

"Yep," said Sam, "and since we know we can count on it, let's use it to our advantage. Let's send him away after dark tonight, thinking we're headed down the south pass sometime tomorrow. But we'll head out of here tonight once we've got the cover of darkness."

"These high switchback trails will be hard to travel in the dark," Summers commented, considering.

"That's why nobody will think we'd go in that direction," Sam said. "How far will you have to take us before we can circle around and get headed back the right direction?"

"Thirty miles maybe," said Summers. "There's an old mining trail that cuts down." His eyes went up, searching the sky to the north of Cold Devil. "We could be pushing our luck going that way. These high passes can fill with snow pretty quick with almost no warning this time of year."

"All the more reason they'll think we headed south," Sam said. "But you're the one who knows this country. Is this too foolish to consider?"

"Ordinarily, maybe so," said the young marshal. "But I say we give it a try. So long as the weather holds, it's no more risky than facing Morgan Waite and his gunmen."

CHAPTER 5

When Ned Rose left the sheriff's office, he walked straight back to the Gay Lady saloon and paid the teamster for the wagon load of beer and paid ten dollars on Spain's past-due account. Smiling to himself, he pocketed the rest of the money Spain had given him. Seeing Rose arrive, Trixie, who was behind the bar again, started to untie the bartender apron and take it off. But Rose stopped her, saying, "You stay right back there! Keep slinging drinks until I tell you to do otherwise."

"Okay," said Trixie. "You don't have to be so bossy about it."

"Yes, I do," said Rose. "You see, *I am* the boss!" He thumbed himself soundly on the chest. "So keep a civil tongue in your head." Turning and heading back for the front door, he said over his shoulder, "I have more business to attend to. I'll be back directly." Raising his voice for all to hear, he flung his hand in the air and shouted, "Everybody *enjoy* themselves!"

"I've never seen a fellow let something go to his head this quick in my life," said Stanley Woods, who stood panting, leaning on a barrel of beer he had just rolled behind the bar. "I don't know . . . how long I . . . can *stand* him being in charge." He mopped a hand across his beaded brow. "I'm not built for this . . . kind of brute work."

"It's good for you, Woods," said the teamster, standing at the bar, folding the money and putting it away. "It gives you an idea how the rest of us live."

"I couldn't give a damn less how the . . . rest of you fools live, Coots," he growled, still out of breath. "I pimp women for a living, and I'm . . . damn good at it. Right, Trixie?" he asked.

Trixie shrugged a thin shoulder and said coolly, "Don't ask me to vouch for you, Stanley. It looks like Rose is the lead bull in this joint."

The teamster chuckled, raised a shot glass and drained it. Giving Woods a disdainful look, he said, "Anytime something like this happens, there's always one person bold enough to step out and take charge, while others stand around leaning on both hands."

Woods straightened up off of the beer barrel and dusted his hands together. "Gawd-damn it!" he cursed. "I'm no stock boy or bar swamper." He stomped away toward the front door.

"Stanley, where do you think you're going?" Trixie called out.

"To tell Rose that from now on he can roll his own barrels! I'm demanding some respect."

"Je-sus!" Coots grinned, as Trixie and he watched Woods disappear through the door onto the boardwalk. As the two spoke, Margo walked down the stairs and behind the bar, giving a look toward the front door.

"What got into Woods?" she asked Trixie.

Trixie only shrugged, but Coots grinned and said, "I believe we just talked him into getting himself an ass kicking."

"Let's hope so anyway," said Trixie, untying her apron and handing it to Margo. "Are we all caught up upstairs?"

"I took care of as much as I could," said Margo, taking the apron and putting it on. "I need a break for a few minutes. I just sent the blacksmith on his way. He's happy as can be."

"Good." Trixie let out a sigh of relief as she walked around from behind the bar. "I'm going to go roll myself a smoke, all right?"

"Sure, go ahead," said Margo. "I want to talk to Coots anyway." She smiled coyly at Coots while Trixie slipped away and out the side door.

"Talk to me about what?" Coots looked curious.

"I never told you this, but I've got a soft spot a mile wide for teamsters," said Margo.

"Do you really?" Coots looked delighted at the prospect.

Margo leaned against the bar toward him. "When Trixie gets back, how would you like to go upstairs for five minutes, do whatever you want to do?"

"You mean free of charge?" Coots asked.

Margo seemed to considered, then shrugged. "What the hell? Why not?"

"Do I have to use the five minutes all at once, or can I make a couple of trips out of it?" Coots asked, half joking.

"You can have five minutes for free anytime you ride through here," she said. "You are driving that big strong wagon of yours, aren't you?"

"It's the only way I ever travel," said Coots.

"That's what I thought," Margo said, looking dreamy-eyed at him. "Is there anything left on it, after the beer delivery?"

Coots shrugged. "Just a stack of buffalo

skins I'm hauling down the mountain."

"Oh, nice thick buffalo skins," said Margo. "That sounds wonderful!"

"It *does?*" Coots just looked at her, seeing the look of suggestion in her eyes.

Outside, Woods stomped along the boardwalk toward the sheriff's office full of heated determination. But when he saw Rose and the town blacksmith, Milo Herns, walk out of Bracket's Restaurant and head toward the blacksmith's shop, he decided to draw back, cool off and see what they were up to.

Ahead of Woods, Milo Herns swung open the door to his shop and complained to Rose, "I had just got there! I finally can sit in Bracket's without anybody making *nigger* remarks at me, and damned if you don't come roust me out before I could order my meal. Do you know how much I enjoy just sitting there, having vittles *brought* to me? Alls I have to do is sit there and shovel it in?"

"I'll make it worth your while, Milo," said Rose. "You can trust me on that."

"The last white man I trusted left me sitting in a stolen buggy with two hundred jars of stolen sorghum molasses."

"I told you this is a good legitimate piece of work, Milo," said Woods.

"I pay you twenty dollars, you cut that

70

"Give Herns a beer while he waits," Rose ordered Trixie, who had come back inside moments earlier and taken over while Margo and Coots slipped upstairs. Trixie stood pouring shots of whiskey into three waiting glasses. Three miners turned a gaze toward the small wiry blacksmith, grinned drunkenly and wrapped their strong, rough fingers around their filled glasses.

"Waits for what?" Trixie asked, in one move corking the whiskey bottle, sitting it on the shelf behind the bar. Snatching up a clean mug, she stuck it under the beer tap and opened the tap with a flip of her hand.

"For me to check the till," Rose said, already reaching below the bar and flipping open the metal cash box.

Trixie sat a foamy mug of beer in front of Herns and watched Rose quickly count out a large amount of bills and coins. The coins he dropped into a leather draw-string bag. The bills he folded and stuck away somewhere behind his vest. "*Check it?* It looks to me like you're gutting it!" she said.

"I'm not leaving a lot of money in the cash box back here, in case somebody decides to rob us," Rose said matter-of-factly. "Now turn around." He gestured toward the shelf behind the bar. "Put your hands there."

"What?" said Trixie. "Jack Spain never

safe loose from the closet floor, bring it down here and open it," said Rose, "and you get your money. It's that simple."

"Um-hmm, I know," said the wiry little blacksmith while he rummaged around on a workbench and found some bastard files and a pair of heavy iron cutters. "But we'll need some help wallowing that safe down here from the Gay Lady. I can't afford to break something in my back."

"There's a teamster at the Gay Lady who brought in a load of beer," said Rose. "We'll get him and Woods to give us a hand."

"Woods? *Ha!*" Herns scoffed. "Be better off getting one of them whores to help us. Least-wise something would get moved. Woods couldn't move his shoes if they was off his feet."

"We'll get it down here," said Rose. "That's all that matters."

Wrapping the files and tools quickly in a large oilstained rag, Milo Herns picked up half of a long, thin cigar and stuck it between his teeth. "I'm good. Let's go get to cutting on this big, fat safe."

They left the blacksmith shop and walked with purpose to the Gay Lady Saloon. Watching them from out front on the sheriff's office, Marshal Summers said to the ranger, who stood beside him, "Looks like

Spain's bartender is up to something. I expect Spain is right in not trusting this man." Considering things for a moment, he said, "Sometimes I almost feel bad, coming into a town, grabbing a man and hauling him away from his home and family or some business he's been trying to build up."

"Saloon owning is a risky business at best," said the ranger. "I expect Spain knew that. Whatever we're pulling him away from here wasn't his to begin with. He built it on stolen money. By rights the Gay Lady should be sold and the proceeds divided among the folks whose money was stolen in that stagecoach robbery."

Summers gave a slight smile. "I said sometimes I *almost* feel bad, Sam. Never bad enough to let a man like Spain go."

"I knew what you meant," Sam replied. "Sometimes I *almost* feel the same way. A town like Cold Devil needs a place like the Gay Lady. Seems a shame to let her go down just because a dog like Spain built her."

"Yeah, but the place will go down," said Summers. "We both know it. As soon as we pulled Spain out of there, the vultures started circling, getting a sense of something about to die." He nodded at Rose and the blacksmith walking along the boardwalk toward the saloon doors.

"It won't be long before everybody will be picking at her bones. Rose there is quicker than the others. He's pouncing on her belly while she's still warm."

Sam nodded. "He was already behind the bar, saw the money coming in," he said. "So he's the one who'll squeeze the life out of her."

"If the town owns the land, maybe they'll stop it in time and put somebody else to running the place," said Summers.

"Maybe," said Sam. "But they better move quick. Once folks realize Spain's gone for good, the picking will start." As if dismissing the matter, Sam turned and walked to door of the sheriff's office. "Let's tell Padgett the good news . . . he's going to be a free man, because the *sheriff* is going to prison."

Across the street, Ned Rose and the blacksmith walked into the Gay Lady and up to the flap at the far end of the bar. Rose raised the wooden flap and started behind the bar, but he stopped long enough to give Herns a dark look when he saw that the blacksmith was about to follow him. Herns stepped back away from the wooden flap and instead bellied up to the bar, laying his oil rag full of tools in front of him.

worried about the cash box getting *robbed.*"

"But he should have," said Rose. "*I'm* looking out for his interest. *I'm* taking no chances. Now turn around." He gave her a nudge as if to get her started.

"Turn around for what?" Trixie asked over her shoulder even as she did as he told her and placed her hands on the shelf behind the bar.

"So I can search you," said Rose, his hands already going up and down her sides.

"Hey!" said Trixie. "You have no right to —"

"Shut up!" Rose snapped, leaning against her, reaching up around her, running his hands down into the low bodice of her dress. He quickly ran his hands all over and under her breasts and under both arms. "From now on, I'm keeping a closer count on the cash box, and I'm taking money from it throughout the day."

"But you didn't write anything down," said Trixie. "How do you know how much was in there?"

"I keep it all written down right here," said Rose, tapping a finger to his temple. "Don't worry about what I write down."

As Rose talked, he continued searching. Herns' and the three miners' eyes widened as he hiked the back of her dress and ran a hand around inside her underwear.

"Damn it!" Trixie wiggled and let out a short shriek as Rose probed between her thighs. "I don't steal!" Trixie shouted. "Who the hell do you think you are, accusing me of taking something —"

"Aha!" said Rose, jerking his hand out and holding up a twenty-dollar gold piece. "What's this, then, you thieving whore?"

"That's my lucky twenty!" said Trixie, her voice sounding frightened, for good reason. "I always carry it there! It's sort of my good luck piece!"

Rose's backhanded slap across her face sent her flying sidelong to the wet, dirty floor. Before she could crawl away, the toe of his boot landed solidly in her stomach, lifting her and sending her three feet farther away. She landed doubled up, gagging for breath, her arms going around her waist. "I'll kill you, you gawddamn motherless —"

Rose stepped forward, ready to kick her again. But Stanley Woods, who had just walked in through the side door, saw what was going on and rushed forward, leaping over the bar. At the same time, Milo Herns scrambled up onto the bar top and flung himself onto Rose's back, seeing that Ned Rose intended to make good his threat. Together, the blacksmith and the pimp wrestled Rose away from Trixie and held him long enough for Margo to hurry around the bar and drag Trixie farther out of reach.

"Take it easy, Rose, please!" Woods shouted, Ned Rose slinging the two back and forth like rag dolls. Herns held onto Rose's back, looking like a jockey mounted on a raging wild horse.

"Easy! I'll give you *easy!* You *sonsabitch!*" Rose bellowed, finally flinging the two away and turning toward them, the big Remington out and cocked in their faces.

"Mr. Rose! Mr. Rose! Hold on!" Herns held both hands up in front of him, saying quickly, "I came here to do a piece of work, not to get my ass shot off! The safe, the safe! Remember?"

"Nobody grabs me from behind!" Rose said, with a crazed stare at Stanley Woods.

"You were killing her, Rose!" Woods shouted. "You would have hanged for murder! Is that what you wanted, to get yourself hanged? I did it for you!" Woods lied. "Jesus, don't kill me!"

Rose cooled down, thinking about the ranger and the marshal only yards away, across the street. He also thought about the safe full of money standing upstairs in Spain's room. "If you ever lay hands on me again, Woods, you're dead!" He took a deep breath, turned his gaze toward the black-smith and started to issue the same threat, but something in Herns' eyes told him to keep his mouth shut if he ever wanted to see the inside of the safe.

"No," said Woods, "I'll never lay hands on you, Ned. You have my word! Let's all just settle down, for our own good. No more threats."

"All right, then, no more threats. I'm settled down," said Rose. He ran a hand all over his face, let out a breath and let the Remington's barrel sag toward the floor, his thumb letting the hammer down.

On the dirty plank floor, Trixie lay gasping in Margo's arms. A trickle of blood ran from the corner of her gaping mouth. "Threats?" Margo said, staring hard and cold at Rose. "Here's a threat for you, you chicken-shit son of a bitch! If you ever lay a hand on one of us again, I'll cut your throat so deep, sun will shine out your asshole!"

"Margo, stop it!" Woods said gruffly. "Let everybody settle down! Get Trixie a wet rag! Please!"

Rose stood gritting his teeth, his big fists clenched tight at his sides. "Gawddamn whores!" he growled under his breath.

"There now, see," said Woods, "no harm done." Seeing everybody hold still, he safe loose from the closet floor, bring it down here and open it," said Rose, "and you get your money. It's that simple."

"Um-hmm, I know," said the wiry little blacksmith while he rummaged around on a workbench and found some bastard files and a pair of heavy iron cutters. "But we'll need some help wallowing that safe down here from the Gay Lady. I can't afford to break something in my back."

"There's a teamster at the Gay Lady who brought in a load of beer," said Rose. "We'll get him and Woods to give us a hand."

"Woods? *Ha!*" Herns scoffed. "Be better off getting one of them whores to help us. Least-wise something would get moved. Woods couldn't move his shoes if they was off his feet."

"We'll get it down here," said Rose. "That's all that matters."

Wrapping the files and tools quickly in a large oilstained rag, Milo Herns picked up half of a long, thin cigar and stuck it between his teeth. "I'm good. Let's go get to cutting on this big, fat safe."

They left the blacksmith shop and walked with purpose to the Gay Lady Saloon. Watching them from out front on the sheriff's office, Marshal Summers said to the ranger, who stood beside him, "Looks like

71

Spain's bartender is up to something. I expect Spain is right in not trusting this man." Considering things for a moment, he said, "Sometimes I almost feel bad, coming into a town, grabbing a man and hauling him away from his home and family or some business he's been trying to build up."

"Saloon owning is a risky business at best," said the ranger. "I expect Spain knew that. Whatever we're pulling him away from here wasn't his to begin with. He built it on stolen money. By rights the Gay Lady should be sold and the proceeds divided among the folks whose money was stolen in that stagecoach robbery."

Summers gave a slight smile. "I said sometimes I *almost* feel bad, Sam. Never bad enough to let a man like Spain go."

"I knew what you meant," Sam replied. "Sometimes I *almost* feel the same way. A town like Cold Devil needs a place like the Gay Lady. Seems a shame to let her go down just because a dog like Spain built her."

"Yeah, but the place will go down," said Summers. "We both know it. As soon as we pulled Spain out of there, the vultures started circling, getting a sense of something about to die." He nodded at Rose and the blacksmith walking along the boardwalk

72

toward the saloon doors.

"It won't be long before everybody will be picking at her bones. Rose there is quicker than the others. He's pouncing on her belly while she's still warm."

Sam nodded. "He was already behind the bar, saw the money coming in," he said. "So he's the one who'll squeeze the life out of her."

"If the town owns the land, maybe they'll stop it in time and put somebody else to running the place," said Summers.

"Maybe," said Sam. "But they better move quick. Once folks realize Spain's gone for good, the picking will start." As if dismissing the matter, Sam turned and walked to door of the sheriff's office. "Let's tell Padgett the good news . . . he's going to be a free man, because the *sheriff* is going to prison."

Across the street, Ned Rose and the blacksmith walked into the Gay Lady and up to the flap at the far end of the bar. Rose raised the wooden flap and started behind the bar, but he stopped long enough to give Herns a dark look when he saw that the blacksmith was about to follow him. Herns stepped back away from the wooden flap and instead bellied up to the bar, laying his oil rag full of tools in front of him.

"Give Herns a beer while he waits," Rose ordered Trixie, who had come back inside moments earlier and taken over while Margo and Coots slipped upstairs. Trixie stood pouring shots of whiskey into three waiting glasses. Three miners turned a gaze toward the small wiry blacksmith, grinned drunkenly and wrapped their strong, rough fingers around their filled glasses.

"Waits for what?" Trixie asked, in one move corking the whiskey bottle, sitting it on the shelf behind the bar. Snatching up a clean mug, she stuck it under the beer tap and opened the tap with a flip of her hand.

"For me to check the till," Rose said, already reaching below the bar and flipping open the metal cash box.

Trixie sat a foamy mug of beer in front of Herns and watched Rose quickly count out a large amount of bills and coins. The coins he dropped into a leather draw-string bag. The bills he folded and stuck away somewhere behind his vest. "*Check it?* It looks to me like you're gutting it!" she said.

"I'm not leaving a lot of money in the cash box back here, in case somebody decides to rob us," Rose said matter-of-factly. "Now turn around." He gestured toward the shelf behind the bar. "Put your hands there."

"What?" said Trixie. "Jack Spain never

worried about the cash box getting *robbed.*"

"But he should have," said Rose. "*I'm* looking out for his interest. *I'm* taking no chances. Now turn around." He gave her a nudge as if to get her started.

"Turn around for what?" Trixie asked over her shoulder even as she did as he told her and placed her hands on the shelf behind the bar.

"So I can search you," said Rose, his hands already going up and down her sides.

"Hey!" said Trixie. "You have no right to —"

"Shut up!" Rose snapped, leaning against her, reaching up around her, running his hands down into the low bodice of her dress. He quickly ran his hands all over and under her breasts and under both arms. "From now on, I'm keeping a closer count on the cash box, and I'm taking money from it throughout the day."

"But you didn't write anything down," said Trixie. "How do you know how much was in there?"

"I keep it all written down right here," said Rose, tapping a finger to his temple. "Don't worry about what I write down."

As Rose talked, he continued searching. Herns' and the three miners' eyes widened as he hiked the back of her dress and ran a hand around inside her underwear.

"Damn it!" Trixie wiggled and let out a short shriek as Rose probed between her thighs. "I don't steal!" Trixie shouted. "Who the hell do you think you are, accusing me of taking something —"

"Aha!" said Rose, jerking his hand out and holding up a twenty-dollar gold piece. "What's this, then, you thieving whore?"

"That's my lucky twenty!" said Trixie, her voice sounding frightened, for good reason. "I always carry it there! It's sort of my good luck piece!"

Rose's backhanded slap across her face sent her flying sidelong to the wet, dirty floor. Before she could crawl away, the toe of his boot landed solidly in her stomach, lifting her and sending her three feet farther away. She landed doubled up, gagging for breath, her arms going around her waist. "I'll kill you, you gawddamn motherless —"

Rose stepped forward, ready to kick her again. But Stanley Woods, who had just walked in through the side door, saw what was going on and rushed forward, leaping over the bar. At the same time, Milo Herns scrambled up onto the bar top and flung himself onto Rose's back, seeing that Ned Rose intended to make good his threat. Together, the blacksmith and the pimp wrestled Rose away from Trixie and held him long enough for Margo to hurry around the bar and drag Trixie farther out of reach.

"Take it easy, Rose, please!" Woods shouted, Ned Rose slinging the two back and forth like rag dolls. Herns held onto Rose's back, looking like a jockey mounted on a raging wild horse.

"Easy! I'll give you *easy!* You *sonsabitch!*" Rose bellowed, finally flinging the two away and turning toward them, the big Remington out and cocked in their faces.

"Mr. Rose! Mr. Rose! Hold on!" Herns held both hands up in front of him, saying quickly, "I came here to do a piece of work, not to get my ass shot off! The safe, the safe! Remember?"

"Nobody grabs me from behind!" Rose said, with a crazed stare at Stanley Woods.

"You were killing her, Rose!" Woods shouted. "You would have hanged for murder! Is that what you wanted, to get yourself hanged? I did it for you!" Woods lied. "Jesus, don't kill me!"

Rose cooled down, thinking about the ranger and the marshal only yards away, across the street. He also thought about the safe full of money standing upstairs in Spain's room. "If you ever lay hands on me again, Woods, you're dead!" He took a deep

breath, turned his gaze toward the blacksmith and started to issue the same threat,
but something in Herns' eyes told him to
keep his mouth shut if he ever wanted to
see the inside of the safe.

"No," said Woods, "I'll never lay hands on
you, Ned. You have my word! Let's all just
settle down, for our own good. No more
threats."

"All right, then, no more threats. I'm
settled down," said Rose. He ran a hand all
over his face, let out a breath and let the
Remington's barrel sag toward the floor, his
thumb letting the hammer down.

On the dirty plank floor, Trixie lay gasping in Margo's arms. A trickle of blood ran
from the corner of her gaping mouth.
"Threats?" Margo said, staring hard and
cold at Rose. "Here's a threat for you, you
chicken-shit son of a bitch! If you ever lay a
hand on one of us again, I'll cut your throat
so deep, sun will shine out your asshole!"

"Margo, stop it!" Woods said gruffly. "Let
everybody settle down! Get Trixie a wet rag!
Please!"

Rose stood gritting his teeth, his big fists
clenched tight at his sides. "Gawddamn
whores!" he growled under his breath.

"There now, see," said Woods, "no harm
done." Seeing everybody hold still, he

scrambled to his feet, dusting his plaid suit and grabbing his bowler from the floor. Herns stood up beside him, dusting his shirtsleeves. "What's this about a safe? Is this something I can assist with?" Woods asked quickly.

Rose continued staring at Margo, the big, buxom blonde staring right back, her cold blue eyes shining like tips of dagger blades. "Yeah," Rose replied to Woods, shoving his revolver back onto his waist sash. "Where's Coots?"

"Up there, where I left him, recuperating," said Margo, grudgingly, answering for Woods.

"Get him up and dressed," said Rose. "Have him meet us in Spain's room." As he turned and walked toward the stairs, Rose looked back over his shoulder at all the curious drinkers staring at him. "What the hell are you looking at? Drink your gawddamn whiskey! Mind your own gawddamn business!"

"Yeah," said Herns, following along behind him, half turned toward the drinkers. "This is serious blacksmith work! Y'all go on and drink your drink. I got it!" He grinned, tipping his ragged flop hat.

Watching Woods hurry up the stairs ahead of Rose and Herns, Margo sat staring, Trixie still cradled to her large fleshy bosom. "I meant what I said, honey," she murmured in a tender tone of voice. "I'll kill him. I'll kill any son of a bitch who ever hurts you. You know that, don't you?"

"I know, I know," Trixie whispered, watching the men all file up the stairs to Jack Spain's room.

CHAPTER 6

In Jack Spain's room, Rose, Woods, Milo Herns and James Earl Coots looked all around, examining the width of the doorway and the steep pitch of the stairs. After a moment, Herns raised the back window, leaned out, looked down, then stepped back in and dusted his hands together. "Shove it out the window," he said with conviction, as if leaving nothing more to be said on the matter.

"Are you crazy, Herns?" Rose growled. "We can't just up and heave this heavy bastard out the window!"

"Why not?" Herns asked jauntily.

Rose thought about it, but came up with no real reason why they couldn't.

"Worse could happen is it busts open, which it ain't going to," said Herns. "If it did, your problem would be solved." He paused with a smug grin that quickly vanished as a realization crossed his mind. "I still get my twenty dollars though, for coming up with the idea that got it to open."

Without answering Herns, Rose turned to the teamster and said, "Why the hell, James Earl, don't you keep a load totter on your wagon for big objects?"

"I do," said the teamster, his shirttail still hanging outside his trousers from dressing in a hurry when Woods came and got him. "I'll get it ready." As he spoke, he walked over, stuck his head out the window and looked down. "I best move my horses and wagon just to be cautious."

"Yeah, you go do that, Earl," said Rose. "Once we heave this thing up and out, we'll need your totter ready down there to get this thing over to Milo's shop."

"Whoa," Herns said, squatting in the open closet door, where the three foot tall safe sat. "No need to get in any *big* hurry. I got to saw through some floor and wall just to get loose the bolts holding this baby to the floor." He sighed and added, "We got eight bolts . . . four holding it to the floor, four holding it to the wall. Spain must've feared we'd be attacked by Huns."

"Jesus," said Rose. Then he said with resolve, "All right, if that's what it takes, get to cutting."

"Don't worry. It's as good as cut already," Herns said, taking off his flop hat and pitching it on a wooden chamber chair. No sooner had his hat landed than he looked at the flies circling the seat of the chamber chair and snatched his hat up with a look of disgust. "Sweet Lord God!" He fanned his hat back and forth. "I bet this thing ain't been emptied all week! Spain is a pig." Keeping the chamber chair at arm's length, he dragged it to the far side of the room, then came back and tossed his hat on a cluttered wooden desk.

Rose stood with his arms folded, giving the wiry little black man an impatient stare. "Is there anything else before we get started?" he asked sarcastically.

"Yep, we need a big filled bucket brought up from behind the bar," said Herns.

"You mean water, to cool your saw blades in?" Rose asked.

"Hell, no!" said Herns. "I mean *beer* so I don't get myself into a too-thirsty-to-work frame of mind."

"Christ!" Rose said, turning, shaking his head. "Woods! Tell one of those whores to get up here with some beer. I'll be out back with Coots." As an afterthought, he said over his shoulder, "Tell them to empty that damn stinking chamber pot beneath the chair too. This room is starting to smell as foul as Spain himself."

"Will do," said Woods. He stood, giving Rose a dirty look as the short-tempered bartender walked out and down the stairs toward the rear door. "Bossy son of a bitch!" he murmured to himself.

Seeing the interaction between Rose and Woods, Herns looked up from where he sat squatted on his ankles and chuckled, saying, "Watch it now! Ned Rose is pumped full of himself. He's done took over here."

Woods gave the blacksmith a look and said, "If I want to hear any noise out of you, Herns, I'll rattle your head for it." He walked out onto the upper level and yelled down to Margo and Trixie, "One of yas bring up a bucket of beer for this blacksmith so he'll keep his mouth shut."

Herns shook his head and turned away, mumbling under his breath. Flipping open his oily rag, he examined his tools and dragged them into the closet with him. Crawling all around the safe, he found an access panel in the plank floor and lifted it. "Good," he said loud enough for Woods to hear. "I don't have to saw all these boards. When Spain's builders put the safe in here, they left an access panel to get to the bolts."

"Yeah, well, have at it," Woods said, unconcerned. He walked over to the window and stared down at Coots and Ned Rose standing beside a big two-wheel dolly they had taken from the freight wagon. "Rose will rob this place blind, and I won't get a damn penny," he whispered to himself.

In a moment Margo walked into the room, carrying a metal pail full of beer with a long dipper stuck in it and four mugs hooked on her hand. Herns had already lifted a small section of floor that allowed him to get to the bolts beneath the safe. He'd taken a file in hand and prepared to go to work; but he stopped cold at the sight of the beer.

"Come and get it, one and all," Margo said, setting the pail on the floor and the mugs on a small table near Spain's unmade bed.

"How's Trixie?" Woods asked, walking over and picking up a mug just as Herns reached in and grabbed one for himself.

"She's better," Margo said coolly. "If you're our manager, why didn't you beat the living hell out of that bastard? Isn't that what a manager does, looks out for his girls?"

"Margo, I got over the bar to her just as quick as I could," said Woods. "You were there. You saw me do my best."

Margo gestured toward Herns, who stood filling his mug with the dipper. "From the looks of it, this two-bit blacksmith got there before you did."

Herns started to take offense, but seeing it, Margo reached out and pinched his thin cheek playfully. "What about it, Milo? Want to manage us gals?"

Herns only grinned and sipped his beer, knowing this was no place for him to say anything.

"You did good, helping Trixie the way you did," Margo said to Herns, all the while giving Woods a sharp critical look. "Remind one of us to ring your bell for you."

"You mean *no charge?*" Herns asked.

"That's right, no charge," Margo replied. She grinned, turned and walked out of the room and back down the stairs.

"Hot damn!" said the little blacksmith. "It always pays to help a woman in distress!" He tipped his beer mug as if toasting himself.

"Get back to work, Herns," said Woods. "The sooner we get this over and done, the better."

The ranger set his plate back inside the large wicker basket that a young boy from Bracket's restaurant had brought over filled with food. Wiping his mouth on a cloth napkin, Sam stepped over to the window and looked out at the long shadows of evening stretching across the dirt street. Looking back around at Marshal Summers, he gave him a nod, letting him know it would soon be time to set their ruse into action. "What do your horses look like?" he asked the prisoners.

"Mine's a brown white face," said Denton, "has a bar T brand on him."

"Mine's a big, black-legged gray geld," Spain said grudgingly. "There's no brand on him, but a lot of brush scars."

"What about yours, Padgett?" the ranger asked when the young gunman made no response.

Giving a wary look, Padgett asked, "Why do you want to know what my horse looks like?"

"Just answer him," Summers cut in. "Nobody is trying to trick you."

"All right," Padgett said reluctantly. "Mine's the mousy-looking gruel standing out front of the Gay Lady."

"You've left that horse out there all this time?" Sam shook his head.

"My horse can take it," said Padgett. "I don't pamper an animal. I like to keep a horse tough."

Without responding to Padgett, Sam spoke to Summers loud enough for the others to hear. "I'm going to walk our horses over to the livery barn for the night and check on theirs while I'm there. I'll be back directly." He turned and walked out the door.

When Sam had closed the door behind himself, Summers waited a full twenty minutes, making sure he allowed Sam time to get Denton's and Spain's horses ready for the trail. Finally Summers stood up with the cell key in hand, took a last sip of coffee from his cup and walked over to the cell door. The three prisoners had finished their meals. Padgett stood leaning back against the wall. Spain and Denton sat on the edge of the cot.

"Don't get too comfortable just because you're fed and sober," he said, giving Padgett a look. "We're heading out of here tomorrow. So we're cutting you loose tonight."

Padgett straightened up from the wall with an astonished look, seeing the key go into the lock. "You mean . . . ?"

"That right. You're getting off this time. There'll be nobody left here to look after you. We don't have time to see whether the town of Cold Devil wants to hold the charge against you — like as not they wouldn't, anyway."

"Ha!" said Padgett, looking bemused at

Denton and Jack Spain. "How about that? I finally get a fair roll from these lawdogs."

"There's nothing fair about it," Spain grumbled. "If fair meant anything, they'd cut me loose too. My saloon helped raise this pig sty of a town from the dirt." He looked at Summers as the marshal swung open the cell door and let Padgett out. "Why the hell are we leaving tomorrow? Why can't we wait another day or two, give me a little lead way toward settling my business affairs!"

"The way the sky is looking, we need to get headed south down the mountain as soon as we can," said Summers, answering for Padgett's benefit rather than for Spain's. He closed the cell door and locked it, keeping an eye on Padgett all the while.

"What about my gun?" the young gunman asked.

"No gun," said Summers.

"What?" said Padgett. "That shooting iron cost me twelve dollars!"

"Consider that twelve dollars to be your fine for trying to kill an officer of the law," said Summers. "It's pretty cheap if you ask me. The ranger could have killed you out there, you idiot. If you had any sense you'd learn something from all this, but we both know you won't, don't we?"

"Any learning I get won't come from no badge-totting lawdog," Padgett growled.

Summers' hand went instinctively to his gun butt, ready to crack Padgett across his already swollen jaw. But at that moment, the door opened and Sam stepped inside, saying exactly what the two had decided on him saying when they'd made their plans earlier, standing on the boardwalk. "It looks like we won't be getting our early start tomorrow. Your horse has thrown a shoe, Marshal."

Summers looked surprised and disappointed. "I just had him shod last month," he said.

"Tough luck," said Padgett, smiling at the lawmen's misfortune. "I can't remember the last time I shod my horse, but you can bet he'll be ready to go when I *am*."

"Your horse is right out front, Padgett," said the ranger. "I grained and watered him and brought him over here. So get on him and get out of town before we change our mind and take you with us."

"I can stop for a drink at the saloon, can't I?" Padgett asked.

"No," said Sam, "not while we're still here. Get on your horse and ride."

Raising a hand toward them, Padgett said, "Okay, okay. I'm gone." On his way to the door, he said toward Jack Spain, "Who knows? Maybe these lawdogs will be around long enough to meet Waite and the boys. Wouldn't that suit you just fine, Spain?"

Spain didn't answer. Instead he stood up and moved to the bars and held on to them, a pleading look in his eyes.

"Well, so long *convicts*," said Padgett. Laughing stiffly through his swollen jaw, Padgett left, leaving the door standing wide-open behind himself.

"Listen, Ranger," said Spain, "since we're not leaving anyway, you've got to take me over to the Gay Lady and let me get prepared to be gone —"

Sam cut him off. "We might have done that for you, Spain, if you hadn't placed a bounty on our heads." Summers and he looked at each other, realizing they would be leaving town shortly after dark. "Everything that's happening to you here is your own doing. All we're going to do is take you in and let the court have you. Don't bother asking for special consideration." His eyes went to Denton as he spoke. "That goes for both of you."

Denton shrugged. "I never said nothing."

"Why don't you both get some sleep?" Summers said. "If the blacksmith can get an early start in the morning, maybe we can still be out of here by noon anyway."

"Yeah, right. Good luck getting *anything* done with this blacksmith," said Denton.

"You mean he does bad work?" Summers asked.

"No, his work is good, if you can ever catch him at his shop long enough to do anything," Denton replied.

"I see," said Summers, not really concerned since the thrown shoe story wasn't true anyway. "Maybe I'll get lucky and catch him in."

CHAPTER 7

Feeling certain that the ranger was watching him from the front window, Riley Padgett stepped down to the hitch rail without so much as a glance toward the Gay Lady Saloon. But as soon as he'd mounted and ridden to the far end of the street, he turned his horse to an alley behind the row of buildings along the main street and rode to the saloon's rear door. In the grainy evening darkness, Padgett didn't see the men struggling with the large object in the second-floor window until he heard the deep solid thud of the safe hitting the ground only a few feet from his horse.

"Look out below," Milo Herns called out in a halfhearted warning, seeing Padgett's horse jump sideways and whinny in fright.

"Jesus!" said Padgett, almost as startled as his horse and grappling to keep the spooked animal from bolting away with him. "You're a little damn late with your warning!"

"Sorry, Padgett," Rose said, standing beside Milo Herns in the open window. He gave a little chuckle. "What are you doing out of jail, anyway? We saw what the ranger did to you. Damn shame, is what it was." He couldn't keep from laughing a little to himself, drawing a peculiar look from the little blacksmith.

"They had to let me out," said Padgett. "They had nobody left here to look after me." Easing his horse a step farther away from the big safe and staring down at it curiously, he asked, "What are you doing, burglarizing Spain's room?" Coots and Woods had turned and walked down the stairs toward the rear door.

"Shhhh! Damn it. Keep it down," Rose said, as if afraid Spain might somehow hear Padgett all the way from his jail cell. "I'm doing him a favor, looking out for his capital, is all I'm doing — the way any good friend and faithful employee would do!" He grinned, knowing Padgett could barely see him in the dim evening light.

Shaking his head, Padgett remarked, "Damn. Don't ever feel like you need to do *me* any favors."

"Where are you headed?" Rose asked. "To get Waite and your friends, no doubt."

"Yeah, that's right," said Padgett. "I think

94

Waite will be interested in colleting that ten thousand, if Spain's *got* ten thousand that is."

"Who can say?" Rose shrugged, looking down from the window, wanting to stall Padgett as long as he could without it looking too obvious. "I'm glad to see you out and about. I was afraid those lawmen would haul you out of here, and you'd have to stand trial somewhere among strangers."

"A miss is as good as a mile. I'm out now," Padgett said. He shrugged, dismissing the matter. "You're supposed to be a hot shot with a gun, Rose. I'd think you was already loading up and oiling your drawing arm."

"I'm too busy keeping this saloon on its feet to worry about collecting the reward," said Rose. "But have no doubt I can take the ranger in a fair gunfight any day of the week."

"Yeah, keep telling yourself that," Padgett said skeptically. Looking at the safe, giving it some quick thought, he said, "I got my head busted, trying to kill that ranger for Spain. Maybe that's not worth the full ten thousand, but it ought to be worth at least half of it — don't you think?"

Looking at Herns before answering, Rose said to the blacksmith, "Get on down there with Coots and Woods. Get that thing onto the totter and let's get it over to your shop."

"Don't worry. Ain't nobody apt to up and run off with it," Herns commented, turning and picking up his mug of beer on his way to the door.

Turning his attention back to Padgett, Rose said, "Hell no, it's not worth half! It's not worth close to half. So, put any crazy notions out of your mind." Trying to sound official, he added, "This safe and its contents are hereby under my custody until Spain gets all of his legal problems straightened out."

"By Gawd, I'm getting something for my trouble," said Padgett. His hand went instinctively to the empty holster on his hip.

Thinking about it, Rose called out to him, "Climb down from your saddle. Help us get it inside. We'll see how much money is in there. I'm sure Spain wants everybody taken care of." He paused, then said, "I hope he's doing all right in that blasted jail, him and our sheriff."

"Yeah, as well as expected, I suppose." Padgett spit and stepped down from his saddle as Coots, Woods and Milo Herns came out the rear door. "I want something to drink before I lift a gawddamn finger. I got a taste in my mouth like I've been chewing on a wet sheep. My jaw's killing me where that sonsabitch ranger cracked me with his pistol barrel."

"Woods there usually carries a dainty-looking silver whiskey flask," Rose said, with a cruel grin. "Woods, give the man a drink. He at least had enough bark on him to make a *try* for the ranger."

"It's not dainty," Woods said in defense of his whiskey flask as he grudgingly shook it a little to judge its contents. "It's the same as everybody *else* carries."

"Yeah, every Saint Louis pimp and dandy man," Rose said with sarcasm. "Anyway, I'm coming down there. Let's get this job done."

Woods managed to keep his mouth shut and overlook the insult. Handing the flask to Padgett, he said, "I don't recall anybody ever turning down a drink from it. What do you say, Riley?"

"Give it here. I'll show you," Padgett said, reaching out eagerly for the flask. Taking it, he looked up and saw that Rose had left the window. "Pay no attention to Rose. He's just one more asshole in a world already full of them." He tipped a long drink, then handed the flask back to Woods. "God, I needed that worse than a boy needs warm socks." He looked at the safe on the ground. "Where are we taking this thing, anyway?"

"We're taking it to my place," Herns cut in, sounding a bit proud of himself. "I'm the one man in town who can open this baby."

"Horse shit," Padgett scoffed and ran his hand across his mouth. "It's almost worth staying sober just to see you try."

"Oh, he's going to open it all right," Rose said, stepping out of the rear door. "If he doesn't, I'll have his head on a sharp stick." Walking to the safe, he looked down at it, then up at the darkening sky, judging the weather. "All right, everybody get their drink swallowed," he said. "We're moving this heavy sonsabitch before it starts snowing."

"Snowing?" Padgett also looked up at the sky. "It doesn't look like snow to me."

Rose gave Herns a look. "You did say snow, didn't you, blacksmith?" he asked pointedly.

"Damn right, I did," Herns said in a cocky tone. "And when my big toe tells me snow's coming, you can get out snowshoes."

"It's never wrong, this big toe of yours?" Rose asked, in the same tone of voice, as if Herns would be held accountable for the weather.

"No! Never!" Herns insisted.

"Jesus," said Padgett, "if you listen to this

wind-blowing *negro* about anything at all, you must be as crazy as he is."

"Enough of this jawing. Let's get to work, snow or no snow," said Coots. He stooped down over the safe and placed his big arms around its edges, seeing how to best get a grip on the heavy cube of iron.

"A dollar says he can roll it onto the totter by himself," Padgett said quickly, feeling the long drink of whiskey ease the pain in his head and wrap him in a warm alcoholic glow.

"Go to hell, Riley Padgett," said the powerful old teamster, standing up. "Don't think I'm falling for that ole trick. That's the sort of thing you pull on a young greenhorn. I ain't trying to impress no-damn-body. Now get in here with me, all of yas. Let's roll it over."

"Can't blame a man for trying," Padgett said, leaning down over the safe with Woods, Coots and Herns while Rose rolled the totter over beside the safe and steadied it there with a foot against its frame.

"Can't we just heft it up onto Coots' wagon?" Woods asked, not looking forward to rolling the big safe all the way to the blacksmith's shop on the load totter.

"Maybe if it was empty we could," said Coots. "But this sucker is so full, we're lucky we can roll it over onto the totter, let alone lift it to the wagon bed."

"Jesus," Padgett said. "Cash money's not all that heavy. What the hell could be in it?"

"Cash is not, but gold dust and gold ingots are," Herns offered, seeing Rose's eyes glitter at the sudden prospect of a safe full of gold.

"You mean like the ingots that were stolen from the Blooming Mine shipment last year?" said Coots, giving a questioning look at the others.

"Watch your language now," Padgett cautioned him. "Let's not go making accusations we can't back up."

"No offense intended," Coots said, realizing Padgett rode with Morgan Waite, and that Waite just might have some ill-gotten gains stashed in Spain's safe.

"None taken," Padgett said, offering a smug grin.

From the window of the sheriff's office, Summers gazed out across the street and saw the torch light move into view from the alley behind the Gay Lady Saloon. Recognizing Rose carrying the torch, Marshal Summers said quietly over his shoulder, "Sam, come take a look at this."

Sam stood up from the desk chair and

stepped over beside the marshal in time to see the three men rolling and steadying a large object along on the load totter. Unable to clearly make out the safe in the darkness, even in the torch's glow, Sam said, "What do you suppose this is all about?"

"Whatever that is they're pushing, they brought it from the alley behind the Gay Lady," said Summers, keeping his voice lowered to keep from waking the sleeping prisoners.

"I see," said Sam, getting an idea right away. He gave a quick glance at the dark cell and said, "It's probably best Spain isn't awake and seeing this."

"Yeah, you're right," said the marshal, suddenly realizing what the men were moving along the stiff, rutted street. After a pause, during which the two of them watched the procession, Summers added in the same quiet voice, "It looks like they're headed for the blacksmith shop."

"That makes sense," Sam replied, watching the men struggle along with their load. "I suppose that's what the key among Spain's personal property goes to."

"This fellow Rose didn't waste any time going after Spain's money," Summers commented.

The ranger only nodded in agreement.

"This will keep them busy for a while . . . long enough to keep them from noticing that we're already gone come morning."

The two stood watching until the men and their load disappeared into the blacksmith's shop. Finally Summers said, "I suppose it's time."

"Yep, it is," said Sam. Walking over to the cell door, he stuck a tin coffee cup between two bars and shook it back and forth vigorously. "All right, prisoners, wake up," he said to Spain and Denton, who lay sleeping, Spain on the cot and Denton wrapped in a blanket on the floor beside it. "We've had a change of plans."

"What the hell?" Spain stirred first, rising sleepily up onto his elbows at the clattering sound of tin against iron. He placed a hand against the side of his bruised head and winced in pain.

On the floor, Denton threw off his blanket and pressed his hands against his ears. "Damn it to hell! Do you *have* to do that?" he asked gruffly.

"Now if you're both awake and paying attention," said Sam, lowering the tin cup from between the bars. "I bet you did the same thing a hundred times when you served as sheriff."

Denton let out a sigh. "Yeah, you got me

there."

"What change of plans?" Spain asked, coming up off the cot, running his fingers back through his tangled hair.

"We're leaving Cold Devil tonight," Sam said.

"Tonight? But for God sakes, Ranger!" Spain bellowed, getting a desperate look on his face. "You said I'd be able to go the Gay Lady tomorrow and settle up what I can before leaving here!"

"If we were still here tomorrow you could have," said Sam. Giving Spain an accusing look, he said, "But since you put that price on our heads, we decided it best to leave under the cloak of darkness."

"But I lifted the price on your heads, Ranger!" Spain insisted. "You've got nothing to worry about!"

"Unless some drunken fool like Padgett gets a lucky shot at us, not knowing about the bounty being lifted, or maybe not caring," Summers cut in.

"What about your horse, Marshal?" Spain said gripping the bars tightly while Denton pulled his boots on and prepared himself for the trail.

"My horse is much better," Summers replied in an offhand manner, gathering his rolled blanket and rifle from atop the desk.

"Much *better?*" Spain said. "How the hell can he be much better? He threw *a shoe!*"

"Don't worry about my horse," said Summers. "Worry about getting dressed. It's turning colder out there, spitting a little snow."

"Come on, Spain," said Denton, "can't you see that thrown shoe was just a story for Padgett to hear?" He chuckled. "They've been planning all along to leave late at night so nobody can see which direction we went. This is all because of you and your damn *reward money.*" He didn't try to conceal the contempt in his voice.

"But the reward's off!" Spain demanded. "You heard me tell Rose it's off, gawddamn it! Are you people deaf? There is no bounty!"

"Get dressed and ready, Spain," Sam cut in. "If you keep stalling and don't do as you're told, we'll dress you. If we have to, we'll tie you down over our saddle and let you ride that way all the way. Do you understand?"

Spain moaned and began getting himself dressed.

By the time both prisoners stood dressed and ready at the cell door, waiting for Summers to unlock it, Sam had carried gear and bedrolls out to the horses at the hitch rail and tied everything down into place. Leaving a lantern burning in the window, the two lawmen quickly and quietly cuffed the prisoners and led them to their horses through a light swirl of snow.

"Damn you to hell, Rose!" Spain growled under his breath, looking over at the rise and fall of the glowing bellows fire through the open door of the blacksmith's shop. "I'll be back, you son of a bitch," he said as if Rose were standing close enough to hear him.

As if in a taunting response, a hearty laugh came from the open door of the shop. Seeing that Spain was on the verge of bolting toward the shop at any second, Sam sidled his horse in close and took Spain's reins from him. "You'll get these back once we're clear away from here." Turning to Summers and Denton, he said, "All right, real quiet like, let's move out."

The four horsemen moved away in silence through a thin swirl of snowflakes, the ranger watching Spain look back every few moments until the glow of the blacksmith's fire became a small fiery glitter dancing in his eyes.

PART 2

CHAPTER 8

Morgan Waite sat tall with a dark aura of power about him, atop a big black and silver-streaked barb stallion. Looking out across the lower clouds from a high rock ledge, his dark eyes studied the content of the sky in a discerning manner, the way some mystic might study the inner depths of a crystal ball.

He wore his black but graying beard divided into two long braids, the ends of which were adorned with Cheyenne bead work. He wore a full-length grizzly-skin coat and a wide flat-crowned hat. A short eight-gauge shotgun whose butt stock had been carved down into a pistol grip stuck out from beneath his left lapel. A brace of matching Walker Colt horse pistols lay holstered on either side of his saddle cantle. A third Colt lay in a tied-down holster on his right hip.

"Beautiful, isn't she?" he said quietly to

Stanton Clark, who had just ridden up to him from where the rest of the men sat their horses awaiting him on a flatter level eighty feet below.

Stanton Clark said in reply, "Yes, sir, she is," yet he had no idea which *she* Waite referred to.

Waite could have been referring to the endless line of tall mountain peaks that lay obscured and ghostlike in a silver swirl. He could have been talking about the Earth itself for having spawned such a wonder as those mountain peaks. Or he could be talking about the weather, more specifically, the storm that lay churning and growing beyond the higher mountain range. Either way, the best answer would be one that agreed with him, whatever *she* he might be talking about.

"We've got a rider coming," Clark added.

"Yes," said Waite, still staring out along the mountains as if in awe. "Prepare the men to ride down and intercept him."

"Uh, they are prepared, sir," said Clark. "They're waiting on us." Looking all around, Clark wondered how Waite could have known about a rider on the narrow trail below. The trail on the other side of this high ledge could not be seen from this vantage point.

Waite turned to face him, as if Clark's words had just brought him out of some trancelike state. "Why didn't you say so in the first place, damn it?" he said. But before Stanton Clark could answer, Waite jerked the reins on his stallion and said, "Let's get under way."

"Yes, sir," Clark said, quickly pulling his horse out of Waite's path, noting Waite's eyes had suddenly taken on the fiery quality that always left Clark and the rest of the men unsure where they stood with their leader. "Damn!" he whispered to himself; he'd never seen a man's mood change so fast. One minute Waite could be composed and easygoing. But the next second, look out! Clark reminded himself, riding along behind Waite.

Without a word to the men, Waite rode through them and gave a swing of his arm for them to follow. His cousin Clement Sanderson sidled up to him. As the rest of the men quickly fell in behind him, a newer man named Ty Hall turned to another new man named George Trubough and said, just between the two of them, "What the hell kind of signal was that? I joined up thinking Waite ran this bunch like some sort of military unit, not a bunch of arm-swinging, sky-watching misfits."

"Luckily you didn't say something like that in front of Sanderson. He'd of already told Waite."

"I don't like this kind of setup, people passing words back and forth on one another," Hall said.

Hearing part of what Ty Hall had said, a man named Eddie Mosley jerked his horse back long enough to say to him, "If you don't like it here, Hall, maybe you best turn heels and ride out! We don't need harpers and complainers. We need men!"

"Yeah, then how the hell did *you* manage to get in?" Hall snapped back at him.

Eddie Mosley, not wanting to lag behind, cursed under his breath, but heeled his horse forward, following the others.

"Stupid little punk," Hall said, spitting as he watched Mosley ride away. Grudgingly Hall gigged his horse forward, Trubough right beside him. "His ma and pa must've met at a family reunion."

George Trubough smiled. "You're going to do all right with this bunch, Hall."

"Yeah?" Huddling deeper into his thick wool coat, a wool muffler wrapped around his neck and covering half of his face, Ty Hall said in a drift of steamy breath, "I don't know about you, but I'm about ready to call this job off. I'm a mercenary — a hired-gun sonsabitch. I can live in any kind of weather that suits me. I don't have to be up here watching my piss turn into an icicle."

"Me neither," said Trubough, "but the fact is I've got some legal matters that need to be straightened out. These big ole Rockies are a good place to lay low."

"Yeah," said Hall, "if you can keep from freezing to death on the way to the jake." He kicked up his horse's pace. "I hate the way everybody keeps saying *Once winter gets here.* Hell, it's already *here,* folks! Look around, you idiots! For God sakes, cold *is* winter! The way they talk makes me wonder just how gawddamn cold it's going to get here the next month or two. I'm freezing my nuts off right now!" He nodded toward Waite at the head of the riders. "And here's this old Rebel bastard dragging us all over these gawddamn mountains like a bunch of gawddamn mountain goats. What is it we're doing anyway?"

"Patrolling, *he* calls it," said Trubough. "I figure we're just staying busy right now, keeping ourselves conditioned and ready for when we make a raid on a wagon train or an army payroll or whatever."

"Yeah, whatever is right." Hall gave him a sharp sidelong glance. "People's got better sense than to come through here this time of year, army or settlers or any-damn-body else . . . except us." He paused, then said, "All right, I see what Waite thinks. He wants men to prove they're with him before he takes them too far into his confidence. But spend a winter up here, dragging around, freezing? Hell, I don't owe my dear old *mama* that much loyalty, let alone Waite."

"I understand we'll be dropping down into Arizona Territory before long, do ourselves some robbing, then duck back up here and lay low," said Trubough. "That would suit me for a while."

"Yeah, me too, if what you heard is the truth," said Hall. "The way this is going, a man could make more stealing chickens."

"I hear you," Trubough said, the two of them hurrying their pace to get up closer to the other riders.

On the winding trail below, still feeling the numbing effects of whiskey, Riley Padgett did not see the nine riders until the sound of their horses' hooves came galloping around the next bend and appeared almost before he had time to slap his hand to his empty holster.

"Damn it," he growled to himself. He quickly tugged at his coat in an attempt to hide the holster from Morgan Waite until such time as he could ask around among

114

the men and borrow a gun. But his move came too late.

"Where have you been?" Waite demanded, riding up close and sliding his big barb to a halt. "Where's your gun?"

Two questions at once didn't rattle Riley Padgett. He kept himself composed and said in a calm, steady voice, keeping any whiskey slur out of his speech, "I've been in jail . . . Two marshals took my gun." As he spoke, he confidently lifted his hat and showed Waite and the men his bruised and still swollen face. "This is what they did to me."

"But they turned you loose," said Waite, not accepting anything Padgett said at face value. "Why'd they keep your gun?"

"Because they are no-good lawdog sons-abitches," said Padgett. "That's the only reason I can think of — that and the fact I would have killed them both like dogs in the street if they gave it back to me."

As Padgett spoke, his eyes moved back and forth from man to man, judging whether any of them showed any sympathy for his situation. Closest to him, Stanton Clark, Eddie Mosley, Ben Hevlon, Lode Stewart and PK Barnes sat listening with no sign of interest in their flat expressions. Behind them Hall and Trubough gave each other a look and shook their heads.

"When was all this, Padgett?" Clark asked, cutting in on Waite's behalf, the way he had started to do more and more lately.

Instead of answering Clark, Padgett asked Waite directly, "Did I miss anything important?"

Waite gave a shrug. "We chased a band of gypsies off the mountainside. Nothing we needed you for." Back to the subject, he asked, "When did you get out of jail?"

"I got out of jail yesterday. I spent the night at the Gay Lady," said Padgett. "Jack Spain is under arrest and headed for prison. So is Denton."

Waite thought about it for a second, then said, "Who's taken charge of the saloon?"

"Ned Rose," said Padgett. "That's who I spent the night helping. It took us and the blacksmith most of the night to crack into Spain's safe."

"Oh?" That piqued Waite's interest. It also brought a look of anger to his face. "That damned Rose, sticking his nose in." But then he seemed to settle and asked more calmly, "What was in it — any big cash to speak of?"

"Nothing worth mentioning," said Padgett, sounding disappointed. "I expected he'd give me a healthy cut of gold dust, is why I stayed and helped. Turns out there was no gold in it." He made a bit of a grimacing face. "Big cash? Hell, no. There wasn't over a couple hundred dollars, all told. Rose didn't give me squat for helping him."

"Serves you right for laying around there instead of getting on back where you belong," said Waite. "Fall in with the others. We're headed down to Cold Devil, anyway. I want to be waiting there when Raymond Curly shows up."

"What?" Padgett just sat staring at him for a moment, then said, "You don't want to go kill those lawdogs for what they done to me?"

"Not if it means letting Raymond get to town before I do," Waite said, giving him a curious look. "What's eating at you, anyway? I can see something's on your mind."

"What if I told you killing them lawdogs was worth ten thousand dollars?" said Padgett. "What would you do then?"

"Padgett," said Waite, stepping his horse closer with a dark serious look on his face, "whatever you're wanting to say, you best get it said. I'm in no mood to tolerate any hangover foolishness."

"All right," said Padgett. "The fact is, Jack Spain is offering ten thousand dollars to whoever kills the marshals and sets him free." He grinned slyly. "Whoever does it has all the way from here to Arizona Territory to do it in."

A murmur of disbelief rippled among the men. "Ten *thousand* dollars?" Stanton Clark asked in disbelief, giving Padgett a dubious look. "You don't know what the hell you're talking about."

Ignoring Clark, Padgett said to Waite, "I wanted to collect it — you know, for all of us. But I was too far gone on whores and whiskey, else I'd have killed them both. For all of us, that is."

"If you'd put ten thousand dollars in your pocket, we'd never have seen you again," Clark said to Padgett.

"Do I have to take all this *mouth* off of him?" Padgett asked, getting more angry by the minute.

Waite stared at him coldly. "Yeah, you do. So don't give him any trouble."

Ignoring Padgett, Clark asked Waite, "Spain doesn't have that kind of money, does he?"

Waite considered it, seeming to weigh his words carefully before saying, "He might, if it means the difference between him running free or rotting away in a prison cell."

"Then what say you?" said Padgett, nodding back along the trail leading to Cold

118

Devil. "It's all ours for the taking. Track them two down, kill them and come on back before Raymond Curly shows up."

"Who are these marshals?" Waite asked.

"A couple of nobodies," said Padgett. "At least nobody any of us are worried about, eh, pals?" he called out to the other men. The men only sat staring at him, awaiting Waite's thoughts on the matter.

"Who are they?" Waite asked again, in a stronger tone of voice.

"Summers is one," said Padgett. "Pe—"

"I've heard of him," Clark said, cutting him off before he'd gotten the name out of his mouth.

"Like hell, you have," said Padgett.

"Like hell, *I have*," said Clark. "Pete Summers is an ace lawman. He rides a white-stocking roan." He looked at Padgett. "You was going to say *Pete* Summers, wasn't you, not Joe or Bob?"

Padgett's face reddened. "All right, so you've heard of him. Does that make him the bad hog at the trough? I don't think so." He looked away from Clark and back to Waite. "The fact is, he didn't even come out and face me. He sent the other fellow — an Arizona Ranger named Burrack."

"Jesus!" Clark cut in. "Sam Burrack! No wonder Summers didn't come out with him. Sam Burrack didn't need no help!"

"If he's so damn tough, how come I'm alive and talking about it?" Padgett asked, his anger ready to boil over in spite of Clark being Waite's right-hand man.

"You want the simple fact?" said Clark, looking at the bruised welt along Padgett's jawline. "He must've figured you wasn't worth killing."

Muffled laughter came from the gathered men. Seeing the rage in Padgett's eyes, Waite cut in, taking control, "You picked a couple of hard sonsabitches to tangle with, Riley. I'll give you that." He looked Padgett up and down with a trace of a smile. "Can't nobody say you're not game for a fight. I've heard a lot of stories about Sam Burrack."

"Yeah?" said Padgett, getting his temper in check. "Are we afraid of him and Summers? All of us against them two?"

"Naw," said Waite. "They're just two more lawdogs, far as I'm concerned." He looked at Clark and said, "Ten thousands dollars is lot of money. I expect a man might have to put in some work to collect it." His eyes went to the other men. "What say, men? Want to go kill a couple of *dogs* before we head down to the ruts? It shouldn't take long to get it done."

"They'll have a big head start on us by

the time we get to Cold Devil," Clark cut in.

"I figure they might," said Waite, seeing the men nod their approval. "But it's a good enough place to start." He reined his horse around on the trail toward Cold Devil.

Clark reined his horse right alongside him. He shook his head and murmured to himself, "Damn Riley Padgett. I hope he ain't getting us killed."

CHAPTER 9

By morning the falling snow had grown heavier and started to cling and gather on the branches of pine and juniper alongside the switchback trails. Traveling through the night, the marshals and their two prisoners had felt a strong rumbling in the ground beneath their horses' hooves. But it was only with the break of dawn when they arrived at the mouth of the pass that they realized what had caused the disturbance.

In the falling snow, instead of seeing the mouth to the pass they needed to take, the marshals sat staring at an insurmountable hillside of broken boulders, loose rock, and freshly snapped tree trunks, all of it covered now with a thin white blanket. "A rock slide," Summers said. "Of all places." Looking around the rocky snow-streaked mountains, he added, "Of all times."

Sam sat watching a small clump of pines less than fifty yards away along the rocky hillside.

"Looks like we're headed out through Cold Devil after all," Spain said smugly, giving Denton a slight grin, the two of them sitting handcuffed in front of the lawmen.

"Over there," Sam said to Summers. "I saw something move."

"Probably a big ole grizzly," Spain cut in with a dark chuckle, finding delight in the two lawmen's sudden dilemma.

"Not another word from you, Spain," Sam warned him, still watching the spot where he had seen something moving up toward them over the rocks. "You might want to remind yourself that whatever fix we find ourselves in, you're right there with us."

Spain's grin faded. The four of them turned their attention in the same direction. In a moment, a long red cape stepped into sight as a young woman with long, raven-colored hair struggled over a broken boulder. "Well, my goodness," said Denton. "What's she doing out here?"

"You keep quiet too," Summers said to Denton, looking all around beyond the woman into the stand of pines. "What do you think, Sam?" he said. "Is this a trick of some sort?"

"I don't think so," said Sam. "It's too soon for anybody from Cold Devil to get around us and set us up." Seeing the young woman's steps falter, Sam gave his Appaloosa a nudge and said to Summers, "Keep me covered. I'll go get her."

Even as he'd gotten a start toward the woman, she stepped up onto a large rock and waved her arms back and forth, calling out, "Hello the trail! Help us over here! Please help us!"

Upon seeing the ranger riding toward her, she dropped her arms and stood weaving unsteadily, watching him until he brought the Appaloosa to a halt beside the large rock, then stepped over onto it from his saddle in time to catch her in his arms before she toppled forward. "Easy, ma'am. I've got you," Sam said.

"Please . . . !" she said in a faint and trailing voice.

The ranger swept her up into his arms rather than take a chance on her losing balance and falling before he could stop her. From atop the rock, he easily stepped over and back down into his saddle, cradling the woman on his lap.

Seeing the badge on his chest, she asked in a tone that Sam found questionable, "You — you are a lawman?"

Sam noted a hesitance about her. Taking the reins in hand and nudging the stallion forward, Sam replied, "Yes, ma'am. Does that present a problem for you?"

Her voice strengthened. Sam noted an unfamiliar accent as she said, "No, it does not." She pointed toward the stand of pine. "My grandzpapa is there, in our wagon. He has been sick, very sick." She hastened to add, "But he is much better now! You will see. Please help us!"

Sam looked down into her dark eyes, and it became clear to him why she had seemed hesitant at the sight of his badge. "Smallpox?" he asked.

"No! It is not smallpox!" she insisted. "They thought it was, but it is not!" She nodded in the direction of Cold Devil. "The sheriff and their regulators made us go away from the town. We were forbidden to take on supplies. We are over a week without food for ourselves or grain for our animals." She gestured a weak hand toward the rock slide. "And now we are stuck here, cut off from our caravan."

"We've sparse supplies, but we'll see to it you and your family get fed," Sam said, riding on slowly toward the stand of pines. Looking back over his shoulder, he signaled with a wave of his gloved hand for Summers to bring the prisoners forward and catch up to him. With a free hand, he

125

reached around the woman, lifted his canteen from against the Appaloosa's warm side and raised it up to her. "Drink some water?"

"Thank you." She held the canteen in both hands while he uncapped it. As she drank, Sam told her, "Don't get spooked when you see that same sheriff from Cold Devil riding up here in a minute."

"What does this mean, *spooked?*" She had stopped drinking and ran a hand across her lips.

"It means frightened," Sam said. "Don't let it *frighten* you."

"Oh, *frightened?*" She still seemed a little confused. Yet, looking back toward the three horsemen coming across the rocky ground, she stiffened and said, "It *is him!*"

"Yes, it's him," Sam said. "But he's in handcuffs now. He won't be giving you any trouble."

"In handcuffs?" she asked as if astonished. "He is now a *yronobho?*"

"Ma'am?" Sam asked, giving her a curious look.

"A *yron*— I mean, a *criminal,*" she said, correcting herself.

"I see," said Sam. "Yes, he has gone from being a lawman to being a *criminal.* He's going with me to face charges for breaking the law."

"It is strange in this country, how one day a man enforces the law . . . and the next day he is in irons for breaking it."

"Yes, ma'am, I often find that peculiar myself," Sam replied, watching Summers and the two prisoners draw closer.

"Well, I'll be horse-whipped," said Denton, riding in in front of Summers, seeing the young woman cowering against Sam's chest. "Now you've gone and killed us all, Ranger. This gypsy's whole band is infected with smallpox."

Feeling the young woman stiffen and tremble, Sam reassured her, saying, "Easy, ma'am. Remember what I told you. Me and this other lawman are in charge now." He turned to Denton. "How long ago did you refuse her and her people supplies at Cold Devil?"

Denton shrugged. "I don't know, ten days, maybe two weeks ago."

"If she and her people were infected with smallpox two weeks ago, she'd be dead by now — they all would." He looked at Summers and said, "Her grandfather is over in the pines. They need food and water."

Summers nodded. "Then let's get to him."

The young woman looked surprised. "You

mean you help us, even though we are not your own people?"

Sam gave her a slight smile without answering. Instead he said to Denton and Spain, "You two keep in front of us." To Summers he said, as the prisoners' horses filed past him, "We'll keep a few yards between us in case this is a trick of some sort."

"A trick?" the young woman said. "It is no trick that my grandzpapa and I are hungry."

"Begging your pardon, ma'am," said Sam. "The kind of company we keep makes us cautious of everybody." Even as he spoke to her, his eyes gave Summers a message to stay on the lookout for trouble. "Now, if you'll allow me to introduce myself, I'm Ranger Sam Burrack." He gestured toward Summers. "This is Federal Marshal Pete Summers."

"Ma'am." Summers tipped his hat as they followed along behind the two prisoners.

"I am Trina Yergizvich," the woman said, her voice taking on another weak tone as a renewed wave of hunger swept over her.

"Where are you from, Miss Trina?" Summers asked, not attempting to pronounce her last name.

"We — that is, my grandzpapa, our caravan and I — have traveled here from Romania and Russia. But we are from no particular place. We travel very much. . . ." Her voice trailed, as if too tired to continue.

"I understand. You rest for now," Summers said, not wanting to encourage any more conversation until she had eaten and regained her strength.

"They're gypsies," Denton injected, sitting with his cuffed hands resting on his saddle horn. "That was as good a reason for chasing them away from Cold Devil as the smallpox, far as I'm concerned."

The young woman only stared at him, her eyes growing blank as another wave of weakness stirred in her empty stomach.

"Pay him no mind, ma'am," Sam said to the woman cradled against his chest. He gave Denton a hard look and nudged the Appaloosa forward.

Twenty yards inside the cover of the towering pines, Sam spotted the ornate but faded travel wagon sitting with its tongue lying on the ground. A few feet away from the wagon two horses stood scraping away a light covering of snow, grazing on a few thin blades of dead wild grass. As the two prisoners approached the wagon, an old man stepped down from a rear door with a shotgun in hand. Standing on wobbly legs, with much effort, he shouted in a language no one except the young woman understood.

"Grandzpapa, please!" Trina called out to him, seeing him raise the shotgun toward Max Denton. Then she called out in their native tongue, telling him what the ranger had told her about Denton.

"A *criminal?*" the old man asked in broken English. He lowered the shotgun a few inches with an astonished look on his gaunt, weathered face. "How can this be?"

"It's a long story, sir," Sam said respectfully. Lowering Trina to the ground, where her frail grandfather took her arm as if he might steady her, Sam stepped down from his saddle. With a gesture from Marshal Summers, Denton and Spain both stepped down. Summers waited until last, then stepped down from his saddle, rifle in hand, keeping close watch on the two prisoners.

"Sit, Grandzpapa," Trina said, gently lowering the old man onto his thin haunches and taking his hand off her arm. "They have food to share with us. I must add wood to the fire."

An hour later Trina and her grandfather had eaten a hot meal of pemmican, beans and jerked meat heated over their crackling campfire. While the two sat sipping their second cup of hot coffee, Sam walked over, grained both of their horses and tied them to a tree to keep them from following the grain sack in his hand. "We'll wait a hour and feed them some more," he said walking back to the campfire through the light swirling snow to where the old man sat telling Marshal Summers what had happened to their caravan. A few feet away sat the two prisoners, Denton listening skeptically, Spain looking sullen and bitter.

The old man, his granddaughter and Summers looked up at Sam and nodded. Then the old man continued, saying to Summers, and now Sam as well, "We were already hungry when the sheriff-*criminal* there denied us the supplies we needed." He gestured a bony thumb toward Denton. "We left Cold Devil hungry, with weak horses."

"Where's the rest of your caravan?" Sam asked, picking up his tin cup of hot coffee and taking a seat on the ground beside Summers.

"They had to go on without us," Trina said. Her hands were cupped around a thick coffee mug she'd brought from their wagon.

"I am old and I needed to rest, so we pulled off of the trail here while the others went on through the pass," said her grand-father. "We would have caught up to them today." He shrugged. "But who knew that in the night the rocks would fall and close off the pass?"

The two lawmen only shook their heads. All around them the snow fell and swirled, growing a bit thicker now than it had been.

"But that moment of trouble has passed," the old man said, grinning. "I give to each of you a blessing for saving the lives of my granddaughter, and myself, and *most importantly,* the lives of our horses, for they are truly *innocent* creatures, the ones who live and die by the will of others." He made a sign in the air with his bony hands, then pressed them to his sunken chest, closed his eyes and murmured something in his native tongue.

Seeing the curious looks on the two lawmen's faces, Trina said, "He is speaking to the good spirits on your behalf. He prays to them that they will protect your path and that each of you will *live* without fear as men . . . and *die* without fear as saints."

Out of respect, and for reasons he could not explain, the ranger reached up, took off his pearl gray sombrero and said to the old man, "We're honored, sir." Beside him Summers took off his battered Stetson and

132

nodded in agreement.

"The part about being saints, is some big boots to fill" — Summers smiled — "but thank you all the same for the blessing."

"Hogwash," Denton growled, just loud enough to be heard. "Sympathy from a fool is an old gypsy ploy. They live for sympathy and charity."

Sam looked over at Denton coldly. "If these people had been allowed to get their supplies, thcy wouldn't be in this shape. So have the decency to keep your mouth shut, Denton."

"Ha!" said Denton. "Cold Devil is lucky this band didn't rob every henhouse and break into every store room in town."

Before Sam could speak the old man cut in, saying, "If I were younger, *yes,* I would have stolen what was denied to me by lawful purchase. A man must eat. If he cannot pay for his food, he must steal his food. What else can a man do?"

Spain cut in, saying with a dark chuckle, "Damn, Ranger, why don't you listen to this old geezer? Cut me loose."

"If you can't see the difference between you and these folks, I don't expect I can explain it to you," Sam replied, sipping his hot coffee.

After Denton and Spain fell silent, Summers said to the old man, "We're going to leave enough supplies to get you down off this mountainside, but how will you get around this pass and join up with your caravan?"

"We will pick our way carefully around the edge of the pass," the old man said, sounding confident. "These horses are weak, but in a day or so they will be strong and ready to travel."

Sam and Marshal Summers looked at each other, the shoulders of their coats wet from snowflakes melting above the campfire and falling like thin rain. "That's dangerous work, even on horseback," said Summers. "I'd hate to try to make it in a wagon."

The old man shrugged. "There is no other way. I must try to get around the edge."

"It takes the ground a while to settle after a big slide like this," Sam said. When the old man offered no reply, Sam and Summers looked at each other again, coming to an agreement without having to talk about it. "Maybe the two of us could travel with you," he said to the old man, not wanting to sound as if he needed their help. "It might be easier on all of us."

"But your prisoners," said Trina. "You must get them safely behind bars?"

"Yes," said Sam, "but we're in no hurry.

Our horses could use a day or two of rest."

The two lawmen knew they needed to keep moving should anybody be on their trail, yet they couldn't leave these two alone and helpless. "We'd appreciate the company," Summers said, keeping an eye on the snowfall, gauging it without allowing himself to look too concerned.

"Then let it be so," the old man said with a spread of his weathered hands. "We travel together."

"Good." Sam nodded, standing up, with Summers standing beside him. "I'll go finish graining your horses." Before walking away, he stopped, leaned in close to Summers and asked, "Is this snow going to keep us from getting around that edge to a trail?"

Looking up at the sky, Summers said, "Two days here will be cutting it close, but we should be all right. Getting around that edge is going to be tricky, snow or no snow."

"I saw elk track coming up. After I grain these horses, I'll ride deeper into the pines," said Sam. "We'll run short on staples, but I can fill us up with fresh game."

"I'll shackle the prisoners and keep them sitting near the fire," said Summers, looking warily once again out through the falling snow. "We're going to be all right," he said, as if reassuring himself.

■ ■ ■ ■

From over a thousand yards away, on a switchback trail of another snow-streaked mountainside, an old prospector shook his partner roughly by his ragged coat sleeve. "Damn it, Ethan!" he said. "If you can't see nothing, give me the lens!"

"Get off my arm, Al!" the prospector said, jerking his sleeve free as he lowered the lens and handed it over, rubbing his eye. "The snow's got too damn thick to see through."

"Yeah, you're right," Al Tabbot said after raising the lens, looking through it, then lowering it. "With a rig like that, at least we saw enough to know they ain't a mining company" — he grinned — "less the mine companies is turned to telling fortunes."

"Damned if them two in cuffs didn't look like Max Denton and Jack Spain," said Ethan Greer.

"Speaking of Spain, let's get the hell down from here and get some whiskey in our bellies," said Al.

"That's what I say," said Greer. He grabbed the lead rope to their pack mule and gave it a tug. "We'll take to the old mining trail."

"It could get awful slick," said Al, follow-

136

ing his partner.

"Then we'll slide into Cold Devil," said Greer. "It's a quicker trail, and I need a bunch of everything the Gay Lady's got to offer." The two trudged along the thin trail, the snow around them falling heavier in a white swirl.

CHAPTER 10

Stanley Woods looked all around as he climbed quietly up the wooden ladder to the hayloft in the livery barn. He high stepped through the loosely piled hay, carrying a clean change of clothes tucked up under his arm. Inside the bundle of clothes, he carried a bone-handled Colt .45 in its soft leather holster. Halfway across the loft, he heard a rough, shaky voice call out, "Who goes there?" from back behind a tall mound of hay.

"Carney! It's me, Stanley!" Woods called out in a raised whisper. "I had your clothes washed. I'm bringing them to you!"

"Come on in, Woods," Carney Blake called out in a hushed tone. "Hell, I couldn't stop anybody anyway, unarmed and in my drawers."

"I'm here to change all that, Carney," Woods said, stepping around the large mound of hay into the low glowing light of a coal-oil lantern. "I brought you clean clothes, clean johns and your gun."

"Thank God," said Blake, his voice trembling. "Have you ever tried staying warm with a lantern?"

Stanley handed the shivering man the bundle from under his arm. "Your gun's inside," he said, "unloaded of course, for now, anyways."

"That was a wise idea," Carney said, dropping the clothes from around the holstered Colt. He shook the chain attached to his ankle by a steel shackle. "I ought to be madder than hell at you for doing me this way."

"It's getting you sobered up," Woods said. "That's what you said you wanted, isn't it?"

"I was drunk when I said it," Carney replied. Laying his gun and holster aside, he took off his long wool coat. "You can't listen to what a drunk tells you." He gave a shaky sidelong grin, then stripped his dirty long wool underwear down as far as his ankle. Woods stooped down, unlocked the shackle from his ankle and stood up. Blake stared at the key in Woods' hand. He stripped his underwear the rest of the way off and pitched them away. Both he and Woods winced at the sudden sour smell in the air. "I need a hot soaking bath to sweat the rest of these snakes and spiders out of my belly.

Can you trust me that far, over to the bath-house?"

"Can you trust *yourself* that far?" Woods asked, toying idly with the key in his hand. He looked at an empty soup bowl and biscuit tray sitting in the hay beside a pile of ragged blankets. "You're still awfully jittery."

"That's because I'm freezing to death here," Carney Blake said, hurriedly putting on the clean long johns, shaking out his trousers and stepping into them.

"Then I expect now is as good a time as any to see how you're going to do *sober,*" Woods said. He put the key away. "If I give you your bullets, I don't have to worry about you shooting me, do I?"

"That's a reasonable question," Blake said, taking a second to consider before answering. Finally, he said, "I did mean it when I said I wanted to sober up. But I swear, if I'd known you had the key on you the other day, I would have choked you senseless to get my hands on it."

"That's why I didn't have it on me the other day," said Woods.

"Oh?" Blake said. "So you came prepared to turn me loose today? You're not afraid I'll go and kill a bunch of innocent people and get the sheriff hunting me for murder?" He gave Woods a sharp accusing stare.

"Sorry about all that, Carney," Woods said, looking sheepish. "I had to tell you *something* serious enough to keep your mouth shut. First day or two, I was afraid you'd yell out and get somebody to come find you."

"Well, it worked," said Blake, continuing to get himself dressed. "I don't know which was the worse: me being so blind drunk I believed I'd murdered a bunch of innocent unarmed people or the fact that I couldn't remember a damn thing about doing it."

"Yeah, that's the time to get yourself dried out," said Woods. "You come mighty close to drinking yourself to death."

Blake looked at him. "But I've got a feeling you didn't just sober me up out of concern for my health."

"You're right," Woods said. Then bluntly he asked, "Do you still think you can take Ned Rose down in fair standoff?"

"I see," said Blake. "You're wanting Rose killed." He rubbed his bristly beard stubble. "Yeah, I can take him, I suppose . . . if I wanted to." He sounded hesitant.

"What you mean, *you suppose?*" Woods asked. "That's no way to go into a gunfight!"

"Neither is this," said Blake, holding out a pale and trembling hand. "And the thing is, the more sober I get, the less inclined I am to raise up a gun and blow a man's head off."

"Jesus," Woods said, sounding let-down. "What about your big-gun reputation, all those men you've killed? How did you manage to do all that? Were you drunk or were you sober?"

Blake let out a breath and ran his fingers back through his tangled hair. "Well, I was 'bout half and half, I reckon. The problem I always had with killing a man is that even after he was dead I kept killing him over and over in my sleep." The expression on his pale face turned even more grim and tortured. "It got to where it took me all night to kill everybody over again. That's why so much whiskey. You could say it laid all the dead to rest . . . for a while anyway."

"Well, damn it to hell," Woods said, sounding disheartened with whatever plan he'd had in mind. "This has all been a waste of time."

"No, it hasn't," said Blake. "Give me just a little while longer. Buy me a box of bullets and let me get some practice with this shooter. I'll work myself up to killing Rose. It shouldn't be too hard. He's a no-good son of a bitch anyway."

"I don't want to cause you to go back to

drinking, Carney," Woods said, "in spite of needing you to kill Rose for us."

"Why are you so dead-set on killing Rose, anyway?" the trembling gunman asked. "I thought you made good running whores, him working the bar? I know for a fact you two weren't turning everything in to Jack Spain."

Woods gave him a look. "You have no idea what's gone on in Cold Devil, do you?"

"Not if it's something that's happened the past couple weeks," said Carney Blake. "I'm doing well to remember my name."

"Spain's gone to jail," said Woods. "Rose is running the Gay Lady, and you and me are going to kill him and take the place for ourselves, for as long as it lasts anyway."

"Whoa! Hold on," Blake said. "What are you talking about? Jack Spain in jail? Hell, he owns the sheriff here!"

"Yeah," said Woods, "but two lawmen just rode in, cracked his head and hauled both him and Sheriff Denton off to prison."

"Damn," said Blake. "I missed all that?" He shook his head.

"You've missed a lot, Carney," Woods said. "Let me fill you in while you get yourself dressed."

In Jack Spain's upstairs room at the Gay

Lady, Ned Rose paced back and forth, red-eyed and angry, slapping a leather-bound blackjack into the palm of his big hand. In a loosely formed line facing him stood James Earl Coots, Margo, Trixie and the blacksmith, Milo Herns.

"Where the hell is Woods?" Rose demanded. "Trixie? Margo?" he asked, looking back and forth between the two women.

"I — I haven't seen him today," Trixie said, her eyes shying down away from Rose's piercing stare.

"How the hell are we supposed to know where Stanley Woods is every damn minute?" Margo cut in. "We're whores, remember? Woods is our manager. He's the one supposed to be keeping up with our whereabouts, not the other way around."

"I wanted him to be here listening too. So later on he can't say he wasn't warned," said Rose.

"Well, that's just fine," Margo said. She placed a hand on her ample hip and jutted her elbow forward. "Come on, Trixie, let's get back to shaking gold dust out of these miners."

"Wait, gawddamn it!" Rose said. "I'll make this short and to the point."

The two whores stopped and listened.

Rose raised a finger for emphasis and said,

"I want everybody to know, if there's anything you've got to tell me, get it done right here, right now, this minute!" He eyed each of the four with suspicion as he spoke. "After today if I find out any of yas knows where Spain keeps his *big* money and you're not telling me . . ." He took a deep breath and let it out slowly. "Well, I'm going to hurt you in places you've forgot you even *had*."

"Tell it, brother," Herns said with a dark chuckle, his words inspired by too much whiskey. A half-full bottle hung from his fingertips.

"That goes for you too, *black*smith!" Rose said, jerking around toward him. "You're not off the hook here. If I find out you've skinned me some way, I'll carve souvenirs off you and sell them by mail order!"

"Hey, that ain't funny," said the wiry little blacksmith. He straightened up; his drunken grin disappeared. "I haven't been out'n your sight since we started on that damn safe. I got nothing to hide here." He stepped forward and looked around at the others. "I don't know 'bout the rest of yas, but I don't like to be accused of —"

His words stopped as Rose snatched him up and in one swift move stepped over and hurled him headlong out the window. Herns let out a short scream that ended in a loud thump as he landed on a pile of buffalo hides on Coots' freight wagon. Margo and Trixie gasped at the sound.

"There, end of discussion," Rose said, dusting his big hands together.

"Damn," Coots said, shaking his head, "if that negro is splattered all over my wagon I ain't cleaning it up." He turned and headed for the door.

"Where do you think you're going, James Earl? I'm not through here!"

"You said *end of discussion,*" said Coots.

"That was for the negro," said Rose. "I'm still talking here."

"Not to me you're not," said Coots. "I've done everything I came here to do. I got other stops to make, if your blacksmith didn't ruin my load."

"All right, go then!" Rose bellowed, seeing that the old teamster wasn't stopping for him anyway.

At the doorway, Coots turned and said to Margo, "Is my *five minutes* going to be good anytime?"

"Anytime, James Earl," Margo assured him.

"What the hell's he talking about?" Rose demanded as Coots walked out the door and out of sight down the steep stairway.

"It's personal," Margo said defiantly.

"There's no personal business allowed here," Rose said. "If it concerns The Gay Lady, it concerns me!" He thumbed himself on the chest. As he spoke, he stepped dangerously close to the two whores. Trixie took a step back, but Margo stood firm, her right hand slipping inside her dress at her fleshy waist line.

"I said it's personal, Rose," she insisted, her hand closing around the handle of a petite lady's straight razor, her thumb sliding the blade open. "I've been tossing men long enough to know the difference. If you're not satisfied with how I conduct my personal life, let me know. I'll go down the mountainside, with Trixie right beside me."

"You can't leave," Rose said in a strong tone, even though he backed a step farther away from Margo's hidden right hand. "You both owe Jack Spain money."

"But we don't owe you a damn thing," Margo said, her voice just as strong.

"I'm running this place for Spain until he —"

"Save that horseshit for the rubes and flat-heads," Margo said, cutting him off. "You're taking everything you can get your grubby paws on until this house of cards collapses." She gave a wink. "Good for you. But get abusive with either one of us again, and you'll be out of the sex business, unless you want to run it by hand."

Rose clenched his fists, but he kept his temper under control. "I'm going to overlook you today, Margo. I know how tough you want to look to little Trixie there, show her that you're her big *bull* girlfriend. We're going to all three manage to get along here, for our own sakes. But I mean what I said about Spain's big money. If I find out you know where he keeps it and won't tell me, I'll do things to you both that you'd never imagine in your wildest opium whore dreams."

Margo chuckled. "If we knew where Spain kept his dust and nuggets, do you think we'd be standing here defending his money from you or headed for San Francisco to spend it?"

Rose cooled, knowing she made sense. "All right, then. Let's partner up," he said. "If I find out where the big money is, I'll share it with you. If either of you finds it, you share it with me — fair enough?"

"Please, Ned," Margo said, "let's not treat one another like fools."

"Listen, gawddamn it!" Rose said, starting to get angry again. "I want that gawddamn money!"

"Okay," said Margo, not wanting to push things any further. "But to tell you the truth, I'm betting Jack Spain never kept his big money around here. I'm betting he keeps it in a bank somewhere: Denver, Missouri, somewhere like that."

"There has to be ten thousand nearby," Rose said. "He wouldn't want me promising Morgan Waite ten thousand dollars unless he knew he could come up with it. He knows Waite would kill him."

Before Margo could respond, they heard James Earl Coots holler up at them through the open window. "Rose! Waite and his men are riding in. Better get out the good whiskey, not that grizzly piss you serve the rest of us."

"Morgan Waite," Rose said, a bemused look on his face. "Well, I'll be damned, speak of the devil."

"Trixie and I are leaving, Ned," Margo said evenly. "We always make pretty good money when Waite and his randy bunch come to town."

"All right, go on, both of yas," said Rose. "But if you know what's good for you, you'll make your money and keep your mouths shut. Don't mess up what we've got going here."

"You mean what you've got going, Ned,"

said Margo. "We always know what's good for us. Just let us do our jobs. You smart boys spend your time looking for the *big money.* We'll take ours ten dollars at a time." Settling an arm around Trixie's shoulders, she said, "Come on, hon. Let's go show them some warm skin."

CHAPTER 11

Morgan Waite and his regulators rode up the middle of the wide dirt street through a steadily falling swirl of snow. Beside Waite rode Sanderson, followed by Clark and Padgett. The last two men rode only a few feet apart, yet neither of them had spoken a word to the other the entire ride into Cold Devil. Behind Clark and Padgett rode Ty Hall, Eddie Mosley, George Trubough, Ben Hevlon, Lode Stewart and PK Barnes.

At the Gay Lady Saloon, Ned Rose saw them coming and stepped off the boardwalk into the falling snow with his arms open wide in greeting. "Mr. Waite! Gentlemen all! Welcome to the Gay Lady. Climb down off those horses and let's get you inside where it's nice and warm!"

Catching a glimpse of Woods and Carney Blake walking toward the mercantile store, Rose shouted at Woods as if Blake were invisible, "Stanley! Get over here and take all these horses to the livery barn! Come on, hurry the hell up!"

"He's got some nerve," Woods said under his breath, seething with anger.

"Hell, he never even sees me," Blake said, evaluating the information as he said it. "That might come in handy when the time comes."

"Well, that time isn't going to be while Waite and his men are in town," Woods said, handing Blake some change from his pocket. "Get yourself something to eat and a box of bullets. I'll jump through Rose's hoop a while longer until you get yourself in shape."

The two split off, Blake heading on to the mercantile while Woods turned toward the hitch rail out front of the Gay Lady. "Come on, Woods, damn it!" Rose shouted. "We can't have Morgan and his men waiting all day!" He turned a wide grin to Waite and said, "You don't mind if I call you *Morgan,* do you?"

"No, Rose," Waite said in a flat dry tone, "not if you don't mind me dragging you up and down this street at the end of a rope."

"Please, Mr. Waite," Rose said, his grin suddenly gone, his brow suddenly troubled. "I know Padgett has told you everything that went on here. I'm just trying to hold body and soul together until I hear something from Jack Spain."

"Yeah, I heard," said Waite. "Padgett told me everything." He looked all around the snowy street, seeing only a few wagons in town, only a few horses at any other hitch rails. Then he looked at the three crowded hitch rails out front of the Gay Lady. "With Denton gone, me and my men are taking over the law in Cold Devil." He gave a slight smile. "Padgett told me 'bout the safe, how you had the negro bust it open for you."

"Yes, I did," Rose said. "I had to. I need operating money. But there was not much in there, nothing at all like I expected. That's the truth!"

"Yeah, that's what Padgett told me. Lucky for you he was here to witness it, else I might think you was lying to me."

Woods walked up to Waite's horse and started to take it by it's bridle; but Waite jerked the horse away and said to Rose, "I'm betting we won't be here long enough to need the livery barn." He stepped down from his saddle, motioning for his men to do the same. "Everybody get themselves some whiskey and something to eat. But stay sober enough to ride. We might be leaving here real quick." He spun his reins around a hitch rail; his men followed suit.

Waite and his regulators spilled into the Gay Lady shaking snow from their hats and coats and stomping snow from their boots. All of the men except for Clark and Padgett went straight to the bar. Padgett gave a longing look toward the shelf full of whiskey, but he stayed beside Clark, the two of them following Waite purposefully across the floor and up the stairs.

"Wher— where are you going, Mr. Waite?" Rose asked, hurrying alongside him.

"Where does it look like I'm going?" Waite replied gruffly, reaching out with an arm, making sure Rose stayed a comfortable distance from him.

"To Spain's office?" said Rose. Then in reply to himself he said, "But, like Padgett told you, the safe is at the blacksmith's. There's nothing up here." They topped the stairs and walked to Spain's room.

"Good. Then you won't mind me taking a look," said Waite.

"Well, no, of course not," Rose said, falling a step behind as Waite stepped through the door into Spain's room. Clark and Padgett followed, pushing Rose aside.

Waite stepped inside the custom-built wall closet and stooped down onto his knees to the open panel in the floor where the safe had been bolted. Reaching all around back

154

under the floor until satisfied there was nothing there, he stood up and slapped dust from his knees. "Empty, just as I suspected it would be," he said in a half growl.

"Is that what Spain did?" Rose asked, stepping forward, looking down into the open panel in the closet floor. "He kept money and gold back there? Under the floor, instead of in the safe?"

Waite stared at him. "Jack Spain figured any idiot would look for gold in a safe. So he put it somewhere that would require a little *thinking* to get to."

A sickly look came to Rose's face. "But there's nothing there. So there's no gold, no *big money* after all?"

"Not here," said Waite, "but somewhere nearby. There better be." He wasn't going to mention that Raymond Curly would be coming to Cold Devil, and they would be splitting up a hundred thousand dollars' worth of stolen gold and greenbacks Spain had been holding for them. "Do you think Texas Jack Spain would be stupid enough to offer *me* ten thousand dollars, knowing he couldn't pay up once I killed those lawmen?"

"No?" Rose said, uncertain of what to say.

"You're damn right he wouldn't," Waite said. "I'd be real upset to find you or some of your riffraff has stolen money that was meant to be mine." He gave him a pointed stare.

"I swear to God, Mr. Waite," said Rose. "Ask Riley! I've been going crazy looking for Spain's money — you know, for operating expenses! I haven't found any!"

"He's right, as far as when I was here," Padgett said. "I saw nothing come out of the safe worth getting excited about. That's all I can say."

"As for this room," Rose said, "nobody has taken anything out of here! I would have seen them do it!"

Waite looked all around the room, stepping over to a door that led to another room. "What's next door?" he asked Rose.

"Nothing, just some stock, some of Spain's personals," Rose said. "But you can see, Spain nailed it shut."

Waite noted the nail heads up and down both sides of the door, holding it solidly shut. He turned back to the nervous bartender. "You realize that if I find out you're lying, I'm going to kill you real slow, *Apache style?*"

"I — Yes, I do," said Rose. "I expect I know that. But I'm not lying."

"What do you two think?" Waite asked Padgett and Clark, without taking his stare away from Rose's eyes.

"I sort of believe him," Padgett said.

"I say he's lying," Clark cut in. "Either him, or his pimp, or his whores, or his *negro friend* took everything and hid it somewhere else."

"The only person who knows for sure is Jack Spain himself," Waite said. "Looks like if we want to know, we will have to go save his sorry ass . . . just like he's wanting us to do." He turned to his cousin and said just between the two of them, "I want you to stay here, keep an eye on things. Somewhere Spain has our gold hidden for safekeeping. I don't want it leaving town on us."

Sanderson nodded and whispered, "Don't worry. Nothing's going nowhere till you get back."

As Waite turned back to the others, Clark said, still staring hard at Rose, "We could start carving on Rose and everybody else here with a skinning knife until we find out."

"No," said Waite. "By the time we do all that, the lawmen will have Spain out of our reach." He turned to Padgett and asked, "Which way did the lawmen tell you they were headed?"

"Straight down the trail, like I told you," said Padgett, "just as soon as they got Marshal Summers' horse shod."

"Horse slipped a shoe, huh?" Waite asked, looking dubious about the matter.

"Yes, that was the jist of it," Padgett said.

"Better go get that negro blacksmith, Rose," Waite said. "We'll see if he really shod a horse for the lawmen."

Rose looked embarrassed. "Uh, Herns is not feeling so good, Mr. Waite."

"He's not? What's wrong with him?" Waite asked in a demanding voice.

"He's — uh — I'm afraid he fell out the window," Rose said reluctantly. "But he didn't shoe any horses. He was with me all night working on the safe, and the next day the lawmen were gone."

"He fell out the window?" Waite looked doubtful.

"He was *thrown* out the window," Margo said, walking into the room, a hand on her broad hip. She nodded at the window on the back wall, then added, "That very window to be exact."

Waite stepped over and looked down at the cold, hard ground below through the falling snow. "That's quite a drop from here." He looked at Rose as if he didn't have to be told who had thrown the blacksmith out the window. "He's lucky to be alive."

"His head's swollen twice its size," Margo cut in, giving Rose an accusing look.

158

"Why aren't you down there taking care of Mr. Waite's men?" Rose snapped at her, hoping to shut her up.

"They all said Morgan here gave them orders to eat up and drink up," said Margo. "I came up to ask why they can't jump in bed with me or Trixie and get the snow shook off their branches — so to speak."

"You call him *Mr. Waite!*" Rose reprimanded her in a harsh tone.

"Why?" said Margo. "I always call him *Morgan.*" She gave Waite a coy smile. "What about it, Morgan? Why can't your men spend a little time with us? Trixie and me have to make a living too, you know."

"I'm sorry, Margo," said Waite, his hard demeanor seeming to soften. "We're on the move right now. Next time through we'll all make up for it."

"What about your cousin Clement here," she asked, sidling up close to Clement Sanderson. "He looks like he could use a good —"

"Sorry, Margo, not this trip," Waite said, cutting her short. "I'm leaving here to look after my interests."

But Sanderson managed to give her a guarded wink that said otherwise as Waite turned to Rose, his hard demeanor coming back to him. "You're sure he didn't shod the lawman's horse for him?"

"Yes, I'm sure," Rose said. "We can go ask him. He's not that broken up. He can still talk."

"No, we're riding out right now before the snow blocks the high passes."

"The high passes?" Padgett asked. "But I told you, they were headed down to the flat lands."

"So they said," Waite replied. "But that was only a ruse. That's what they hoped you'd tell me, to keep us going in the wrong direction. I'm saying they took the high trail long enough to swing around and go down on the other side of the mountain. If I was them, that's what I would do, knowing there was ten thousand dollars on my head."

"But this snow," Padgett said. "It's going to be hard going on the high switchbacks, if that's even the way they went in the first place!"

"Then let's not waste time," Waite said. "I know a couple of shortcuts on the way there." He nodded in the direction of the higher mountain line, then said to both Padgett and Clark, "Get us some grub, some coffee and fresh horses. I calculate we'll catch up to them in a day if we push it."

Even as Waite spoke, Ty Hall pushed the

two old prospectors, Al Tabbot and Ethan Greer, into the room ahead of him.

"What the hell is this?" Waite roared, seeing the two old men stumble to a halt and hold on to each other to keep from falling.

"I don't want to interrupt here," Hall said, "but these old goats come in talking about seeing Spain and the sheriff up in the high passes yesterday. Thought you'd want to hear it."

"You're damn right I want to hear it!" Waite said, getting excited. "How far up?"

"We didn't say it meaning to cause any trouble!" said Al Tabbot, looking shaky and scared. "All we meant was to pass along the latest news!"

"All right, all right!" Waite said. "There's no trouble. Start talking."

Ethan Greer said reluctantly, "We saw two lawmen and Spain and Denton. A rock slide had them stuck at a blind pass — them and a gypsy wagon."

"Stuck at a rock slide, eh?" Waite said, a slight grin coming to his face. "You mean Thunder Pass?"

"Yep," said Tabbot, "that's the pass all right. From the looks of it, they'll be there for a spell."

"Those same gypsies," Clark said, recalling their last encounter with the caravan.

161

"Now they've teamed up with the law."

"No, this is just one wagon," Tabbot said, "not a whole caravan."

"Just one single wagon?" Waite contemplated, scratching his chin.

Rose cut in, saying, "A few days back, Sheriff Denton chased a caravan of gypsies away from here. Said he sent them on their way because one of them was down with the smallpox."

"Smallpox," Waite said. "A band of gypsies carrying smallpox up over the mountains . . . and a couple of no-good lawdogs helping them spread the disease." He looked at Clark, then at Padgett. "I think that alone gives us regulators good reason to be on their trail."

"Sounds right to me," Clark said firmly.

Waite cut a hard stare at Padgett. "Well, then, Riley, any more doubts on which way the lawmen headed when they left here?"

"No." Padgett shook his head in submission. "It looks like you were right."

"You're damn right, I'm *right!*" Waite roared. "Now what are you waiting for?" he demanded. "Get those supplies and horses rounded up. Get the men gathered up and in the saddle." His grin widened. "We'll ride all night and be down their shirts come morning. We've got the best reason in the world to hunt down and kill these disease-spreading lawdogs."

CHAPTER 12

The ranger sat quietly behind the cover of a large sunken boulder that lay half covered by snow. He watched a herd of elk sixty yards away move in a line from one stand of pine to another, making its way silently, ghostlike through a white snowy mist. When a young stag came into his sights, Sam squeezed the trigger on his repeating rifle and watched the animal falter, drop down onto its front knees, then roll over on its side.

Standing from behind his cover, Sam looked all around as the echo of his shot resounded off into the endless distance. In the snow before him the young stag lay as still as stone, the only movement a flutter of fur in a light passing breeze. The rest of the herd had vanished, without a sound, without a second of hesitation. Before walking over to claim his kill, the ranger went first to the edge of a thin wood line, unhitched his Appaloosa and led the big stallion by his reins.

A half mile away, Max Denton looked toward the sound of the shot and said, "I hope that means what I think it means. A good hot meal of venison or elk would smooth out some rough spots in my belly about now."

Jack Spain looked over at Summers, who sat sipping a cup of coffee on the other side of the fire. "While you and that ranger go giving out our supplies like we own a storehouse, I hope you realize that anything could happen going down these slopes this time of year. We could get laid up and need every bean and crumb."

"Sam is bringing us something in," Summers said. "He wouldn't pull the trigger if there wasn't something in his sights." He raised his tin coffee cup toward Spain as if in a toast. "You two put some more wood on the fire."

Hearing the wagon door creak open, Summers glanced over to where the young woman stepped down to the snow-covered ground and walked toward the fire. "I heard gunfire," she said, looking off in the direction of the rifle shot.

"Nothing to worry about, ma'am," Summers said, seeing the troubled look on her face. "I expect that was our dinner calling out to us." He offered a smile but the woman did not seem to understand his meaning.

Trina walked up close to him and stooped down, pulling her wool blanket snug around her. "I thought perhaps it was the regulators we came upon — the ones who chased our caravan across the valley." She gestured a nod off toward an unseen valley in the distance.

Summers had reached out and filled a cup with steaming coffee. "No, ma'am, I doubt that," he said, passing the cup to her.

She wore fingerless gloves and wrapped both hands around the hot cup for its warmth. "Always it is the same wherever we go," she said. "There are always regulators, sheriffs, night riders." She shook her head slowly, staring into the dancing flames as if searching for answers in the fire's glowing belly. "It is our curse, the curse of the *Romas.*"

To change the subject, Summers asked, "How is your grandfather today?"

"He still rests, but his strength is back," Trina said, acknowledging his attempt to lighten her spirits. She gave a tired smile. "He is most grateful to you and the ranger for all that you have done for us."

Summers only nodded and sipped his coffee. Around them the snowfall increased.

By the time Sam led the Appaloosa into sight with the young stag lying across the saddle, night had seeped across the sky. Meeting him inside the dome of firelight, Summers helped him pull the stag to the ground a few yards from the fire. "How does the trail look around there?" Summers asked.

"There's a foot of snow in some places where its banking up," said Sam. "I'm afraid it's not going to get any better for a while." He pulled a long knife from his boot and threw it, burying it in the ground near Jack Spain's feet. "You two get this elk dressed out," Sam said to the prisoners. "What we don't eat, we're taking with us."

Spain grumbled, but reached down and picked up the knife with his cuffed hands. "How the hell do you expect us to dress an elk, cuffed like this?"

"You'll manage," said Sam. "Keep in mind, if you lose that knife, it's going to be awfully cold standing naked in this snow while we search your clothes for it."

"The way this snow is falling, you're right," Summers said to the ranger. "We've waited as long as we can. Their horses had all day yesterday and today to get rested. Trina says her grandfather has his strength back. We won't be doing them any favor keeping them on this mountainside any longer than we have to. Once winter sets in, it'll be spring before these passes and trails thaw out."

"I know," said Sam. "Let's break camp come morning and get that wagon around the edge of the pass before noon. Maybe the snow will have let up by then."

"Let's hope so." Summers gazed off into the white swirl.

An hour later the party had gathered around the fire and had their fill of roasted elk and hot coffee before retiring for the night. When the utensils had been cleaned and put away, Trina and her grandfather went off to the faded ornate travel wagon. The lawmen and their prisoners spent the night near the fire beneath two canvas-draped lean-tos they'd constructed the night before out of downfall pine limbs. Sam and the marshal took turns keeping watch on the prisoners, who slept beneath the other lean-to a few feet away.

During the night the snow stopped falling. An hour before dawn, Sam watched the first glow of sunlight seep upward, closer to the edge of the horizon. When he awakened the marshal and pointed out the quick change in the weather, Summers breathed a slight sigh of relief and stood up from beneath the low lean-to. "This could be the break we needed," he said, studying the grainy sky. "The snow's not finished with us yet, but while it's stalled, maybe we've got time to get around the edge and get these people and their wagon onto a safer trail."

"Yep," Sam agreed, also standing, his rifle hanging loosely in his hand. "We need to be packed and moving as soon as there's enough light."

While the lawmen and their party prepared their horses and the wagon team for the trail, three miles down the snow-swollen switchback trail, Morgan Waite and his men rested their horses on a rocky point. Staring upward across a wide stretch of mountainside at the glow of campfire light, Waite said as he patted his horse's steamy neck, "There's the entrance to Thunder Pass."

"Damn, we made it," Clark said, as if surprised.

"Yeah," said Riley Padgett, uttering the first words he'd said to Clark since they'd started riding up from Cold Devil, "and almost in time for breakfast."

But as Waite and his men sat watching, they saw the firelight grow dimmer and dimmer until the ridge finally turned dark. "Looks like they're heading out this morning," Waite said. "If we hadn't rode all night, we'd have missed them altogether." He gave both Clark and Padgett a look.

"That's a fact," Padgett said, agreeing with him.

Clark nodded. "If Thunder Pass is rocked under, they'll be all morning getting up the ridge and the rest of the day getting around it."

"That is, if the snow will let them get around it at all," said Waite.

"But so will we, won't we?" Padgett asked.

"No," Waite said. "We're taking one of the shortcuts I told yas about." He nodded toward a thin, steep path to their left as he backed his horse a step and turned toward it. "We'll split off here, swing around and be up above them before they reach the ridge above Thunder Pass." He grinned to himself. "I want Jack Spain headed back to Cold Devil and under my thumb just as soon as I can make it happen." He gigged his tired horse forward onto the steep path. "I know just the place to hit them."

At midmorning the lawmen and their party stopped in the middle of the snow-covered elk path they'd followed slowly since dawn. Steam puffed from their tired animals' nostrils. Upward, less than a hundred yards ahead of them, lay the rocky, snow-streaked rim of Thunder Pass. Sam looked sidelong to Max Denton, who he'd had walk alongside him while Summers and the other prisoner stood down beside the wagon, resting their horses.

"This is where it's going to get tricky," the ranger said, more to himself than to Denton. He stopped and adjusted the two lariats he'd taken from his and Summers' saddles and draped over his shoulder. He followed the elk path upward with his eyes, seeing only the trace of it beneath a foot of snow.

"Tricky?" the prisoner said. "I'd call this plain crazy!" His and the ranger's eyes turned to their right, looking out across a more than two-hundred-foot drop into the rock-filled pass. "These people should have had better sense than to head up here this time of year."

No sooner had Denton spoken his words than he looked as if he hoped the ranger had not heard him. But it was too late. Sam turned to him with a cold stare and said in a blunt tone, "You put them here, Denton." He lifted the rope from his left shoulder and began feeding coils of it from one gloved hand to the other. "These people would have set up outside of Cold Devil for the winter had you not taken it on yourself to chase them away."

Denton's face reddened. "I thought they carried smallpox. I was looking out for all the residents of Cold Devil. That was my job."

"Yeah, your *job*," Sam replied skeptically. "Strange how things can take a change. In Cold Devil your job was to harass these folks, accuse them of carrying disease and chase them away. Now your job is to step down here and help us get them out of the mess you put them in."

Denton clenched his cheeks to keep from saying something else he might regret. Looking away across the obstructed, snow-covered pass he murmured under his breath, "Damn gypsies."

Beside him Sam looked farther up the steep path for a strong pine tree. "Hold your hands out," he said to Denton.

"What?" Denton looked surprised, as if he couldn't believe what Sam was about to do.

"I'm taking your cuffs off long enough for us to rig up," Sam replied. "Don't think I won't shoot you if you try to make a break for it."

"Make a break in this weather? Hell, no," said Denton holding out his cuffed wrists, "not me."

Sam unlocked the cuffs and shoved them down behind his belt. While Denton rubbed his freed wrists, Sam took the other rope from his shoulder and handed it to him. "Go wrap it around that tree." He nodded toward a pine on the inside of the path. "I'll get the one along the outside." He nodded toward another tall pine, this one standing twenty feet ahead of them, clinging dangerously close to the rocky edge.

"You get no argument from me there," Denton said, eyeing the deep rock-filled pass beneath them.

Sam kept watch on the prisoner while the two made their way to the respective pines. Picking his way carefully along the snow-covered edge, Sam swung his rope around the pine, caught it and led both ends back down to where he and Denton both met again on the path. Their breath steaming in the cold, Denton glanced back and upward and said, "It's not only going to be tricky — it's going to be slow going, twenty, thirty feet at a time."

"Yep," Sam said, eyeing the prisoner, "slow and cautious. We should top up about noon, I figure, with any luck." The two trudged down the trail to where the wagon sat with its brake on and rocks propped behind the rear wheels as an extra precaution. "If you're ready, Grandpapa," Sam said, since Trina had told him that the old man answered to no other name, "pull forward on the ends of the ropes and we'll tie off to the frame."

Without answering, the old man nodded from the driver's seat of the wagon. He raised the traces in both hands, eased the brake handle forward and slapped the traces to the team's backs at the same time. Stepping clear of the wagon, Trina and the rest of the party watched the wagon rock backward only an inch before the strength of the horse team took hold and pulled it forward.

At end of the ropes lying in the snow, the wagon stopped. The old man sat back on the brake handle and locked it expertly. Carrying the two rocks, Summers and Spain chocked the rear wheels; Sam and Denton tied one end of the ropes firmly to the wagon frame and wrapped the other ends around the saddle horns of Summers' roan and the ranger's Appaloosa.

"Don't start getting homesick on us, Spain," the ranger warned the prisoner as he took off his cuffs so he and Denton could walk alongside the wagon, carrying the rocks they would use to chock the rear wheels.

Spain only grumbled under his breath, rubbed his wrists and stooped down beside the wagon, ready to pick up the rock when it came time to do so.

"All right, Grandpapa," said Sam, stepping back into his saddle. "Nice and easy does it." He and Summers turned their horses and put tension on the ropes as the old man released the brake and coaxed his horse team forward.

CHAPTER 13

At noon the ranger dropped onto a rock and sat slumped for a moment, too spent to bother brushing the snow away. "We made it," he said to Marshal Summers, who sat down on his haunches, coiling one of the ropes in his wet gloved hands.

"Yes, and I never want to do something like that again," Summers said. He nodded toward the two prisoners, who had shouldered the rear of the wagon on the last pull in order to get the vehicle over the two-foot rise at the crest of the ridge. "What about those two? Think we ought to leave the cuffs off them for a while . . . show our appreciation?"

Looking over to where Spain and Denton leaned against the side of the wagon, Sam said, "Yes. Why not? Them and their horses are both too tired to make a run for it right now."

In the front of the wagon, Trina and her

grandfather stood checking the team of horses. When they had finished, they walked over to the two lawmen. "Grandpapa and I will never forget all you have done for us," said Trina. "But now that we have crossed Thunder Pass, we must hurry and meet our caravan down there." She pointed out and down at the snow-covered land that lay far below them.

"We understand," Sam said. Summers and he smiled and nodded at the old man, who stood silently by, letting the woman speak for both of them.

"We will say a special prayer for the two of you, to protect you both on your way to where you are going," said Trina.

"Obliged, ma'am," the two lawmen said in unison, tipping their hat brims.

"You folks have a safe journey," Sam added.

"What she says, she says for both of us," the old man cut in. His voice sounded stronger; his face had regained some of its color. He reached out a weathered hand and shook hands with them hand-to-wrist fashion. "And the prayer of a gypsy is a *powerful* prayer. We cannot pray that you have no hardships, because toil and trouble are man's destiny. But we will pray that whatever hardships you have, you will overcome.

And you will!" He raised a finger for emphasis and smiled proudly. "On this you have my *sacred* oath!"

"What more could we ask for?" Sam said sincerely.

The lawmen and the prisoners watched the old man and his granddaughter step aboard the wagon and roll away steadily through the snow. "His oath, ha!" Denton commented. "His *oath* is worth about as much as —"

"As the *oath* of a sheriff who was on the run from the law?" Summers cut in.

Denton fell silent, but Spain cut in, saying, "Okay, now that you two tin stars have done your good deed for the day, can we get somewhere and build a fire? I'm freezing here." He blew his breath on his shivering cupped hands.

"Where's those wool gloves I gave you from my saddlebags?" Summers asked.

"I misplaced them over there somewhere," Spain said, looking embarrassed.

"Then go look for them," Summers said in a strong tone of voice. "You, go help him," he said to Denton, who stood huddled inside his coat.

Denton grumbled and walked away with a sour expression on his wind-reddened face. Steam rose from his shivering lips.

"These two are going to be a pain in the neck the whole trip," Summers commented.

"Yes, I'm afraid you're right," the ranger said, standing up from the rock and brushing snow from the seat of his trousers. "So let's keep moving. The sooner we get them behind bars, the better I'm going to feel."

The two lawmen gathered the tired horses and stood waiting while Spain found his gloves half buried in the snow. He shook them off and came trudging through the snow, Denton right beside him. "Time to get cuffed," Summers told them flatly.

The men grimaced, but held their hands out. When they were cuffed, Sam led their horses' reins while Summers mounted. Only then did he hand over the reins to the prisoners' horses and move back and step up into his saddle. Mounted, the four made their way along the meandering ridge line that only three days before had been a well-worn trail. Now that trail lay collapsed and crumbled, having filled the pass with thousands of tons of earth and rock.

They stayed in the fresh wagon tracks and followed them away from the broken ridge line until they came to a fork in the trail. "Well, there they go," the ranger said, nodding at the two furrows in the snow. To their right, they saw that the gypsy wagon had traveled downward around the side of the taller snow-streaked mountain lying before them.

"Yeah, they should be all right now," Summers said, gazing down and out across the rolling mountainsides to where three separate columns of campfire smoke rose from within a stand of pines. "There's their people waiting for them." At the edge of the pines stood a tiny figure waving a blanket back and forth at the mountain, as if seeing the wagon roll along high above him.

"Good," said the ranger. "Now we can move on." He nudged the Appaloosa, sending it up the other fork.

The path the lawmen and their prisoners took ran upward and parallel above the gypsy's trail. For nearly a mile, they could look down and still see the ornate wagon winding the trail beneath them before it finally disappeared and began its trek down the other side of the mountain. By then the sun stood halfway down the western sky and could only be seen through a low deepening gray. The snow beneath the horses' hooves lay thicker than it had been coming up the mountainside.

"We'll be lucky if we make it across this rim before nightfall," the marshal estimated, standing in his stirrups and looking out ahead of them across the unbroken snow.

"We'd best keep riding past dark until we do," Sam said. He also scanned the land before them, but it was the higher ridge to their left that drew his close attention. He looked along the ridge warily, noting that it ran the length of land they still had to cross. "I've never seen better ambush country." He gave Spain a harsh look and pushed the Appaloosa forward, pulling Spain's horse right along beside him, keeping the saloon keeper between himself and the long ridge line. Ahead of him, Summers jerked on Denton's reins, both lawmen keeping the prisoners close.

Atop the long ridge line, staring down through a field lens, Riley Padgett chuckled and said over his shoulder to Morgan Waite, "For a second there, it looked like *Mr. Arizona Ranger himself* stared me straight in the eyes."

Hearing Padgett's cynical tone, Clark said, "Don't get yourself seen, or you'll wish the ranger was all you had to worry about."

Padgett turned his eyes from the field lens to Clark. "You should've been born a woman, the way you fret so much."

Clark's temper flared. His fists clenched tight at his sides.

Seeing trouble about to rise between the

two men, Waite cut in quickly. "Both of yas, quit nipping and growling at one another. I'm sick of it." To Clark, he said, "It wouldn't matter if he was seen up here. There's nothing the lawdogs can do about it now."

"Yeah." Padgett grinned, handing the field lens to Ty Hall, who stood huddled beside him in the cover of a snowcapped boulder. "We've got them dead to rights anytime we want them! We could wave a flag and fire a cannon. It wouldn't change nothing."

Waite stepped forward from beside his tired, steaming horse and held his hand out for the field lens. "Let me see how our ole pal Spain is holding up." He grinned. "He'll be so happy to see us he'll likely fill his boots."

The men waited quietly while Waite looked down on the struggling lawmen and their prisoners. "I'll say one thing for them. They're smart enough to use those two for cover." A cruel grin came to his face. "But that's not going to do them much good," he commented, the lens going from Summers' face to the ranger's, both lawmen's faces partially obscured by the prisoners. "We'll give them about thirty more yards. Then we'll cut them down. We'll collect Spain and go home."

"What about Denton?" Padgett asked. "Don't we want to collect him too?"

"Yeah. Why not?" Waite said; he shrugged as if having all but forgotten about the sheriff. "If he's lucky enough to make it." He took the lens down from his eye and collapsed it between his gloved palms.

The ranger felt trouble coming as clearly as he'd ever felt it in his life. Yet there was nothing that he and the marshal could do, he reminded himself, except to keep pushing toward the other end of the exposed stretch of mountainside. He knew that had they not stopped and spent the two days with Trina and her grandfather they would have been beyond reach of anybody following them from Cold Devil. But leaving the old man and the young woman stranded at the closed pass had not even been open for consideration. The lawmen and their prisoners struggled on.

Halfway across the open land, Sam sidled his Appaloosa up beside Summers' roan and called out to him, "Let's trade prisoners."

Summers gave him a curious look, at first not understanding why Sam would make such a request. Then the realization dawned on him. Of the two prisoners, Spain would be the most important one to keep alive for the sake of anybody interested in collecting a reward. That made Spain the least likely to be fired upon. "No trade," Summers said, shaking his head. "Denton and I are getting along good. You keep Spain beside you." He nodded ahead of them toward the far end of the ridge line, which could now be seen. "Besides, we're halfway there and nothing's happened." He gigged his tired horse forward, pulling Denton alongside him.

Even as Summers' horse pulled away from him in the snow, Sam saw the back of the marshal's coat puff out as a shot hit him from a long, high angle, slicing through his shoulder and flinging him from his saddle. The sound of the shot trailed a split second behind. But the ranger had already jerked his rifle from its boot and yanked back hard on Spain's reins, causing his tired horse to rear and turn sharply in the snow, sending its rider to the snowy ground.

"Good shot!" Clark said, huddled by Waite's side as Waite levered another cartridge into his Winchester repeater. Along the high ridge, the rest of the regulators began firing, taking close aim through the growing afternoon gloom.

Clark, Padgett and the others fired at the ranger's Appaloosa as it bounded away in the snow, responding to a hard slap from Sam's gloved hand. A few feet behind the Appaloosa, Denton's horse bounded along as he lay balled down in his saddle, shouting up at the regulators, "Don't shoot! It's me! It's Denton!" Bullets kicked up snow all around him.

Having ordered his men not to fire in Spain's direction, Waite took careful aim toward the ranger and waited, watching for his opportunity. "Smart move, lawdog," he murmured to himself, seeing Sam drag Spain through the knee-deep snow to where Summers' blood had left a long red streak. "But it won't last long. You'll slip up and give me the shot I want."

Meanwhile, in the snow, Sam held an arm clamped around Spain's neck, using him for cover. He gave a quick look toward the Appaloosa, seeing the animal gaining distance between himself and the riflemen. Reaching down with the same hand that held his rifle, he grabbed the wounded marshal by his collar and began dragging him toward a boulder standing dangerously near the edge of broken land.

"Lea— leave me, Sam," Summers gasped, blood spilling down his chest. "Get on out of here."

"Hang on, Marshal!" Sam shouted, ignoring the lawman's words. "You're going to be all right!" He dragged him hurriedly, knowing that at any second a rifle shot could finish the helpless man. "We came here together, and we're leaving here together!" Yet, even as he spoke, he saw steam rise and curl from Summer's bloody shoulder as he pulled him behind the cover of the snowcapped boulder.

"Damn it!" Waite said, watching the long red strip lead across the snow to the boulder. He raised a hand to silence the riflemen, then turned to Clark and Padgett and said with a disappointed look, "It looks like we're going to have to ride down there and finish these two off firsthand."

"Yeah," Clark said, standing, brushing snow from his elbow. "He's going to do whatever he can to drag this thing out."

"It won't do him any good to fight us now," Waite said. He gestured his rifle barrel toward Denton and the fleeing horses. "We've killed his pard and set him afoot. We'll meet Denton on our ride down and get this thing over with before the snow starts again."

Ty Hall also stood up from his position on the edge and brushed snow from his coat sleeve. Standing at the edge, he looked down onto the blood-streaked snow. "The man can't have much fight in him . . . down there, surrounded, cold, no horse. He might just as well —" His words stopped as he bucked backward a step and staggered in place, clasping his hands to his stomach.

"Jesus!" Padgett shouted, hearing the rifle shot, following the immediate sting of Hall's blood across his cold face.

The regulators dropped quickly along the ridge and scurried back away from the edge. Hall turned on the spot, looking stunned, his lips spewing blood as he tried to talk but couldn't form the words.

"Lay down, gawddamn it, Ty!" Waite shouted in disgust at the dying man. "You've got nothing left to say! You gut-shot sons-abitch!"

As if following an order, Hall sank to his knees in the snow. "I hate . . . this," he managed to growl, making his last complaint before pitching forward and landing with a soft *plop.*

Without venturing any closer to the edge and giving up cover, Waite shouted out, "All right, you got one of us! So what? That won't change anything! If you're smart, you'll turn him loose! Either way, he's coming with us when this is over!" His words echoed out across the snowy mountain canyons.

A silence followed. Waite stood for a moment as if listening for a reply. When none came, he stepped toward his horse.

"Maybe he's hit too," Padgett said.

"Maybe he's thinking it over and deciding to let Spain loose," Clark said. "That would make sense, given the odds against him."

Waite had started to reach for his saddle horn when he stopped at the sound of a determined voice rolling up from the edge of the pass. "Come down and take him, Waite." Sam's voice echoed, seeming to gain strength as it rolled across the barren snowy canyons. "I'll be ready for you!"

"Hardheaded *lawdog*," Waite growled, shaking his head and stepping up into his saddle. Looking around at the men as they mounted, he said, "Mosley, Barnes. You two stay up here and keep them pinned down for us until you see we're closing in. Then come join us."

Eddie Mosley and PK Barnes nodded, drew their rifles from their saddle boots and stepped back away from their horses.

CHAPTER 14

"One false move and you won't live to see the outcome of this, Spain," the ranger warned as he attended to his fallen partner. He had leaned his rifle against the boulder, keeping it close at hand while he opened Summers' shirt and examined the bloody shoulder wound.

"How . . . bad is it, Sam?" Summers asked, craning his neck and trying to look down at the shoulder wound.

Sam noted that Summers had not lost consciousness even for a moment — a good sign, he thought, as he untied the marshal's bandanna, wadded it and pressed it against the wound. "It's hard to tell. The bullet's still inside you, Pete," he said, wiping his bloody fingers back and forth in the snow. "But you're alive — just stay that way until I can get you off this mountain and get you some help."

"Where's . . . the other prisoner?" Summers asked in a strained voice.

"He got away, but don't worry. He'll keep." Sam took off his own bandanna and cradled it in his palm while he filled it with snow and made an ice pack. "Waite and his men are riding down. Think you're able to hold a gun?"

"I can lift my sidearm," said Summers, running his right hand down to his holster and slipping his Colt upward with a shaky hand.

"That's good." Sam lifted the bloody bandanna from the wound and replaced it with the one filled with snow. "It's going to take both of us to hold them off." He quickly filled the bloody bandanna with snow and placed it back on Summers' gaping wound.

"Hold *them off?*" Spain said in a surprised tone of voice. "Are you out of your mind, Ranger? You've got to let me go! Can't you see that? There could be a dozen men or more riding with Waite. He saw through your diversion and came and found us! I win, you lose!"

Summers' Colt cocked and pointed at Spain from ten feet away. In his anger his hand appeared steadier, his voice stronger. "Don't count your winnings yet." His finger squeezed the trigger.

Sam shoved the gun away just as the shot exploded. Spain ducked over against the boulder, cringing, having felt the sharp draft of the bullet whistle past his head. "My God, don't let him kill me!" he shrieked, his face white behind his trembling hands.

"There'll be time for that later, Pete," the ranger said, giving Spain a cold stare. "Right now we best save our bullets for Waite and his men." He looked back and forth between the two men, then said to Summers, "Can I trust you to keep a gun on him while I check out there for our horses?"

Summers stared at Spain as he nodded. "You can trust me," he said, "so long as Spain keeps his mouth shut."

Sam stood in a crouch and moved around the side of the rock until he could look off in the direction Denton and the horses had taken. Seeing no sign of the horses other than their hoofprints trailing out across the snow, he moved back behind the cover of the boulder just as a rifle shot ricocheted off it. "If Waite is coming down, he's taking no chances," Sam said, huddling back down beside the wounded marshal. "He's got us pinned here."

"Did they kill our horses?" Summers asked the ranger, still staring hard at Spain.

"No," said Sam, "but they're gone." He

looked down the long jagged dropoff not more than six feet away. "Horses wouldn't help us. This place is nothing but a bare shooting gallery from up there." A hundred feet beneath them, on the steep, freshly broken land, he saw fallen pine and spruce stretched downward among rock, dirt and snow. Root balls larger than houses stood upturned from the crumbled mountainside.

As if trying to be helpful, Spain ventured in a careful voice, "If you had a rope you could climb down a ways." He gestured down to where a straight drop turned into a steep slide for another five hundred feet.

"Shut up, Spain," Summers said, giving him a hard, smoldering look.

Spain shrugged and tried to look sympathetic. "Sorry," he said timidly.

"Is that them, so close?" Summers asked the ranger, hearing what he thought to be the rumble of horses' hooves in the snow-covered ground. He leaned and looked out across the snow. At the far end of vision, he saw the horsemen began to ride down off the higher trail onto the long stretch of land. He saw Max Denton pushing his tired horse toward Waite and his men.

"Yes," said Sam. "They're wanting to get this over and get out of the weather, I expect." As he spoke, the rumble in the ground grew more intense. "But that's not horses' hooves we're feeling," Sam said, placing a hand on the boulder in order to steady himself.

"What the hell is it, then?" Spain gave the lawmen a puzzled, fearful look.

"I don't know," said Sam, "but it's powerful." He felt the large boulder tremble against his hand. Giving a glance toward the broken edge of land, he said, "We can't stay here. This edge feels like it might break away beneath us." He spoke in a calm voice, but the look on his face relayed the seriousness.

At the bottom of the trail, Waite and his men felt less of the rumble beneath them as they gathered and looked toward the large boulder in the distance. Dismissing the tremor beneath their horses' hooves, Waite grinned, nodding toward the solitary boulder. "Hiding places have gotten a little scarce since the landslide. There was a whole pine forest standing there our last trip through here." He drew his rifle from his saddle boot. "So much the better for us," he added, nudging his horse forward, seeing Max Denton drawing closer to them.

Denton felt nothing strange going on in the ground beneath him as he goaded his horse through the snow. Nor did he immediately notice the earth quaking when he brought his horse to a halt ten yards from Waite and his men and began waving his hands in the cold air. "Morgan! It's me, Max!"

"Yeah, Denton, we see you," Waite called out, waving him forward.

Denton pushed his tired horse the remaining few yards and reached his cuffed hands out. "I can't tell you and your men how obliged I am," he said, almost tearful in his gratitude.

"All right," Waite said, "don't make a big thing of it. We came for Texas Jack Spain. You just happen to be part of it."

"All the same," Denton said, collecting himself, "I'm obliged." For the first time he noticed the tremor in the ground. "Did you feel that?"

"We've been feeling it," Waite said in a matter-of-fact tone.

"The whole damned mountain is shaking!" Denton said, stepping his horse back and forth and looking down, as if to find more information in the snow.

"Yeah, the whole mountain is shaking," Waite conceded impatiently. "Now talk to me about the lawmen? Is the one I shot *dead*?"

"I'd say so," Denton replied. "I didn't

stick around to find out. Soon as I heard the shot and saw the blood fly, I lit out."

"Yeah, he's dead," Waite surmised for himself, gazing confidently toward the large boulder in the distance.

"To hell with Spain, huh?" Clark cut in, saying to Max Denton. "Your only interest was in saving your own hide."

Denton gave him a quizzical look. "Well, yeah, something like that. What would you have done, stayed and checked the man's pulse?"

"Forget what he'd of done," Waite said. "How well heeled is the other one? How's his ammunition?"

"He's in good shape, both counts," said Denton. "He always has a rifle in hand. Now he's got his ammunition and the other one's. But I don't know what kind of shot he is, far as that goes."

"Ride up that ridge and ask Ty Hall what kind of shot he is," Waite said. "He just opened Ty Hall's belly for him."

"Damn," Denton said, wincing a bit. "He's dead?"

Waite didn't answer. Instead, he dismissed the question with a derisive toss of his head and said to the men who had gathered around, "Everybody spread out, get ready to ride right over this lawman."

"What about me?" Denton asked.

"What *about you?*" Waite asked, noting the cuffs on his wrists. "You're cuffed. You've got no gun. Your horse is staggering underneath you."

"Can somebody get me loose here?" Denton asked, looking from face to face.

"Maybe later," Waite said, nudging his horse away from Denton.

Maybe later . . . ? Denton sat staring in disbelief as the regulators rode away.

Behind the boulder, Sam watched the horsemen spread out and move forward, at a run, or as much so as was possible through the thick snow. Beside him, Pete Summers lay against the side of the boulder, his Colt in hand, his coat closed over the snow-packed bandanna covering his wounded shoulder.

"I'll pick some of them off until they ride into your pistol range," Sam said, taking aim with his repeating rifle, the long-distance sight raised and ready. He tossed a glance toward Spain. "Which one is Waite?"

"I can't see that well from here," Spain said, defiantly.

"All right, have it your way," Sam said. "As soon as they're close enough, I'm putting you between us and them. Seeing that ought to give them something to think about."

"You can't do that, Ranger," Spain ventured. "That's inhumane!"

"Tell it to the judge, Spain," the ranger said. "Here's another way we can do this. I can send your body to them, tied over a saddle with a bullet in your head. That would put a quick stop to all this."

Spain didn't reply. He sat brooding.

"Which one *is Waite?*" Sam asked in a stronger tone, looking out along his rifle sights.

"The one on the black-silver barb," Spain said reluctantly.

Sam's eyes and rifle barrel made a quick sweep and came to rest on the tall figure riding in the middle of the horsemen. "He's wearing the flat crown and the bearskin?" Sam asked.

"Yeah, that's him," Spain said, grudgingly.

As Sam locked his sight onto the chest of the bearskin coat, the ground shook so violently he had to stall his shot for a moment. When the tremor passed, his eyes went to the base of the boulder, and he saw a fresh three-inch gap in the snow. "I better make this quick," he said to Summers. "We've got to get out of here."

"To where?" Spain whispered under his

breath, looking all around the stark land with a trace of a bitter smile.

Riding through the snow, Morgan Waite felt his barb stallion sway beneath him before catching itself and correcting its path. "Damn, this is getting worse!" he said aloud to himself, the rest of the men having put as much as ten to fifteen yards between them. His eyes turned to the high ridge, where tall pines quivered in place, spilling snow from their heavily laden branches.

Bringing the barb almost to a halt, he looked back and forth at the quaking land, his vision as out of control as that of a drunkard. "Whoa, boy, easy!" he said to the rattled stallion.

With much effort, he managed to focus on his men, seeing their horses also swaying and stumbling on the unsteady ground. Looking ahead of him, he caught sight of the rifle barrel and the determined face looking out at him from behind the rifle sights. "Damn you, Spain," he growled to himself, realizing how the ranger had managed to recognize him and single him out.

Waite tried to duck down quickly and swing his stallion away; but his action came too late. He felt the bullet strike him hard in his upper left shoulder. At the same time, he felt the earth rock and sway with renewed violence, back and forth like some large beast shaking its loose coat. "Good God!" he shouted, realizing the world had suddenly come undone before his eyes.

He clasped a gloved hand to his shoulder and saw the puff of gun smoke. He heard the single blast of rifle fire. Yet, even as he felt the hard bite of the bullet, he stared in rapt fascination as the ranger and the large boulder turned slowly sideways in a world that had suddenly lost its bearing.

Through a loud, deep rumble, Waite heard a scream and saw Jack Spain leaping desperately toward solid land, grasping with his cuffed hands at whipping tree roots that sprang out of the mountainside like the tentacles of some submerged beast. "Good God!" Waite repeated. Dumbstruck, he saw a wide slice of land more than a hundred yards long crumble away, dropping man, boulder and all into the gaping mouth of Thunder Pass.

CHAPTER 15

To Waite's right, Stanton Clark's, George Trubough's and PK Barnes' horses had fallen to the ground with them when the earth broke away. The three struggled hurriedly to their feet, hanging on to their reins, stunned by what they had just witnessed. Their horses rolled up onto their hooves, terrified, and tried to bolt free. The men held the frantic animals in check.

"What the hell was that?" Stanton shouted, his reaction to the landslide being that of rage, to keep his fear from showing. Above the canyon, a boiling wall of dust surged upward more than a hundred feet and seemed to hang suspended in the sky.

"An earthquake, gawddamn it!" Waite shouted back at him, also choosing rage rather than fear. "Get back away from that edge. It could still break some more!"

"Whoa!" said Ed Mosley, who had nudged his fearful horse forward for a better look down over the edge. He yanked back on his reins and started to turn and ride back. But the sound of Jack Spain's coughing, choking voice stopped him.

"Somebody help me! Please!" Spain cried out from the jagged new edge of land.

"Waite!" Ed Mosley shouted, stunned, staring into the thick dust. "Spain's hollering over the edge. He must be hanging on!"

"They're all dead!" Waite said. "Get the hell away from there!"

"I'm not dead! Help me!" Spain cried out. "I'm holding on! The lawmen are dead!"

Waite spurred his barb quickly, joining Ed Mosley. The other men ventured closer, but at a much slower pace, staring down cautiously as if to make sure the land was not cracking and crumbling beneath them. "Hear him over there?" Mosley asked as Waite sidled up to him.

"Morgan, *please!*" Spain sobbed, unable to control his terror.

Waite gave Mosley a look of disbelief, then snatched a coiled rope from his saddle horn and jumped down from his saddle. "Tie this off!" he demanded, favoring his wounded shoulder. He tossed Mosley one end of the rope. As the men arrived around them, Waite looked back and forth, then held the rope out to Riley Padgett. Shaking the rope impatiently, he said, "Come on, Padgett! Hurry it up! Spain's out there hanging on for life."

"Me? Why me?" Padgett asked, his eyes widening at the thought of going any closer to the fresh edge of land and its wall of dust.

Waite threw the rope into his chest and shouted, "Why *not* you?" He jutted his wounded shoulder. "Do you think I wouldn't do it myself if I wasn't shot?"

Padgett didn't push the issue. He threw a loop around his waist and began tying it with shaky hands.

"I never seen a man shake so bad," Clark commented under his breath.

Turning a cold stare to Clark, Waite demanded, "Get a rope around yourself. Show him how it's done!"

Clark looked hesitant. PK Barnes took rope from his saddle horn and tossed it to Clark.

"You heard me, gawddamn it!" said Waite. "Tie off and get out there with him! Barnes, loop his rope around your saddle horn. Hurry up now. This place could drop out from under us any minute!"

"Jesus!" Padgett said, staring down at the ground under their feet.

As soon as Clark tied the rope around his waist, the two men walked out slowly toward the edge of the broken land, each of them stepping lightly. Ten feet back from the edge, they dropped onto their bellies and crawled to the edge, where dust still rose upward. "Spain, where the hell are you?" Padgett asked, raising his bandanna up over his nose. Beside him Clark did the same.

"Right down here!" Spain said, his voice raspy from the dust.

"Lord!" Padgett looked down, seeing Spain's cuffed hands wrapped tightly around a wad of long broken tree roots, no more than two feet down the wall of dirt and rock. Reaching down together, Padgett and Clark took him by his wrists and dragged him quickly up over the edge onto more solid ground.

Choking on dust, Clark said, "There, you're saved. I'm getting out of here!" Yet before Padgett and he could turn around and crawl back, Spain scrambled away ahead of them, making a terrified whining, sobbing sound.

"Settle down, Spain!" Waite demanded, catching the saloon owner and shaking him, keeping him from running past them as soon as he rose to his feet. "You're safe! Get yourself in hand!"

Spain took a deep breath but continued shaking uncontrollably, grasping Waite with his cuffed hands. "I thought I was dead! I've never seen anything like it!" he said in a trembling voice. "You — you saved my life!" He looked all around, seeing Padgett and Clark arrive, yanking down their dust-covered bandannas. "Every one of yas saved my life!" he said, raising his cuffed hands. "I won't forget this! You're all drinking free at the Gay Lady. That's my *sworn oath* to yas!"

Padgett and Clark hurriedly untied the ropes from their waists and pitched them to the men holding them wrapped around their saddle horns. Spain tried grabbing both men in gratitude, but they slipped away from him and hurriedly mounted their horses.

"Come on, Spain, damn it. Stop fooling around!" Waite said, stepping into his saddle and reaching a hand down to him. "We're not safe here. This whole mountainside could collapse!"

"Right, you are!" Spain said. He grasped Waite's gloved hand and climbing up quickly behind him. "But I mean what I said. I'm not forgetting this! Free drinks for all!"

"Forget the free drinks, Spain," Waite said. "You know damn well what brought me up here." He gigged the horse away from the edge, the other men doing the same.

Spain grew quiet. Taking note of it, Waite changed the subject for the moment and asked, "Are both the lawmen dead?"

"They are, indeed!" Spain said, collecting himself some, feeling better now that he realized he was on horseback instead of hanging above a bottomless swirl of dust. "I saw them both falling with that big boulder right above them. Wherever that rock lands, it'll have them two mashed against its bottom, *forever.*" He looked back and managed a smile toward the high boiling dust. "Good gawddamn *riddance to them!*" he shouted toward the broken rim.

As the regulators rode away, on the bottom of the other side of Thunder Pass, the old man and Trina had looked up and along the ridge line at the first sound of gunfire. The other members of the caravan had hurried forward from the pine woods to meet them, rejoicing at their return. But upon the sound of gunshots, the entire camp had fallen silent and looked warily upward. When they'd seen the earth and the large boulder give way and spill down into the already earth-swollen pass, a gasp went up among them.

"Grandpapa!" said Trina in a worried tone. "Those were men falling along with the rock! I think one of them was Sam, the ranger."

The old man did not answer her. Instead he stared up for a moment longer before turning his faded eyes to a young man standing beside his wagon. "What do you say, Django?" he asked the young man in their native tongue, giving him a questioning look.

"It does not matter what I have to say," said the younger man. "You alone must decide whether or not to go see if these men are alive." He studied the tree-strewn mountainside and the dust rising above it. As he spoke, he noted that snow had begun to fall again, sparsely now, yet he knew it would grow heavier. "I must tell you honestly," he said, "I see no way anyone can live through what we just witnessed." He gave Trina a sympathetic look and said softly, "I am sorry."

"No, no," the old man said, shaking his head. "You misunderstand what I ask you, Django. I do not ask if Trina and I should go. *Of course we* are going! These men saved our lives! I only ask if you and the others will be joining us?"

"It is rare for our people to ever find kindness among the *gadje*." The young man looked upward again for a moment, as if considering something. "When these men saved your and Trina's lives, they saved the lives of every one of us." He nodded. "Yes, we will all go and search for them." He turned to the others gathered around them and said, "Bring rope, shovels, and drinking water." As if in afterthought he added, "And bring torches. This search could last long into the night."

The blackness that engulfed him was deep and impenetrable. When he drifted back into consciousness, Sam reached out a weak, languid hand and felt the surface of the boulder not more than two feet from him. The familiar feel of it reassured him he was still alive. "Pete?" he asked quietly, his hand searching the ground around him, finding nothing.

When he and Summers had slid down onto the rocky ledge in a fall of dirt and rock, the last thing he'd seen had been the big boulder lumbering down end over end above them, as if at any second it would crush them into the mountainside. But it hadn't, he reminded himself. No sooner had the two lawmen landed on the rocky ledge than the boulder slammed down in front of them and tipped backward, capturing them in a narrow space between it and the mountainside.

How long ago had that been? He had no idea. "Summers?" he asked quietly, feeling a dull pain coming back to life in his leg, in his head, throughout his battered torso.

This time he heard his partner moan on the other side of him. "Yeah?" Summers answered in a weak, wheezing voice.

"Thank God," Sam rasped. He reached out with his other hand and found the marshal lying balled in the dirt.

At first there had been dusty gray light on either side of the boulder where the two of them landed. But as more dirt and rock poured down and began filling both sides around the boulder, light disappeared, replaced first by crumbling earth, then by pitch-darkness. "Are — are you hurt?" Sam asked.

"I don't know," Summers said, choking on dust. "You?"

"My leg's banged up, but it doesn't feel broken," Sam whispered haltingly. "My head is bleeding. . . ." His words trailed off.

"The boulder *saved* us?" Summers asked, his senses coming around.

"For now," Sam said. "Let's hope we can claw our way out of here. The whole mountainside might be on top of us."

"Spain," Summers asked, "are you all

right?"

"Spain's not with us," Sam said. "I didn't see him while we fell." He turned stiffly and dragged himself along on his belly until he found the mounded dirt and rock at the edge of the boulder. Dragging a rock down, the first thing Sam noticed was a thin, cold stream of air on his hand. A good sign, he told himself. He dug another rock down with his hands and rolled it to the side. "Pete, crawl over here if you can," he said over his shoulder to the darkness. "Get some fresh air."

"Fresh air?" Summers scooted on his back until he found himself beside Sam. "Maybe we're not buried too deep after all."

"Maybe," said Sam, "but it won't matter how deep if we can't move what's got us covered. If it's mostly dirt, we'll just keep scratching away at it . . . long as we've got air."

"Yeah, we keep scratching," Summers said, rolling stiffly over onto his stomach and reaching in to help Sam dig.

Breathing in a lungful of the cold, dusty air, the two continued to scrape and dig at the rock and dirt until at length a bead of dusty light appeared suddenly in the darkness. The two stopped and stared for a moment, their eyes following the faint light down their hands and arms. "We'll make it!" Sam said, gulping dryly, but sounding more confident. They looked at each other's shadowy face and dug at the rock and dirt with renewed hope.

Beyond the boulder, snow had begun to fall heavier, quickly starting to cover the freshly upturned earth. Climbing up the steep mountainside over loose dirt, rock and downed trees lying strewn around from the first landslide, Django Brilhowitz adjusted the rope on his shoulder and gave the other men from the caravan a dubious look. "Are you certain that is the boulder where they had taken cover, Trina?" he called out to the young woman, who had managed to get in front of them.

"Yes, I am certain," Trina replied. "I saw them fall with it." She raised a hand above her eyes to shelter them from the falling snow.

"It will soon be dark," Django called back to her. "Stay close to us. Losing you up here in the cold will not help matters."

"I will stay close," Trina replied. She looked all around the boulder standing above them and along the rocky ledge. Instead of the ledge standing straight up above them as it had before, the land beneath it had now turned into a long steep sloping hillside. Looking back behind her she called out to a man who picked his way along the rough ground with a large wolf hound at his side. "Up here, Brunal!"

Breathing heavily, leaving a trail of billowing steam, the man reached down to the wolf hound, petting the animal affectionately, and said, "Well, you heard her! Back to work, you lazy dog! Find these men so we can all go back to our fires." He gave a gesture of his hand that sent the big hound barking and bounding up the slope. Trina watched the dog pass her, traveling zigzag, its wet, steaming nostrils searching first the ground beneath its hairy paws, then the air above its head, its nose tipping high toward the boulder itself.

Behind Trina her grandfather came forward with the use of a long walking stick. "Don't worry, my granddaughter," he said. "This dog can find *anyone,* anywhere, *anytime!*" As he spoke, he raised the stick and stirred the air. "Let me see no doubt in your eyes. Are you not the one who gave them a blessing that they would overcome any hardship they meet on their journey?"

"Yes, Grandpapa," Trina said, "but sometimes I fear that a blessing is only —"

"Shhh, hush now," the old man said, cutting her off quickly. "A *Roma's* blessing is only as strong as the *Roma* believes it to be! Have faith! The evening is young. See how the snowflakes still dance?" He gestured all about the devastated land with a weathered hand.

"Yes, Grandpapa," Trina said with a soft smile.

No sooner had the old man finished speaking than, farther up the slope beside the boulder, the big hound flew into a barking frenzy, bouncing back on the white-streaked ground.

"Ah! You see!" said the old man. "The dog has found something! Let us hope now that it is the young lawmen!" Trina and he hurried up across the rough terrain.

Behind the boulder, Pete Summers scraped with his good hand, his wounded shoulder rendering his other arm almost useless. The thin bead of light had grown as more rocks were moved and rolled back behind the lawmen. Yet as the bead of light grew larger, evening gloom had begun to lessen its brightness. In the shadowy darkness, when Sam watched his partner stop digging, he said, "What is it?"

"I heard something out there," Summers said, looking with caution toward the fading light. "Think Waite's men are searching for us? They couldn't see us, so they figured we're behind this rock?"

"I doubt it," Sam said, listening intently himself, catching the distant sound of rock being rolled away from the other side. "But I wouldn't swear to it." He felt for the Colt still resting in the holster on his hip. "There's somebody out there, though. I hear them working. Whoever it is, they're digging us out."

"It's a good thing," Summers said. "My shoulder is bleeding bad again."

"You didn't say anything," Sam replied.

"What good would it have done?" Summers asked.

Sam considered for a moment. Then, as if coming to a decision, he drew the Colt from his holster and said, "Duck down from the ricochet. Whether that's Waite or somebody else digging, I'm letting them know for sure we're in here."

"Fire away," Summers said, sinking farther against the ground, shielding his head with his good arm.

Sam held his Colt out arm's length. "Here goes," he said, cocking it. "Whoever's there will either kill us or save our lives." He squeezed the trigger, recocked, fired and recocked again. Then he settled down for a moment, succumbing to the pain in his leg and the throbbing along the side of his bloody head.

On the pile lying upward along the boulder, Django stood holding a large rock in his arms. At the sound of three well-spaced gunshots, he grinned down to the old man and Trina, who stood beside the big wolf hound while the young men labored. "Someone is alive," he said. *"Good!* Now we work harder, knowing we are uncovering the *living* instead of the *dead!"*

Trina kissed her thumbnail and whispered a cautious prayer of thanks, watching the men step up their pace, pitching away rocks and dirt with their shovels. An hour later, stepping up closer on the side of the half-cleared boulder, she followed the torchlight Django held down toward a narrow opening in the remaining rock pile.

Two of the men stood stooped down, pulling a dusty gloved hand upward from the pile. Trina gasped a little at the sight of Pete Summers' bruised and battered face hanging limp but alert, as the men dragged him the rest of the way up and passed him from arms to arms until he lay on the ground staring up at the sky in relief. "Help . . . Sam . . ." he said in a faltering voice, his hand pressed to his bleeding shoulder wound.

"Don't worry," Trina said, kneeling

quickly at his side, raising his head onto her lap as someone passed a small gourd of water to her. She glanced at the opening and saw the men pull the ranger up from the ground. "They are helping him up right now." She brushed Summers' dusty tangled hair from his face. "Here, drink some water. You and Sam are safe now. Me and my people will look after you as if you are both one of us."

PART 3

CHAPTER 16

Margo stood atop a ladder leading up into the hay loft of the livery barn, holding a lantern up over her head, giving Ned Rose light as he searched all around among piles of pitched hay. "If I find out Carney Blake has found Spain's money up here, I'll beat his head against a barn timber."

"Now you're talking crazy," Margo offered. "Carney was living up here while he dried out, is all. As drunk as he's been lately, he wouldn't have known what to do with Spain's money if he'd found it."

Rose kicked a blanket across the floor of the loft, then did the same to a pile of ragged clothes Carney Blake had discarded the day Stanley Woods had brought the sobered gunman a clean change. "His friend Woods knows what to do with it, though," Rose said gruffly.

"This is too much," Margo said, taking a step down the ladder. "I'm leaving, before you go nuts and accuse me of having it."

"Naw," Rose said, dismissing the idea, "if you whores had Spain's money, you wouldn't be able to keep your mouths shut about it this long."

"That shows just how little you know about us," said Margo.

"I know more about you and Trixie than I care to," Rose said suggestively. He walked back over to the ladder and said, "Get out of my way. I'm coming down." He kicked a boot out at her near her face. Margo didn't flinch, but she did step down the ladder to the ground and wait until Rose joined her.

"Where do you want to search next, in the jake behind the saloon?" she asked scornfully. "Maybe Texas Jack sank all his money and gold in shit, just to see who would dip down into it."

"Don't look down on me as if you have no regard for money, Margo," Rose said. "After all, you sell yourself for it every day of your worthless life."

"I don't sell myself," Margo snapped back at him. "I rent something of mine out a little, here and there. But I'm not running all over Cold Devil scratching like a dog looking for bones, making a damn fool of myself over somebody else's *money.*"

Rose murmured under his breath, "Stupid

whores. No wonder you all die broke in the streets."

"I'm not going to die broke in the streets. I can promise you that." She gave him a look of total disdain.

But Rose hadn't heard her last few words, nor had he seen the look on her face. His thoughts had followed his eyes to the blacksmith's shop, where Milo Herns stood inside the open door busily turning a long pole back and forth in his hands. "Next we're going to the blacksmith's," Rose said without facing Margo. "You can put out the lantern."

"Why don't you leave the little negro alone, Rose? Herns doesn't know anything about Spain's money. Christ, you've nearly crippled the poor man as it is!"

Rose chuckled, already starting toward the blacksmith shop. "He had no business shooting his mouth off the way he did," said Rose. "Tossing that uppity little negro out a window now and then is the best way I know to keep him respectful."

Margo shook her head in disgust and followed him to the shop through a falling snow that had grown heavier over the past two hours when it had moved down from the mountains. "The blacksmith's is my last stop for the day," Margo said. "My feet are freezing."

"You'll stop when I say you'll stop," Rose growled over his shoulder.

"All right," Margo said with defiance. "Then you explain to the miners why I'm digging these icy heels into their backbones. Talk about killing the business. Nobody I ever knew wanted to ride a whore who had cold extremities."

"Soon as we're finished with Herns, go on back to the Gay Lady and warm yourself before the evening crowd starts showing up," Rose said, seeing her point. "Tomorrow we search around some more."

"That comes as no surprise," Margo said. She blew her warm breath on her free hand. "We've searched every damn day this past week."

"The money is here somewhere," said Rose. "I've got to have it." Changing the subject, he asked, "Has anybody seen Clement Sanderson?"

"No! That's the strangest thing!" Margo looked bewildered. "I haven't seen him since Waite and the others rode out. Woods looked for him, said his horse is still in the livery barn. What the hell do you suppose could have happened to him?"

"Who knows what a man like Sanderson might be up to?" Rose said, shaking his head. "I'm just glad he's not in my way."

At the open doorway of the blacksmith shop, Margo hurried a few steps ahead and called out through the sound of a roaring fire in the smelting furnace, "Yoo-hoo, Milo. It's Margo. I have Ned Rose with me."

Rose caught up to her and, shouldering her aside, stepped through the open door. "I don't need no introduction to enter a damn forging shop!" he said angrily to both Margo and the blacksmith. Rose noted that in his right hand Milo stood holding a long wooden pole with an iron hook on one end. Herns' left arm was in a cotton sling. "What's that?" Rose asked, a bit leery of Herns wielding such an instrument after Rose tossed him out the window.

Milo gave him a dark stare. "It's a special hay hook I made for one of the sodbusters. He never came back and paid me for it. I'm fixing to break it up for firewood and reuse the iron."

"Well, get it out of your hand while I'm here," Rose demanded, his fingers tapping idly on the big Remington in his sash.

Milo said in a sour tone, "You come into *my* place of business and think you can tell me what I *can* or *can't* hold in my hand? Is that what you think you can do?"

"Exactly," said Rose, "and for your own

good. Everybody knows you and I aren't getting along well. One wrong move and I might think you intended to use that metal hook on me. Any judge in the world would call it self-defense if I killed you." He stared at Milo; his fingers stopped tapping the gun handle and wrapped around it. "Now *corner* it."

"I wouldn't want this lovely *innocent* bystander getting herself hurt," Herns said. He looked at Margo, then let out a tense breath, limped to the nearest corner and propped the long pole against the wall. "Now what is it you want from me, Rose? I'm in no shape to do much, as you can see." He made sure Rose got a look at his swollen face, his bandaged ribs behind his open shirt and his injured left arm in its sling.

"I don't need your help, Milo," Rose said, ignoring the tone of the blacksmith's voice. "I'm shaking this town down from one end to the other until I get my hands on Spain's money."

"You mean his gold?" said Herns.

"Gold, cash, whatever," Rose said. "But that's what I'm here for."

"Oh?" Milo said in sarcastic mock surprise. "And here I am thinking you might have come to *inquire* about my health."

"Don't start with your mouth," Rose warned. "I can't throw you out a window here." He nodded toward the outside. "But I can break the ice off the water trough with your head and give you a cold water bath."

Knowing full well that Rose was capable of doing such a thing caused Milo to soften his attitude. "You want to look around here for gold, be my guest," he said with a sweep of his right hand. "I wish you *would* find some. I'd like to think that all this time there's been gold right here under my nose."

Ignoring Herns' words, Rose stepped over to a closed wooden door. "What's in there?"

"What's in there?" Herns looked at Margo, then at Rose. "The same thing that's always been in there! More of my tools, some scrap iron." He stopped, then reached for the closed door and said, "Hell, go on inside and look around. Make yourself at home. If I had any gold, I wouldn't be stuck in Cold Devil another winter — that's for damn sure! Not when my bones are crying out for San Francisco!" He gave Margo a pained grin.

Rose opened the door a few inches, looked all around the cluttered room, then closed it soundly. "Don't mock what I'm doing, Herns."

Herns' grin disappeared quickly. "No, I'm

not mocking you, Rose," he said, once again looking at Margo as Rose turned on his heel and stomped out of the shop.

"Come on, Margo," Rose called back from the other side of the door. "We've wasted too much time here."

"Coming," Margo said. On her way out, she stopped and nodded toward the long hay hook in the corner, saying in a whisper, "You better wipe the end of the hook off if you don't want to be answering more of his questions."

Herns gave her a worried look. "Yes, ma'am!" he said, jerking a ragged bandanna from his hip pocket. While Margo turned and followed Rose, the little blacksmith grabbed the pole from the corner and vigorously wiped the end of the hay hook.

Across the street from the blacksmith shop, Stanley Woods and Carney Blake walked along the edge of the street through the falling snow toward the saloon. Seeing Rose appear before them fifteen yards away, Blake said to Woods in a lowered voice, "This would be a good time to stop Ned Rose in his tracks, then stop his tracks altogether."

Woods gave him a look. "You mean right now, this minute? You just call him down and shoot him?"

"Why not?" said Blake. "It's what I've been sobered up and practicing for." As he spoke, his hand raised and lowered the big pistol in its holster, loosening it. "Can you think of a better time and place? He's out here where I want him. He can't refuse me." Blake stopped and stood with his feet shoulder length apart.

"Well, yes, but —" Woods' words stopped.

"Ned Rose!" Blake called out in a strong, purposeful voice. "Stop where you are!"

"Oh, Jesus!" Woods said. He hurriedly stepped away from the gunman's side, up onto the nearby boardwalk.

Rose stopped; so did Margo, a few feet behind him. Rose heard the tone of voice and noted the stance Blake had taken. Yet, even as he adjusted his own stance, he called out through the falling snow, "What is it, Blake? I'm in a hurry here."

"Your hurrying is over, Rose," Blake replied. "It's time you and I had a reckoning."

"Uh-oh," Margo said. She stepped back out of the way.

"I see," Rose replied. He stood calmly, letting his heavy coat fall open in front. His right arm crooked just enough to keep his hand poised near the handle of the big Remington in his waist sash. "I suppose this explains all the target shooting I've heard every morning outside of town?"

"Yep, that was me, Rose," said Blake. "I've shot you a thousand times this past week. Now I'm here to do it in person."

Margo stepped slowly up onto the board-walk out of the falling snow. She gave Woods a look as if to ask if he couldn't do something to stop this. Woods only returned her look with a faint smile of satisfaction, letting her know he was the one behind it.

"I'll kill you, of course," Rose said matter-of-factly, his demeanor comfortable, yet poised. "But I suppose you already know that." Steam swirled in his breath.

"Waite!" Woods called out, seeing Morgan Waite and his men ride into sight out of the falling snow at the far end of town.

Without taking his eyes off Rose, Blake replied to Woods, saying, "I've waited long enough. You want him dead. I'm giving him to you."

Rose's interest piqued upon hearing that Woods had something to do with this — not that the information surprised him.

"No, damn it!" Woods said, feeling a bit ill at hearing Blake tell Rose that he wanted him dead. "I mean here comes Morgan *Waite!* Him and his men!"

"Oh," Blake said, uncertain where this put

the situation. "Well, that doesn't change anything," he added, not wanting to turn loose of what he'd started, especially after mentioning that Woods wanted Ned Rose dead.

"Like hell it doesn't," Rose said, raising his right cautiously away from the Remington. Taking a step to the side, he said to Blake, "I'm not fighting you." To Woods he said without turning his eyes away from Blake, "We'll have to settle this another time . . . unless you both want to answer to Waite. He *is* the law around here, now that Denton and Spain are gone."

Seeing the riders draw closer, Margo breathed a sigh of relief. Then relief turned into surprise as her eyes widened and she said, "It's Spain! He's back!"

Woods stared at the riders in stunned disbelief, seeing Spain gig his horse ahead of them and jump down at the hitch rail out front of the Gay Lady saloon. "Damn," he whispered to himself.

In the street, Carney Blake circled wide of Rose and stepped up beside Woods as Rose sidestepped away a safe distance before turning and hurrying toward the livery barn.

"This is the second time Morgan Waite has showed up and kept us from killing this tin horn son of a bitch," Blake said.

"You might not have to kill him now," Woods replied, watching the regulators also pull their horses up to the hitch rail. "Texas Jack Spain might kill him for us."

CHAPTER 17

Jack Spain walked inside the Gay Lady Saloon, shook hands all around and stepped behind the bar, catching Trixie as she squealed and ran to him, thrusting herself into his arms. "Texas Jack!" she cried out in elation. "I'm so happy to see you! It is you, isn't it? I'm not dreaming this, *am I?*"

"Hell, *no,* you're not dreaming! It's me, sure as hell!" Twirling the thin young woman and holding her up in the air against him, Spain called out jubilantly, "I said I'd be back, and by God, here I am!" Lowering Trixie to her feet, he said, "Drinks all around! Whiskey for everybody! Make it my Kentucky reserve!"

"Uh, that might not be a good idea, Jack," Trixie said under her breath. "We've run low on the good stuff since you've been gone."

"What? How could we?" Spain demanded. "I never run short . . . on *any-damn-thing!*"

"Rose didn't order any," Trixie offered in a whisper, seeing the eyes along the bar watching her. She lowered her voice even more and said, "He hasn't been ordering any beer like he should either. I don't think he believed you'd ever be coming back."

"That son of a bitch! Where is he?" Spain demanded, just between him and Trixie. But before she could even answer, he called out in a louder voice for everybody to hear, "Give them all a double shot of whatever you've got opened! Give me one too! It's not important *what* we drink, but who we drink *with,* eh, men?"

"Rose left here earlier with Margo," Trixie said. Seeing Spain's mood darken, she hurried away, grabbed an open bottle of whiskey from an almost bare shelf and stepped over to a row of shot glasses held in thick callused hands along the bar top. "Here we go, boys! Bottoms up!" she said, sloshing whiskey from one shot glass to the next.

"I can't wait to see the look on his face," Spain growled under his breath.

"Uh-oh," Trixie said, nodding toward the front door, which suddenly flew open. "It looks like you won't have to wait long."

Morgan Waite gave Ned Rose a shove forward and walked in behind him, flanked by two of his men, Ben Hevlon and Lode

Stewart. Waite carried Rose's Remington in his gloved hand. "Look who Lode and Ben here saw slipping into the livery barn," Waite said, shaking snow from his bearskin coat.

"Do tell," Spain said, jerking a billy bat from under the bar. He hurried around the corner of the bar, asking on his way, "And just what was my bartender doing in the barn?"

Receiving a prompting look from Waite, Lode Stewart spoke up, saying, "He looked to us like he was about to saddle a horse."

"No kidding," Spain said. He slapped the billy bat in his palm, barely able to control himself. "And where might you have been heading once you saddled yourself a horse? Out of town, no doubt."

"No, sir, Texas Jack!" Rose said, seeing the killing rage in Spain's eyes. "I wasn't headed anywhere. I've been busy running this place until your return, just like I promised you I would."

"And now that you've returned," Lode Stewart cut in with a laugh, "he wanted to keep on running, *period!*"

"Give me back my gun and we'll see how funny you think things are," Rose said to Stewart, his temper taking over in spite of his situation.

"Don't go making threats, Rose," Waite

warned him. "I'm back now. It's time we see how well you've taken care of things while I was gone." He held out his hand, palm up, and said, "Hand over the operating roll."

"Oh." Rose looked sheepish as if he'd forgotten. Reaching down to a large bulge in his pocket, his hand came out clutching a thick roll of cash. "I carried it to purchase stock with, same as you always did."

"But you were leaving town with it, if these men hadn't caught you," Spain said.

"No, that's not true," Rose protested.

"Don't call these men liars, Rose," Waite warned, wagging the gun in his direction. "Where's my cousin Clement?" he asked suddenly, as if the question might catch Rose off-guard.

"I don't know," Rose said. "The fact is, I haven't seen him since you left Cold Devil. He must've rode on after you left."

"His horse is in the livery barn," Ben Hevlon said.

"Is that so?" Waite gave Rose a suspicious look, then said to Hevlon and Stewart, "Go find him. Have the rest of the men help you search. I don't care if you have to turn this town inside out! Find Clement."

As the men turned and left, Spain and Waite both turned to Ned Rose. Pointing at him with the billy bat, Spain said, "Let's get upstairs. I heard what you did to my safe no sooner than I was out of sight."

"I — I had to have all the operating cash I could lay my hands on, Jack!" Rose said as the billy bat nudged him toward the stairs. "Still, I never found enough!" He sounded worried. "I never found any big money, and that's the gospel truth!"

"That's the same thing he told me when I rode in here last time," Waite said to Spain. "I decided I best bring you two face-to-face and hear what you've got to say about it." He leveled a look at Spain. "I better have ten thousand coming from somewhere, not to mention the money you've been holding for me."

Spain replied confidently, "You'll get the ten thousand, *plus* everything else you have coming." He shoved Rose up the stairs toward his office. "Just follow me. We'll get things sorted out here."

Waite gave a slight grin. "I should have known you had things under control here, Texas Jack."

They climbed the stairs and walked inside the open door of Spain's office. Motioning toward the door as he walked through it, Spain gave Rose a dark look and said, "I still don't know how that door came to be unlocked. I've never left it unlocked in my life."

"It wasn't me," Rose said. "I swear I never had the key to it."

"*Somebody* had it," Spain said. "It wasn't in my pockets when the ranger searched me down."

"Well, it's open now," Waite said, eager to collect his ten thousand and see the gold from the robbery with his own eyes. "Let's get on with the matter at hand."

"Yeah, that's what I say." Spain gave Rose a smug look and walked to the open closet door, behind which the safe had been removed. "As you can see, when I had this place built and had the safe installed, I took great pains to make sure that not just any *ordinary fool* could slip in here and rob me." As he spoke, he swung his hand back and forth, gesturing in a superior manner, then tapped his finger to the side of his head. "So I did some sharp thinking."

At the open door, Max Denton walked in and stood a few feet behind Waite.

"Get on with it, Spain," Waite said.

"As you wish," Spain beamed, letting his gaze go from one face to the next, enjoying himself.

He stepped out and away from the closet and over to a large oaken dresser. Scooting it out from the wall, a small braided rug sliding along with it, Spain nodded at the floor. "Knowing that someday a situation like this might present itself, I had this secret trap door built here for just such an emergency." He rubbed his hands together proudly and kneeled down.

Rose stared in silence, yet he cursed himself for not having thought of looking under the braided rug.

"Pretty damned slick of you," Waite whispered under his breath.

"I say it pays to always keep one step ahead of the game," Spain said, grinning. "Wouldn't you agree, Rose?" He gave Rose a cold, sharp stare, seeing by the look on the bartender's face that he hadn't gotten his greedy fingers on the private cache of treasure.

Reaching down with both hands, Spain lifted two metal handles, gripped them tightly and jerked a three-foot-square section of the floor up and laid it aside. Spreading his hands, he said, "And now, without any further ado —"

Watching him stare down beneath the surface of the floor, Waite, Rose and Denton all three saw the grin fade away quickly as they moved forward for a better look.

"What's wrong, Spain?" Waite asked.

"It's — it's empty!" Spain gasped. He batted his eyes as if they had failed him. But looking again, he saw no bags of gold dust, no shining gold coin, no bound bundles of cash. "Oh, my God! It's all gone!" Spain's voice trembled.

"It better not be!" Waite said in a menacing tone. But even as he spoke, he hurried forward and looked down into the gaping empty hole in the floor. Rose and Denton also looked down, standing on either side of Waite.

Looking up from the empty hiding place, Spain rose stiffly and said to Waite with an outstretched hand, "Give me the gun."

"I swear to God I didn't take it!" Rose shouted, backing away a step, looking ready to turn and bolt out the door.

Instead of giving Spain the big Remington in his hand, Waite took a step away from everybody, waved Rose back in with the long barrel and said, "Nobody is killing anybody just yet." He singled out Spain and said, "Calm yourself down. When Raymond Curly gets here, you're going to need every able gunman you can come up with."

"Calm down?" Spain said. Yet even as he questioned Waite's advice, he followed it, dropping his hand away from reaching for the Remington. "You sure are taking this

238

awfully damn well. This missing money is yours as well as mine and Curly's."

"I'm not taking it well at all," said Waite. "But we're going to find out what's going on here before we go unloading guns in one another's bellies." Turning to Rose he asked, "Who's been in and out of here since the lawmen left with Spain?"

Considering it, Rose said, "Nobody! That is, nobody has been up here long enough to slip a load of gold and cash out of here without being seen."

Waite walked to the window and looked down through the falling snow. "Padgett said you moved the safe by throwing it out the window. Where's the teamster who helped you move it?"

"He's long gone," Rose said. "But he couldn't have had anything to do with it. I was with him the whole time."

"It sure as hell didn't carry itself out of here!" Spain bellowed. He looked all around and asked, "Where's Margo?"

Just as he asked, Margo walked through the door, followed by Woods and Blake. "I'm right here, Jack," she said, stopping and placing a hand on her ample hip. "But don't start accusing me of anything unless *accusing* is the sort of thing that meets your fantasy." She winked at Waite and said,

"How goes it, Morgan?"

Waite let the gun slump an inch in his hand. "Not so good, Margo," he said, staring at Spain and Rose. "I expect the next time I need something looked after, I'd do better to come to you and Trixie."

"*Looking after things* is what we do best," she said and smiled. "Remember you promised we could look after you and your men the next trip through here?"

"Yeah, I remember. But this ain't the *next trip,* darling," Waite replied. "This is the same trip. We haven't gotten it sorted out yet."

"Who has been up here since I left Cold Devil?" Spain demanded, sharply cutting in to Waite and Margo's conversation.

"Well, now let me see," Margo said mockingly, tapping a finger to her lips as if having to think carefully. "Everybody and their brother, I suppose, is the best answer."

"Don't fool around, Margo," Spain warned her. "This is a serious matter. There's a fortune missing here! I need to know who's been up here! Somebody is going to die before this is all settled."

Margo took a more serious air. "Sorry, Jack. There's been the teamster Coots, Trixie, myself, Herns." She paused and pointed at Woods. "He's been up here . . .

so has Clement," she said to Waite, "since you and your men left him here."

"My cousin wouldn't dare steal from me," said Waite.

"I never said he would," Margo said. "I'm just telling who all has been up here. But, to tell the truth, nobody has been up here enough times to tote out anything much bigger than the chamber pot."

Spain turned from Margo and looked at Carney Blake standing beside Woods. "Were you up here at any time, Carney?"

Blake looked him in the eye and said, "If I was, it would've been before I sobered up. I would've been too drunk to remember it."

"What are you doing sober anyway?" Spain asked, giving him a curious look.

"I got him sobered up, Jack," Woods said, "not long after the lawmen took you away."

"Oh? And since when did you become such a damned do-gooder?" Spain asked.

"I did it for a couple of good reasons," Woods said. He gave a glance toward Rose, seeing him unarmed, the big Remington still in Waite's hand. "First of all, I saw the way he was treating the Gay Lady. I couldn't stand it. He was robbing her blind. I knew I was no match for him, so I figured I'd sober Carney up to help me take this place away from him."

Rose cut in with a sneer, "I would've killed this drunken idiot quicker than a cat can scratch its —"

"Shut up, Rose!" said Spain. To Woods, he said, "You said there was *a couple* of good reasons. What's the other one?"

"Well, I wanted us to come set you free," Woods said.

"For the ten thousand, of course," said Spain.

"That would have been good, but the money wasn't what it was all about for me. I wanted to set you free even if there was *no money* involved. Like I said, I hated seeing him strip the Gay Lady down to nothing."

"I'll kill you, Woods, you ass-kissing worm!" Rose said, opening and closing his big fists.

"Not unless you kill me first," Blake said. "This man dragged me up out of the street. From now on, anybody bothers him, they bother me."

"Woods, from now on, you've got Rose's job. Can you handle it? Take care of the bar and oversee Margo and Trixie while I search this town top to bottom?"

"I can handle it, Texas Jack," Woods said boldly.

"What about me, Jack?" Rose said. "You can't believe this pimp. I looked out for this place like it was my own! Don't fire me for doing what I thought was best for the place!"

"Don't worry, Rose," said Spain. "I'm not about to fire you." He turned to Woods and Blake and said, "You two make sure he doesn't try to leave Cold Devil." He looked at Blake. "Can you stay sober and keep him busy, cleaning, sweeping, polishing spittoons while Woods helps me search the town?"

"I'll do my best to," Blake said.

"Make sure he works like his life depends on it" — Spain glared at Rose — "because it *does.*"

"Whatever you say, Texas Jack," Blake said. He turned to Rose. "You heard him, Rose. Let's get started. I'm going to see to it you keep this place cleaned and shining."

CHAPTER 18

James Earl Coots knew the hazards of traveling the high trail at any time of year, let alone during the first snows of winter. *Not to mention with a wagon bed full of gold dust, gold ingots, cash . . .* He considered his situation, looking down through the trees at the band of Ute Indians traveling along the switchback trail below. Had they seen him? Of course they had! Utes saw everything up here. This was their terrain.

"All right, now what?" he murmured to himself, looking all around, having noted the small band were women, children and a couple elderly round bellies. Who could say there weren't a few warriors with them? What if those warriors had seen him and slipped up around him? The Utes were peaceable enough, but up here, with nobody around? The buffalo skins alone were valuable, he reminded himself.

He held the shotgun at port arms and

walked cautiously back to the wagon. Stepping up into the driver's seat it dawned on him *these were trade Indians returning from the town of Closely.*

Now that he'd thought of it, he'd seen them there a dozen times, selling pots, pans, beadwork. He let out a breath of relief and chuckled to himself, feeling a bit foolish. Still, it would have been a shame to make it this far — no more then eight or nine miles from Closely — and get robbed.

He started to shove the shotgun under a faded red blanket on the seat beside him, but he stopped and thought for a moment longer. Maybe seeing the Indians had been some sort of sign, something meant to caution him. The last five miles into Closely would be flat, barren and slow-going, especially so with the foot and a half of fresh snow covering the trail. Anything could happen on that last five miles. "Damn . . ." he murmured, looking all around again.

Casting a glance upward into the falling snow, he judged how long it should take before his wagon tracks and footprints would be covered. An hour, maybe less, he told himself. Then, shotgun in hand, he stepped back down and trudged to the rear of the wagon. He flipped back the top two hides covering the cache of stolen treasure and began carrying it over into the thin strip of trees along the ridge line. Better to make two trips these last eight miles, rather than take a chance of getting waylaid and lose the full amount.

When he'd estimated that roughly half of the bags of gold coin and ingots lay at the trunk of a tall snow-covered spruce, Coots scraped the snow back carefully, keeping the top layer clean. Beneath the snow he pulled up a heavy frost-stuck rock and rolled it over, exposing a sunken spot in the earth. "Perfect," he murmured.

Filling the impression with the bags of gold, he rolled the rock back over the spot, covering the treasure, and spread the snow back into place. "Don't you worry," he whispered down to the cache of gold, as if it were some living thing. "I'll be back for you before your toes get cold."

Back inside the wagon, Coots pushed on slowly for the next hour, covering no more than two miles of the slick steep downhill trail. At the last sharp elbow turn, Coots looked back up the trail and let out a sigh of relief for having made it. "There's an extra dip of oats waiting for everybody tonight," he said to the big wagon horses.

As he reached inside his coat for his briar pipe and tobacco pouch, five horsemen walked their mounts into sight around a high edge of rock and stopped abruptly, facing him from less than twenty feet. "What have we got here?" said the closest rider, gigging his horse a few steps ahead of the others. All five looked mildly surprised at finding a wagon on the steep trail.

Coots' first instinct was to reach for the shotgun lying beneath the blanket. But he caught himself in time and sat tensed, his gloved hands held chest high as five pistols sprang from their holsters and pointed at him, cocked and ready to fire.

"Keep your hands right there where we can see them," said the lead horseman.

"You got it, mister," said Coots, already looking to throw the men off from the gold in the wagon bed. "I ain't risking my life for a stack of stinking buff' hides."

The lead rider, a tall lean man wearing a full black beard, looked at his companions, then back at Coots. "Tell me something, teamster," he said. "What is it about us that makes you think we're going to rob you?"

Coots looked them over warily. "Force of habit, I reckon," he said. "I don't run into many white men in these high uppers, especially this time of year, this kind of weather. What ones I have run into was all up to no good." He paused, then asked, "So was I wrong? You fellows are not out to rob me?"

"Oh, we *are* going to rob you," the leader said with a shrug. "I was just curious about how you knew it." He looked past Coots, up the steep snow-covered trail. "How bad is it between here and Cold Devil?"

"It's a tough run of work," said Coots. "But you can see, I brought down a load of stinking half-cured buff' hides in this old Studebaker. I expect you fellows will make it on horseback."

"Yeah, I expect we will." The rider grinned, scratching his beard idly. "You know that's twice you've mentioned them stinking buffalo hides."

"Is it?" Coots said matter-of-factly. "I hadn't noticed."

"I bet you didn't," the lead rider said. He nodded toward the long brake handle. "Jerk that brake back good and tight." Then to one of the riders, he said, "Mike, come take a look at these hides for me."

"Damn it," said a young man wearing a patch over a badly scarred left eye. "I never should have let it be known that I once shot buffalo for a living." He stepped his horse past the lead rider, to the rear of the wagon.

"Mister, I never meant anything about those hides," Coots said in a last effort to dissuade the thieves. "Far as I'm concerned, take them, and good riddance to them. All I hope to do is to finish this run in one piece." Having come upon these men by surprise, catching them without masks covering their faces, and hearing one of them called by name, Coots realized the seriousness of his situation, gold or no gold.

Watching the one-eyed man step down from his saddle and begin inspecting the hides, the lead rider turned his eyes back to Coots and said flatly, "We don't always get what we *hope* for."

The words sent a warning chill up Coots' spine. He sat silently, but giving a cautious sidelong glance along the edge of the trail, judging his chances at making a leap out into the cold air and snagging onto something on his way down the rocky mountainside.

"He's telling the truth about these hides," said One-eyed Mike Flutes, having thrown back the top hide and looked closely at it. "They're only about half-cured. Somebody got into a hurry and sold them cheap before they cured proper. That's a damn shame," he added, reverting back to his days in the hide business.

"Yeah, it sure breaks my heart," the lead rider said with a sarcastic twist. "Before you get too depressed, suppose you might look around under a few of them, see what there could be —"

The lead man's words stopped short as Coots hurled himself up from the driver's seat and out across the back of his horse, actually taking a step on the horse's rump for momentum. "Gawddamn!" the lead man shouted, seeing Coots sail out onto the cold snow-filled air and plunge downward out of sight.

Coots felt tops of short pine and spruce whip him furiously as he rolled and tumbled in a spray of snow, ice, loose rock and broken tree branches. Above him he heard a shot ring out; but he had no fear of it. His hands grasped wildly as he rolled and bounced and slid, gaining speed on his way down.

"What a crazy sumbitch!" said Mike Flutes, hurrying over and looking down the silvery-gray mountainside. "I'd take a fast bullet in the head any day over jumping off a damn cliff!"

"Well, that's you," the lead man said, easing his spooked horse back away from the edge of the trail and holstering his smoking Colt. "Now what about those buff' hides? I don't want to sit here all day." He stepped his horse back to where the other two riders sat looking down in the direction Coots had taken over the edge.

"Maybe he thought he could fly," one man commented, spitting out over the edge.

"Maybe he didn't mean to jump," another said. "Maybe a flea bit his ass." He grinned at his own humor.

One-eyed Mike turned back to the stack of hides, flipped another one over and looked all around under it. Seeing some of the bags of gold dust, he reached out and pulled one to him, opened it carefully and looked inside. "My goodness!" he murmured under his breath. Before saying anything else, he pulled back a bag of gold dust and nuggets and turned it upside down, letting the contents spill onto the course buffalo fur. "Raymond! Damn it, *Raymond!*" he shouted at the lead man. "You've got to see this! The Curly gang has hit the mother lode!"

The lead man, Raymond Curly, gigged his horse to the rear of the wagon and jumped down from his saddle. The other three men were right behind him.

"I pulled back the next hide and damned if all this didn't just jump out at me!" Mike Flutes said, suddenly out of breath, having thrown the heavy snow-laden hide all the way over, exposing all the bags of cash, gold dust and ingots beneath it.

"Whoa!" said Raymond Curly, staggering a bit as if having grown dizzy. Grabbing up a handful of loose gold nuggets from the buffalo hide, he gasped at the sight of them and said, "Whoooeee! Mike, ole pard, ain't you glad you flipped over that buff' hide!"

Fletcher Mays and Crazy John Beck shouldered in beside Raymond and Flutes, their eyes growing wide upon seeing all the loose gold ingots and the bags of dust and nuggets piled farther up in the wagon bed. Ben Bernsten walked first to the front of the wagon, then reached up and pulled the sawed-off shotgun and faded red blanket from the driver's seat. He stuck the shotgun under the blanket roll behind his saddle and threw the red blanket around his shoulders. Then he joined the others at the wagon bed, shoving himself in between Mays and Crazy John.

"Look at all this, Ben!" Mays said as he reached into the wagon bed with his gloved hand and picked up a large nugget.

Before he could stop himself, Raymond Curly instinctively knocked the gold nugget from Mays' hand. But seeing the stunned look on Mays' face, Raymond said, "Damn, I don't know why I done that, Fletcher." He picked the nugget up and put it back into

Mays' waiting hand. "No offense intended."

"None taken." Mays grinned and looked closely at the nugget.

Also inspecting a gold nugget, Ben Bernsten snapped at Crazy John Beck, when the wild-eyed man stepped in too close, "Get your own gold, John! There's a whole gawddamn wagon full. You don't have to breathe in my face!"

Crazy John backed away, but gave Bernsten a vicious look, his hand tightening around the butt of his drawn Colt.

"Who the hell you suppose this belongs to?" Flutes asked, studying a nugget with his good eye. When Raymond Curly just stared at him, Flutes remarked, "Must be that stupid driver's. Only a person stupid enough to jump off a mountain would be stupid enough to carry his gold around in a damn freight wagon under a buffalo. . . ." His words trailed to a halt. He fell into a studious silence for a moment while Raymond and the others stared at him. Finally, Flutes said sheepishly, "Aw, hell, he stole this somewhere, didn't he?"

"That *would be* my guess," Raymond said, giving the one-eyed gunman a look. Picking up the empty gold bag, Raymond looked up the trail in the direction of Cold Devil. "This bag looks familiar." He flipped it to

Crazy John and asked, "Does it look familiar to any of yas?"

The gunmen studied the mine bag. "You're damn right it does," Crazy John Beck said before the other men began to get the idea. "This is our gold! The gold we stole! The gold Spain is supposed to be looking out for! That *snake* son of a bitch!" he shouted and fired two shots into the falling snow, unable to control his boiling temper.

"Easy, Crazy John!" said Raymond. "There's no need in wasting bullets. Let's think about this a minute and see how we turn it to our advantage."

The men looked at one another. Then Raymond gestured toward the bag of gold and grinned. "This looks like only about *half* of what was there. That makes it just about how much we're traveling to Cold Devil to get. This gives me an —"

"Yeah?" Bernsten interrupted. "So we can take this, turn around and go south? Get over into Mexico where there's sand instead of snow? I'm all for that."

Raymond stared at him for a moment, then continued. "As I was about to say, as long as Spain doesn't know we've got this money, he's still got to make good on our share when we get to Cold Devil."

The men thought about it for a second; Crazy John, One-eyed Mike and Mays chuckled at the idea. "Yeah," said Crazy John, "and Spain and Waite is both scared to death of us. They have been ever since we skinned and killed that whiskey peddler last summer for being unsanitary."

Raymond grinned, turning the gold nugget back and forth in his hand. "It pays to keep folks a little bit scared. Makes them politer, easier to deal with."

"You've all lost your damn minds," Ben Bernsten said harshly, standing wrapped in the red blanket. "There's nothing to say this is the same gold."

"No, but it would damn sure be a strange coincidence if *it's not*," Raymond replied. "Anyway, all we've got to do is show up in Cold Devil and keep our mouths shut. We'll know quick enough if it's the robbery gold or not."

"It's not right turning against our own kind," said Bernsten. "Spain has taken care of our gold. We shouldn't turn against him."

"If he's *taken care of it*," Raymond said, "how the hell come it's meeting us halfway down the mountainside? For all we know, this could be Spain's doings, slipping it out of town before we get there. I'm for seeing what we can squeeze out of Spain and Waite when we get there."

"I still say it's bad business, turning against our own kind. I'm not going along with it," Bernsten added, shoving his Colt down into his holster and crossing his arms in a stubborn pose.

"I agree it's a bad thing going against our own kind," said Raymond, stepping around toward his horse and picking the reins up from the ground. "It'll get a man killed if he's not careful."

"Damn right it will," Bernsten said grudgingly.

Crazy John took a quick step backward as Raymond grabbed a handful of the red blanket, raised his pistol with his other hand and shot Bernsten squarely in the back of his head. Bernsten slammed forward onto the icy ground in a spray of blood and brain matter.

"Damn!" Fletcher Mays said. "I sure didn't see that coming!" He and One-eyed Mike looked bewildered, clutching the reins to their spooked horses. Bernsten's horse wheeled quickly on its hind hooves and bolted away down the slick trail.

Raymond tossed the red blanket over his shoulder and let his smoking Colt drift toward the two as he looked at them, making sure there were no objections. "I've seen it coming for the past week," he said. "Have you, Crazy John?"

"Damn right I saw it coming," said John. "He's been getting cross and irritable with me. I couldn't have took much more of it. I'd of shot him myself."

"So has anybody got any problem with me blowing his head off?" Raymond asked, the Colt still poised and smoking in his hand.

"None here," Mays said. He and One-eyed Mike stooped down, picked up Bernsten's body by the heels and shoulders, and carried it to the edge of the trail. Swinging the corpse back and forth, they hurled it out into the falling snow and looked down after it as it disappeared into a silver-gray swirl.

"What was you saying about keeping our mouths shut and seeing what we can squeeze out of Spain and Morgan Waite?" Mays asked.

Raymond grinned and nodded toward the wagon. "Come on, let's get this Studebaker turned around. We'll talk about it on the way to Cold Devil."

CHAPTER 19

Coots had broken several smaller snow-coated branches in his fall down through the interior of the tall pine tree. But as his fall had broken the branches, so had the branches broken his fall. Clinging to the cold trunk of the swaying pine, he looked down at the body of the gunman that had fallen past him only moments earlier, leaving a splatter of blood as it skimmed past an outreaching limb. Seeing the body impaled on the broken branches of a large spruce standing sixty feet below him, Coots realized he'd made the right decision by taking the leap.

He whispered a quick prayer of thanks for his good luck. *Now to get down . . .* Unpinning his trouser leg from a short spike of pine at the tree trunk, he took a careful step down from one large limb to the next, ever mindful of the sharp limbs of the spruce lying below, and the long rocky drop beneath it.

At the bottom of the pine, he leaned against its trunk and took some deep breaths. *So far so good . . .* he told himself. But upon looking all around, he realized that the ledge where he stood had no path leading off the steep mountainside. "Aw, man!" he murmured, looking at the streaks of snow and icicles clinging to a jagged wall of rock.

As he looked upward at the mountainside, he heard a commotion in the spruce tree beneath him and looked down over the edge just in time to see the broken limbs break free of the trunk and send Bernsten's body sliding and bouncing the rest of the way to the thin trail at the bottom of the mountain. Watching the body land limply, Coots winced; but then he looked back and forth and noted the outline of an elk path meandering in and out of the rocks.

Batting his gloved hands together, feeling the cold in his fingertips, he looked once again up the mountain, knowing he would have to make a decision soon or risk freezing to death once the mountainside fell into afternoon shadow and left him stranded for the night. "All right, here goes," he said in a steamy breath. He took his first steps through a long, thick lip of snow that capped the edge of the trail.

To his relief and surprise, once he got himself onto the elk path and headed down, he found the trip safer than he had expected. The snow lay calf deep in spots between rocks, but it was dry and billowy and didn't cling to his heels or turn slick beneath him. Before an hour had passed, he stepped out onto the trail and stood over the dead gunman.

After only a moment of hesitation, he stooped down, slipped the big Colt from its holster and held it in his hand, looking it over. "You won't need this, but I might, if I run into your pards." He rolled the body onto its back and unbuckled the man's gun belt.

Coots took a quick count of the ammunition in the gun belt, then buckled it into a loop and slung it over his shoulder. He stuck the Colt back into its holster. He quickly searched the dead man's coat and trouser pockets and found a few dry wooden matches, a pair of bone dice and a half twist of chewing tobacco. He took a bite of the tobacco and shoved the matches into his coat pocket.

Shaking the dice in his gloved hand, he started to roll them just to see how his luck was running. But then he thought better of it, threw the dice away and stood up, dusting snow from his knees. He looked down at the dead man, then up at the sky, as if trying to think of something to say. Finally, reaching up to remove his hat before he realized he'd lost it, he ran his fingers back through his wet, tangled hair.

"Lord," he said, "I don't know what to say for this man. We met under bad circumstances. Amen." Turning, he walked away along the narrow trail, huddled inside his coat against the renewed snowfall.

Before he'd gone twenty yards, Coots saw his hat lying upturned in the snow beside a rock. The sight of it took him aback for a moment, as if this might be some sort of trick. But after looking back and forth quickly, he cast his suspicions aside, hurried over and gratefully snatched it up from the ground. "Whooeee!" he called out to himself.

Slapping the hat against his leg, he put it on his wet head and pulled it down snug, immediately feeling warmer. "Coots, you're going to be all right," he said to himself. "Just keep doing what you're doing."

Twenty minutes later, he came upon the trail leading up the mountainside. He ducked down quickly and scurried off behind a rock when he caught a glimpse of the lineback dun horse walking into sight from around a turn in the trail. Instinctively he jerked the Colt from its holster; but, upon realizing the horse was riderless, he let out a breath of relief, shoved the pistol back into the holster and stood up, a trace of a smile coming to his cold face.

He reached into his coat pocket, took out a piece of rock candy he carried for his wagon team and walked forward slowly, saying, "Easy, boy," holding the candy out in his gloved hand. "You need me as much as I need you, so don't go nuts on me," he purred, getting closer and closer, seeing no sign that the animal might bolt away. "That a boy . . ."

Only when he felt the reins safely in his hands did he let his tension ease down. Watching the horse lip the piece of candy up from his glove, Coots looked the animal over good, noting the rifle butt sticking up from a saddle scabbard. Then his eyes widened in surprise as he recognized his own sawed-off shotgun butt sticking out from beneath a blanket roll.

"Well, I'll be . . ." Coots whispered, stretching an arm back to the shotgun butt without letting go of the reins. He drew the sawed-off, looked it over good and grinned in his joy and disbelief. "If all this ain't a sign, I don't know *what is!*" He swung up into the saddle with lifted spirits and said to the horse, "Come on, *ole cayuse,* they're not taking that gold away from me."

Turning the horse back to the trail, he rode upward at a cautious pace, the pistol and his reins in his left hand, his shotgun cocked and ready in his right. But there were barely even wagon tracks left by the time he stopped the horse and looked over at a streak of frozen blood that had splattered on the side of a rock. Beneath the rock Coots saw paw prints from where some creature of the wilds had ventured out and licked and scratched at the snow, uncovering its gory contents.

Coots gazed upward along the trail through the falling snow and the waning evening light. The sight of blood served to remind him that although his luck had been holding strong, luck was something that could leave a man flat at any second. With a more solemn look on his face, he nudged the horse forward. He uncocked the shotgun and lay it across his lap, but kept the Colt drawn and ready.

Darkness had all but claimed the sky when he reached the tree where he'd buried part of the gold. His and the dun's were the only tracks on or around the narrow trail; but that fact brought him no comfort until he'd slipped down from the saddle, walked over and uncovered enough of his hidden treasure cache to realize nobody had disturbed it. Then he whispered a silent thanks upward to the darkening sky and sank back against the pine trunk for a moment.

Moments later he'd moved twenty yards up the trail and built a fire behind the cover of four-foot-high rocks that half circled a protruding overhang. "We've both slept in worse, I'll wager," he said to the horse, watching it crunching hungrily on the remains of the rock candy and a handful of grain Coots had found in the dead outlaw's saddlebags.

Coots sat in silence for a long while, feeding small twigs and branches into the fire and staring into the licking flames. "What a day this has been," he said quietly, shaking his head as if in disbelief. He wondered what he should do come morning. There was enough gold here to last him the rest of his life wherever he wanted to live it, he reminded himself.

Yet, seeing Margo's face in his mind, recalling the scent and feel of her, he realized that the gold alone had never been what brought him into this. Curling down onto a blanket from behind the dun's saddle, he smiled, picturing himself pulling his wagon up beneath the window the way he did and catching bag after bag of gold as Margo and Herns threw it down to him.

"Hell, if I know you, Coots," he said, picturing the words coming from Margo's lips instead of his own as he drifted to sleep, "you're going to do whatever suits you."

On the first day, Sam had lain near a fire beneath a ragged lean-to the Romas had prepared for him and Summers in a sheltering pine forest. Trina had insisted the two lawmen move into the wagon long enough to recuperate, but neither of them would hear of it. The fact of the matter was Summers knew that Sam had no intention of lying around the fire for long watching the snowfall close off the passes while the escaped prisoners were on their way back to Cold Devil.

"I'll be up and around by tomorrow morning," Summers had told him, both of them wrapped in blankets near the fire, sipping hot broth Trina had made for them. "I heal fast. Don't leave without me."

"I won't," Sam said, and he meant it. But Summers noted the restraint in his voice. They both knew the marshal's wounds needed more time to heal. "Tomorrow

265

morning I'm searching for our horses."
Thinking of the big Appaloosa stallion, the
ranger's voice softened with the weight of
his loss. "Black Pot never left me stranded
all the time we rode together. I owe him the
same."

"Maybe I can help search," Summers offered.

Sam shook his head. "The best thing you
can do is keep still and get mended. We'll
just take it easy here a while longer," Sam
replied. "I'll find the horses if they're alive.
Spain and Denton will keep."

But even as Sam spoke, Summers saw him
gazing out through the falling snow toward
Cold Devil with a look of urgency in his
eyes.

The next morning, in a false show of
improvement, Summers struggled to his feet
and managed to walk out into the snow-
covered woods behind the lean-to, saying
over his shoulder, "I'm feeling pretty fit.
Maybe I can go searching with you."

Trina had cooked a small pot of oats for
the two. She gave Sam a questioning look
as she stirred a wooden spoon around in
the pot.

"No," Sam said quietly, "he's not going
anywhere."

"I am glad to hear you say this," Trina

said. "If he does not let the wound in his shoulder heal stronger, he will bleed to death out there."

"I know it," Sam said, standing up stiffly. One leg was badly bruised. His torso, front and back, had been battered and cut by tumbling rocks. He walked in the direction Summers had taken and found him stooped in the snow, clutching his shoulder wound. Blood seeped through the blanket around him.

"This isn't the way I want things, Sam," he said in a weak voice. The ranger helped lift him to his feet and looped an arm carefully across his shoulder.

"I understand," Sam said, limping himself as he helped the wounded marshal back to the campsite.

When Summers had settled down and Trina had checked his wound and found it still healing sufficiently, she turned to Sam and said, "Django and some of the men are out searching for your horses. You do not have to do anything but rest." As she spoke, she examined the deep cut on his forehead, which she had pressed together and carefully stitched with a needle and thread.

"Obliged, ma'am," Sam said, "but all the same, I best get out there with them and help out. Black Pot won't take to a stranger."

"No horse ever thinks of Django as a stranger," Trina said confidently; yet she knew that the ranger was going to search no matter what she said.

Moments later, the snow fall had slackened to a halt and let a long ray of sunlight spread down through the low gray sky. On a wagon horse he borrowed from Trina's grandfather, Sam rode out through the knee-deep snow in the direction of the fallen mountainside. He had borrowed a long woollen muffler to replace his lost sombrero. Wrapping the long muffler around his head and the tails of it around his neck in the fashion of the Roma men, he left prepared to spend the entire day if need be in search of Black Pot and Summers' white-stocking roan. But as his mount labored to the crest of a short, steep hill and stopped, Sam looked down into the deep valley and saw Django and three other Romas leading both horses upward toward him on a long, winding trail.

"Oh, my, look at this," Sam said to himself. Black Pot loped along beside Django in the snow, the breath of both man and animal steaming in the cold air. Behind Black Pot, Summers' roan bounded along in the same fashion. Neither animal appeared any worse for the wear. Sam heeled the wagon horse forward, unable to wait for the big Appaloosa to reach him.

At the bottom of the hill, Django and the men stopped as Sam sidled up to them. "We found these fellows in the draw up in the canyon," Django said with a gold-capped smile. "I believe they were happy to see us."

"Obliged," Sam said, unable to say much more for fear his voice would falter. He stepped down from the wagon horse, looked Black Pot over and rubbed his muzzle.

"I checked him for you," said Django. "They are both fine." He sat with his wrists crossed, watching Sam shake his saddle, testing it before stepping up into it.

"I have to ask another favor of you," Sam said, turning Black Pot in the snow and sidling up to Django. He patted the big stallion's neck. "When we get back to the camp, I need for you to keep the roan out of sight for a few days until the marshal is strong enough to ride."

"Ah, yes, I understand," Django said. "We will do that for you."

"Again, much obliged," the ranger said. "Tomorrow I have to ride to Cold Devil to recapture the prisoners."

"You will kill the escaped prisoners and the men who helped them," Django said, a look of regret coming to his dark eyes.

"If that's how it must be," Sam replied; he stopped patting the stallion. "And I'm certain that is how it *must be.*"

Django's dark eyes looked him up and down. "And you will do all of this alone?" he asked in a manner that suggested an offer of help if Sam wanted it.

"You and your people have taken good care of us. You saved our lives," Sam replied. "But I'll take it from here."

CHAPTER 20

Raymond Curly, Fletcher Mays and Crazy John Beck rode into Cold Devil through snow reaching nearly up to their horses' knees. They had left One-eyed Mike Flutes and the wagon in the shelter of a cliff overhang on the other side of the flatlands, five miles away. Halfway across the flatlands, the snow fall had come to a lull, and the sun had once again peeped through the gray sky, making the three riders appear as dark spots on an otherwise glittering white horizon.

"There goes one of the whores carrying a bucket of water," said Mays, gazing at Cold Devil through a field lens. He studied Trixie as she struggled to carry a wooden bucket up onto the boardwalk through a cleared pathway in the snow. With her free hand, she held a heavy coat collar closed at her throat.

"Is she looking our way?" Raymond Curly

asked, barely seeing the tiny figure with his naked eye.

Paying no attention to Raymond, Mays murmured, "*Whoeee!* She looks good, her cheeks all rosy red from the cold." He smiled, watching Trixie's steaming breath waft around her loose ringlets of hair. "I want some of that," he said as she stepped out of sight into the front door of the saloon.

"Gawddamn it!" Raymond said. He reached over and grabbed the lens out of Mays' hand. "You're supposed to be seeing what's going on there — if anybody's watching us ride in or not!"

"I was!" Mays said, rubbing his eye. "All's I saw was the whore carrying the bucket! I would have said it if I saw anything else."

Raymond Curly raised the lens to his eye and looked through the glare of snow and morning sunlight for a moment, seeing no one on the snowy street. "Damn!" He lowered the lens and rubbed his eye. "I don't know how you could see anything anyway."

"Which one was it?" Crazy John asked, looking over at Mays as the three rode on.

"The one you're in love with," Mays said with a thin, crafty grin, staring straight ahead. When Crazy John made no reply, Mays went on. "I remember her from

Abilene, must've been three, four years ago."

"Don't start," Raymond warned.

But Mays continued. "Some of the drovers there bet that she wouldn't lay up on the bar and take on a —"

"Shut up, Mays!" Crazy John shouted. His hand clamped around his gun butt.

"Oh, sorry." Mays chuckled. "I must've already told you the story."

"Both of yas, cut it off!" said Raymond, giving Mays the hardest stare. "When we get in there, I want both of you on your best game. We've got about half or more of the gold. But now that we've already got our share, let's see what's happened, see what else we can shake out of Spain and Waite."

"We've got you, Raymond," said Mays. "Me and John are just poking sticks at one another, right, John?"

Crazy John didn't answer. Instead he stared at Cold Devil and asked Raymond, "Any harm in me spending some time with her?"

"Not until we see what's going on here," said Raymond, nudging his horse a step forward ahead of them. "There'll be enough whores in old Mex to wear all the hair off your belly."

Inside the Gay Lady, Trixie carried the bucket of snow behind the big glowing wood stove and set it out of sight to thaw. Taking off the big coat, she hung it on a wall peg and walked to the bar, where Woods and Carney Blake stood drinking hot black coffee. "It's cold in here," she remarked, rubbing a hand up and down her arm.

"You think so?" said Woods. Looking off toward the far corner, where Rose sat polishing one of the many spittoons piled around him, Woods said, "Rose, what say you get some more firewood into the stove? Trixie's cold."

Without reply, Rose stood up and walked to the stack of firewood along the back wall.

"I'll make a good bar swamper out of him yet," Woods said just among himself, Trixie and Blake.

"I feel sorry for him," Trixie said.

"Yeah, you would." Woods shoved his cigar into his mouth and took a puff. He pursed his lips and let out a smoke ring. "That's why you'll always be nothing but a dumb whore. You can't even realize who's your friend and who's your enemy."

"Take it easy, Stanley," Blake said, wincing at how harshly Woods had spoken to the woman. "Trixie's all right. She treats everybody the same."

"Yeah, that's what I mean," said Woods.

"Rose used to backhand her all over this place, and now she *feels sorry* for him. If that's not stupid, what do you call it?" He took another puff and made another smoke ring.

"I never believed in carrying a grudge," Trixie said with a shrug. "Is that so wrong?" She looked at Carney Blake as she asked.

"No, that's not wrong," Blake said. "Don't pay any attention to Stan. He's got a high horse under him now that Spain put us both over Rose."

Woods grinned. "I've got to admit it feels pretty good not to have to jump every time somebody says my name." He puffed the cigar and added, "From now on, I don't jump up and down for nobody. I take my time, doing whatever I damn well please."

"There's riders coming," Trixie threw in casually.

"Anybody thinks I'm going to get in a big hurry, they can just kiss my —" He stopped; his eyes widened. "What did you say?"

"Yeah, three of them, on horseback," Trixie replied matter-of-factly, nodding her head, casting a finger in the direction of the flatlands.

"Aw, Jesus, Trixie!" said Woods. "You waited all this time to tell me? What's the matter with you?" He straightened his coat and snatched his bowler hat up from the bar. "You heard Spain and Morgan Waite tell me to keep them informed if anybody rode in!"

"Well, now you can go tell them," Trixie said, calmly, with a thin smile.

"Damn it! Watch the bar!" Woods commanded her. "Come on, Carney!" he shouted over his shoulder on his way across the floor. Snatching his heavy wool coat from a wall peg, he disappeared out the door.

Blake whispered, "I swear, Trixie," giving her a secret smile. "I'm right behind you, boss!" he called out to Woods, snatching his new broad-brimmed Stetson hat from the bar top.

No sooner had the two left the Gay Lady than Trixie poured herself a cup of coffee and stepped around behind the bar. As she picked up a rag and began wiping the bar top, Rose walked up and said humbly, "Trixie, I heard what you just said about not holding a grudge. I want you to know that I feel the same way. If I can do anything for you, I will. And I'm hoping maybe you'll feel the same way, if you can do anything for me. Maybe we could let bygones be bygones? What do you say?"

"Go fuck yourself, Rose," Trixie said,

continuing to wipe the bar without so much as a glance toward him.

"Is this your best work, Woods?" Waite growled as he shoved his shirt down into his trousers and stepped away from the window that looked out across the flatlands. On the thick feather bed Margo lay flat on her back, naked except for a thin sheet thrown across her belly. She smoked a cigarette, rocking a knee back and forth, staring idly at the ceiling.

"No, sir. I — I came running as soon as I saw them. The snow glare must've kept them hidden."

Swinging up off the bed, Margo stood fully naked in front of the two men for a moment, cocking a hand onto her hip. "My God, what a weak, simpering turd you are, Stanley," she said, shaking her head, then slowly reaching for a soft plush robe lying over a chair back.

Seeing the flushed look come to Woods' face at the sight of the buxom naked woman, Waite chuckled mirthlessly and said, "Yeah, I know what you mean. That's *why* she can call me by my first name." His gaze turned bemused by Woods' expression. "What? You mean you two never . . . ?"

"Poor Stanley isn't able to keep my interest up, if you know what I mean," Margo said with a thin, cruel smile, wrapping the robe snuggly around herself.

"Pitiful," Waite said under his breath, picking up his hat and bearskin coat as he stepped past Woods and into the hallway of the overcrowded hotel. Woods scrambled to keep up to him.

Along the hallway, a few late risers still lay wrapped in ragged wool blankets, most of them having fled to Cold Devil to get out of the snow. "Where's Jack Spain?" Waite asked, looking around as if Spain might appear.

"Him and Blake are both waiting out front of Bracket's Restaurant," Woods said. "We found him having breakfast there. Your men are gathering there right now. They've been searching the town all morning, just like you told them to."

"No sign of the gold, ingots or otherwise, eh?" Waite asked, walking down the stairs to the hotel lobby.

"No progress that I know of," Woods said. "All signs of guilt seem to point to the teamster Coots."

"I'm starting to think the same thing," Waite said, "but he couldn't have done it by himself. He had to know somebody who could get him into the office, into the gold,

and out with all it before anybody saw him."
His gaze narrowed on Woods' eyes.

Feeling uncomfortable, Woods said, "Then
it would have to be one of the whores, either
Trixie or Margo or both. They have always
had free roam of the place, except for
Spain's private office."

"Or you," Waite said. "You seem to get
around wherever you please in the Gay
Lady."

"No, sir, Mr. Waite. It's not me, so help
me God!" Woods said. "I don't want you
thinking I had anything to do with it!"

"Then back off the womenfolk!" Waite
snapped at him. "I have a soft spot for
Margo. Trixie too since she's Margo's
friend."

"Mr. Waite, those two whores are *much
more* than friends," Woods ventured. "I've
caught them with my own eyes going at it."

Waite stopped dead in his tracks. He
turned, grabbed Woods by his shirt and
lifted him onto his toes. "Are you willing to
bet your eyes on that, Woods?"

"I'm only telling you what I know from
my personal exper—"

Waite cut him off. "Because that's what
you'll be doing the next time you open your
mouth about Margo or Trixie — either one!
That's the most disgusting low-down lie I've

ever heard." He glared hard at Woods. "Wouldn't you *agree?*"

"Yes, sir, you are absolutely right! It's all one big lie!" Woods said. "I'm sorry I ever repeated such a terrible story. I must have lost my mind!"

"Yes, you must have." Waite turned him loose and continued down the stairs and out the door, grumbling under his breath, "Lying son of a bitch."

On the boardwalk out front of Bracket's Restaurant, Waite and Woods found Jack Spain standing amid Waite's men, his checkered linen breakfast napkin still hanging beneath his chin. Spain stared out toward the approaching riders with a troubled expression on his face. Beside Spain, Stanton Clark and Max Denton took their eyes off the riders and walked up to Waite.

"We barely saw them in time to get some of our rifles atop the roof line." As Clark spoke, he nodded along the roofs of the hotel and the mercantile store. "I can't say if Raymond Curly and his men saw them getting into position or not."

"Well, I expect we're about to find out, Stanton," said Waite, stepping over beside Jack Spain.

"How come none of your *regulators* saw them coming sooner?" Spain asked, his voice sounding nervous and agitated.

"Beats me," said Waite, calmly. "If you don't like the way me and my *regulators* are doing things, this is a good time to let me know. I'll pull them out of here."

Spain settled down and said, "Don't mind me, Morgan. I'm all wound up over this." He stared off toward the three riders as they pushed through the snow and within the town limits.

"As well you should be, Spain," Waite said, also staring at the three riders. Along the roof line, sunlight glinted off a rifle barrel.

Upon seeing the glint of sunlight, Mays said to Raymond Curly, "We're riding straight into a trap, Raymond! At least let us draw our rifles and let them know we're putting up a fight!"

"No!" Raymond demanded. "Leave them booted!" He raised a gloved hand toward Spain and Waite, and the men gathered on the boardwalk. "A man is never trapped if he's got something everybody wants." He gave a friendly grin and veered his horse over toward the waiting men. "Look at those worried faces," he said under his breath. "I've got a feeling that gold has been the talk of the town."

"Welcome, Raymond Curly and associates!" Spain called out heartily as the horses drew up to the hitch rail, where the snow had been cleared away by two old miners for the price of a hot breakfast. "We've been expecting you fellows."

"I see you have been *expecting somebody,*" Curly said, nodding toward the roof line. His grin widened, but kept a sharp edginess to it. "I'm glad you didn't mistake *us* for them." He stared flatly at Spain and Waite.

"No, indeed," Spain said, thinking fast. "I had some damn lawmen come drag me out of town for a while. But Waite and his men came to my rescue. We've kept men posted ever since in case the lawmen come back."

"What?" Raymond looked puzzled. "You mean some lawdogs dragged you out of your own town, and they're still alive to tell about it?"

"Oh, no, they're dead," Spain said quickly. "But you never know. There could be others coming." He wasn't able to keep the nervousness out of his voice.

"More lawmen coming?" Raymond said, enjoying seeing Spain in a tight spot. "Sounds like you've been running a loose ship here, Texas Jack." He looked back and forth along the boardwalk, then said, "I hope you have looked after what I left here for your safekeeping."

"I've done my best, Raymond," Spain

said. "But I'm afraid I've got some bad news."

"Bad news? Uh-oh," Raymond said, feigning a troubled frown. "I don't like the sound of this." He looked at Mays and Crazy John.

"Neither do we," Mays said, speaking for himself and Crazy John.

"Wait a minute!" Spain said, holding his hands out in a show of peace. "Don't jump to conclusions. Climb down. Let's have a drink. Any problem we might have can be settled."

Raymond slipped down grudgingly from his saddle, as did Mays and Crazy John. "We didn't come here to settle a problem," he said. "We came here to get our gold."

CHAPTER 21

Inside the saloon, Raymond Curly, Crazy John and Mays listened to Spain's story about his and Denton's arrests, and how they had come back to Cold Devil and found out the gold had been stolen. At the end of the story, Raymond Curly looked back and forth calmly from one tense face to the next. "That's a hell of a story, Texas Jack," he said in calm voice. He slid his empty shot glass across the bar for Trixie to fill it.

Spain watched Raymond's eyes intently as whiskey poured in a thin braid into the shot glass. "And every word of it is true," Spain added, gesturing a nod at the men surrounding him and Waite.

Beside Raymond, Crazy John slid his empty glass forward and said politely, "Me too, Miss Trixie, if you please." He stared at Trixie longingly, not seeming too concerned with the conversation or the atmosphere around him.

Mays shook his head, finished his drink of rye and said to Spain, "But still, I guess what I don't understand is why somebody's head ain't stuck on a pole out front wearing a sign that says, *'This son of a bitch is dead! Now where's my gawddamn money'?*"

The men all turned their attention to him when he'd finished. "Oh?" Waite took a step forward and asked pointedly, "And whose head might that be, Mays? I'd like to know."

"For starters, your gawddamned cousin Clement," Mays said bluntly, his expression and demeanor telling Raymond Curly that he might have forgotten that they already had their share of the stolen gold and were simply playing for something extra.

"Spain just told you we're looking *all the hell* over town for my cousin!" Waite said.

"Maybe you should forget all the hell over town!" said Mays in the same raised tone of voice. "Maybe you should be looking *all the hell* down the trail!" He looked at Raymond for support. "Are you believing this shit? Who's to say that ole cousin Clement ain't in this with some help of family members?" His angry stare cut back to Waite.

"Easy now, Mays," Raymond cautioned, seeing Waite growing more and more angry himself. "Let's not start chopping heads till we know which head to chop." He turned the heat of the conversation to Spain and said, "It seems to me that no matter what's happened to our gold, Texas Jack has to be good for it."

"Whoa, hang on now," Spain said. "I'm not standing good for that kind of money! I can't! I don't even have that kind of money!"

"You've got the Gay Lady," Raymond said without having to give it a thought. "She ain't worth the kind of gold that we've got coming. But I say you either come up with the gold or start packing your personals." He gave a tight smile, but not at Spain. Instead, he turned his gaze to Waite. "What do you say, Waite? Is the man who holds money for a fee responsible for it or not?" His smile said that he already knew the answer.

Waite said, "That's true, Texas Jack. You knew the responsibility you took on when you agreed to hold that gold for us. If you didn't mean to take it on, you should have made it clear right then, not now." Waite saw this as a chance to shift the conversation away from his cousin Clement. If Clement had slipped out of Cold Devil with the gold, Waite knew he'd show up. When he did, Waite would get a lion share for himself, not to mention the ten thousand

Spain had promised.

Leaning over the bar closer to Trixie, Crazy John whispered as he laid his hand over hers, "Hear that? You'll soon be working for me."

"Nothing would suit me better," Trixie whispered, smiling coyly but listening closely to every word the men said to one another.

"There's another son of a bitch I'd shorten from the neck down!" Mays said, still raging, barely under control. He pointed an accusing finger at Ned Rose, who stepped in through the side door out of the snow and walked forward with a grim look on his face.

"I found your cousin, Mr. Waite," Rose said, standing slump shouldered. "He's dead."

"Clement? Dead? No!" Waite looked stunned. "Where is he? What happened to him?"

"I'll show you," Rose said, turning mechanically and walking back out through the side door.

Spain and Raymond gave each other curious looks, Raymond's less sincere than Spain's. He and Mays fell in behind Spain and followed him and Waite out to the wood stacks behind the Gay Lady. Looking back, seeing Waite's men behind them, Raymond asked between him and Mays, "Where the hell is Crazy John if we need him?"

"Looks like he stayed to do some moon eyeing with that whore," Mays whispered. "I told you he's in love with her."

"Gawddamn it!" said Raymond.

Stopping at the wood stacks and looking down at the frozen body lying facedown in a dirty stretch of trampled snow, Waite shook his head slowly in grief and anger.

"I drew back the tarp to get to a new stack and he just dropped over on his face," Rose said.

"Get him up from there," Waite demanded, clenching and unclenching his fists.

Lode Stewart, Riley Padgett and George Trubough hurried forward, lifted the planklike figure from the ground and leaned him back against a stack of seasoned wood. Dirty snow clung to the wide-open eyes and filled the gaping mouth. Waite saw the purple bullet hole in the center of his cousin's forehead. The corpse held its frozen right hand chest high as if a gun might have been pried from its stiff fingers.

"God, I hate seeing ole Clement like this," Riley Padgett said, trying in vain to wipe dirty ice from the dead man's face.

Staring at the corpse, Waite quickly realized that any prospects he'd had about Clement and him sharing the stolen gold were now gone. "I want the no-good bastard who killed him," Waite growled, "and I want him fast!" His dark stare turned to Spain.

"Morgan, this has nothing to do with me! I was with you on the trail coming back here, remember?"

"You swing weight in this shit hole of a town!" Waite said. "You better start swinging it in a way that comes up with Clement's killer!"

Seeing Waite's anger starting to boil, Ned Rose withdrew a few feet from the gathered men and eased away toward a shed standing behind the saloon.

"Look at this," Woods said to Blake. The two men stood out front of the hotel, where they had watched the men leave the saloon through the side door. "See him?" Woods nudged Carney Blake, directing his attention to Ned Rose.

"Yes, I see him all right," Blake said, turning his gaze to Rose. "I told him to get those spittoons shined."

"Forget the spittoons," said Woods. "It looks like he's hiding something up under his coat."

"It sure does," Blake said, seeing Rose

struggle with the shed door until he shoved enough snow back to slip inside. "Let's see what he's up to."

The two stepped down off the boardwalk and trudged to the shed, hearing the angry raised voice of Morgan Waite resound around the side of the Gay Lady Saloon. "Wonder what that's all about," Woods said before they reached the shed.

"I don't know," Blake said. "But I've got a feeling these boys are going to be shooting holes through one another anytime now."

"Yeah," Woods said, looking back over his shoulder toward the sound of Waite's and Spain's voices. "We're known as Spain's men now. We'll be okay if Spain comes out on top, but we could be in big trouble otherwise."

"I'd feel much better if we had more guns in our corner," Blake said. As he spoke of more guns, he swung the door to the shed open and saw Rose holding an ice-coated gun cocked in his face. "Uh-oh," Blake said, stopping suddenly.

"Don't shoot him, Rose!" Woods pleaded.

"What are you two turds doing following me?" Rose demanded, his voice back to its same old hateful tone.

"We saw you come in here! We came to check and see if you're all right! What's going on around the corner?"

"Get inside! Shut the door!" Rose demanded. "Did anybody else see me come in here?"

"No, I don't think so," Woods said. "What's going on around the —"

"I found Clement Sanderson, shot deader than a plumb bob," said Rose. "That's what's going on." As he spoke, he gestured the icy gun barrel toward his Remington sticking up from Blake's belt. "Hand it over, Blake."

Looking at the ice-coated gun on Rose's hand, Blake said calmly, "I doubt that gun will fire, Rose, so settle down."

"If it's cocked, it'll fire," Rose said, making sure Blake saw the hammer pulled back on the big Colt.

"All right," Blake said. Reaching slowly and pulling the Remington from his gun belt, he handed it to Rose. "I take it that's Clement's gun."

Rose gave a nasty smile; but he lowered the ice-coated gun from Blake's face, uncocked it and shoved both guns down into his waistband, having left his customary waist sash in his room. "That might be the first time you've been right all day, *rummy.*"

Blake bristled. "There's no cause for name calling, Rose. If you've got trouble with me, we can settle up right. We're both armed."

"Hold it, both of you!" Woods said, coming dangerously close to stepping in between them. "We might all three need to think about how we're going to stay alive if things take a wrong turn here!" He looked at Rose and asked, "Why have you always had it in for Blake, anyway? He's never wronged you that I know of."

Blake cut in, saying, "He's down on me because he knows I've already *had* something he craves, but can't get ahold of. I've been a top gunman most of my life. All he's done is slung beer and wished he could shoot somebody famous."

"*Been* is the right word for it too," Woods said. "Look at you. You're a once-was, a *has-been,* a broken-down whisky-soaked saddle tramp. Yeah, you had a name for a while. But you didn't deserve it and you couldn't keep it. So don't compare your worthless self to me."

For a moment, Woods and Blake stood in rapt silence, just staring at Rose, seeing if his rant was over. Finally, Woods shook his head slightly, as if to clear it, and said, "Jesus, Rose, Carney's right. You're ate up with envy!"

"So what if I am?" Rose said, letting out a breath of relief. "You asked me. I told you.

Now what about the situation here? What makes you think we need to side up and help one another?"

Blake had settled, not allowing himself to be affected by the hot-tempered bartender. But he kept a cold, flat stare on him as Woods said, "I'll tell you what makes me think it. Spain is running out of string with both Waite and Raymond Curly. Being known as Spain's men makes us all three walking targets."

Rose seemed to consider everything. "Raymond already told Spain he's taking over the Gay Lady if Spain doesn't come up with the money he owes him. I heard him say so when I walked through the door."

"See?" Woods said. "Everybody is sitting on a powder keg here. All it's going to take is one small spark to send us all up in smoke. Where does that leave us if we don't side together?"

Rose looked at the two closely, tapping his fingers on the butt of the big Remington, glad to have it back within his reach. "What will it mean to us if we *do* stick together?"

"Staying *alive,* for starters," said Blake, but that by itself didn't seem to be enough for Rose. He looked at Woods, as if expecting more.

"Once, Spain, Curly and Waite all go at

293

it," Woods ventured, "if we're still standing when the smoke clears, we could all three become saloon owners. That's something I always wanted."

Blake added, "If you're looking to gain a reputation with a gun, I don't know what better chance you'll have than right here in Cold Devil."

"We keep Spain thinking we're his men," Rose murmured, thinking out loud.

Blake and Woods both nodded in agreement.

Rose continued, tapping his fingertips as he thought things through. At length, he said flatly, "Count me in. But don't get in my way once the killing starts."

During one of the lulls in the snowfall, the ranger spotted the smoke from One-eyed Mike's campfire spiraling up into the gray sky. He followed the smoke until he found himself stopping the Appaloosa and looking down on a wide ridge seventy yards below. He'd been two days on the snow-filled trails from the other side of Thunder Pass. This would be the morning when Django told Marshal Summers that they had found his horse, Sam reminded himself, looking back along his trail as if the wounded marshal might be following him.

Sam hoped the marshal would continue to lie low and recuperate with the Romas even after they gave him his horse. But he doubted that would be the case. If things had gone the other way around, he wouldn't have waited, Sam thought to himself, gazing down at the blazing campfire. He hadn't *lied* to Summers the night before he'd left. He'd simply told him the gypsies had found Black Pot. Then he told him he believed the roan would show up in a day or two.

Summers would have done him the same way, Sam decided, allowing himself a trace of a smile behind his woollen muffler, as he thought about it. His eyes followed a set of wagon tracks leading out of sight into the mountainside. "Now, then," he whispered to Black Pot, as if getting back to business, "why would anybody be up here freighting in this kind of weather?"

As he backed Black Pot and turned him on the trail, he thought about the freight wagon and the gray-bearded teamster he and Summers had spotted from afar on their way to Cold Devil. They'd seen the kegs of beer in the big Studebaker wagon as it had struggled along the high trail. Could this be the same man? If it was, he'd sure taken a long time finishing his run. Sam looked west at the setting sun as he rode down carefully and quietly through the smooth, undisturbed snow.

On the ledge, One-eyed Mike Flutes had spent most of the afternoon clearing his share of the mountainside of any visible deadfall wood sticking up from the snow. By dark he had the fire licking high into the night in spite of Raymond having ordered him to keep a low flame. Yeah, sure, what did Raymond care . . . ? He wasn't the one up here freezing his nuts off, Mike reminded himself.

Finishing the last drink from a whiskey bottle he'd kept hidden in his saddlebags, Mike let out a belch and threw the empty into the fire. He sat on the remaining pile of deadfall that he'd saved for the long night ahead. Tomorrow he'd have to go a little farther away on his horse and drag back enough to make it through another long night.

"Hello the fire," Sam called out, seeing the man clearly from behind a rock along the edge of firelight. He'd watched the campsite long enough to know that the man was alone.

"Hello, yourself," One-eyed Mike said, looking back and forth, trying to find the direction the voice had come from. "Come in and make yourself seen." A rifle lay three feet away, to his right side. The ranger knew what had just crossed his mind as the man rubbed his palm up and down his trouser leg. He'd just wished he'd laid the rifle a little closer.

But it was too late for him to wish it now. Sam walked into sight with his rifle in hand, the barrel slumped a bit, but his hand in place on the small of the stock, his finger inside the trigger guard. "Sonsabitch," One-eyed Mike growled to himself, seeing the badge on Sam's chest through his open coat.

"How'd the beer run go?" Sam stepped forward into the firelight and closer to One-eyed Mike.

Mike, having no idea what the ranger meant by such a question, didn't answer. He gave Sam's muffler-wrapped head and face a curious look and said, as his hand slipped off his leg and closer to the rifle, "Do I *know you,* lawdog? Are you some kind of A-rab?"

Realizing this wasn't the teamster he and Summers had seen on the trail, Sam replied, tipping his rifle barrel up, "You don't know me yet, but I'm the man who shot your hand off, if it keeps crawling."

Mike's hand stopped suddenly, halfway to the rifle stock. But his right hand lay poised near his holstered Colt. "I don't know who you think I am, but you've got the wrong man," he said. Then he asked, looking closer with his one eye, "Besides, ain't that an Arizona badge you got there?"

"Yes, I'm an Arizona Ranger," Sam replied, "but I'm a U.S. federal marshal assigned to this territory." He loosened the muffler and pulled it down off the bridge of his nose.

"Oh, you're a ranger. No, you're a marshal." Mike shook his head and said, "That's all just confusing as hell. Where the hell did you get such head gear as that?"

"Listen to me close because I'm only going to tell you once," Sam said, speaking slow and distinctly. "Raise your Colt with two fingers and let it fall."

"Am I under arrest?" Mike asked, even as he slowly did as he was told. "Can't we talk about this?"

"We can talk," said Sam. "First of all, where's the teamster I saw driving that Studebaker?" He nodded at the wagon sitting behind Mike against the mountainside. A few yards away, the team horses and Mike's riding horse stood tied to a jagged rock.

"That wagon? *Pa's* wagon? Is that what this is about?" Mike looked relieved. "Hell, why didn't you say so? That was my pa!"

Mike grinned, as if clearing up a misunderstanding. "Hell, I sent him home! He's there right now, warming his toes, safe and sound with Ma and the kids!"

A rifle shot exploded, kicking up splinters of wood just beneath Mike's rear end. "Jesus!" he shrieked, quickly clamping his spread knees together. "I wasn't reaching for nothing!" He stuck his hands in the air. "See?"

"No more family fire-side stories," Sam said, jerking another round into his rifle chamber. "If I kill you and leave you for the varmints, nobody will ever know we met."

"I'm One-eyed Mike Flutes," Mike replied, speaking in a more serious tone. "What do you want to know?"

CHAPTER 22

After handcuffing the outlaw, Sam sipped hot coffee from a tin cup while he listened to the other man tell him everything that had happened with the teamster and the gold. Sam realized One-eyed Mike hadn't intended to mention the gold; but once the ranger had found it in the wagon, he came clean on how Texas Jack Spain had been holding the gold for them. Still, he didn't say anything about where the gold had come from.

When Mike had finished, Sam sat staring at him for a moment, the long wool muffler unwound from his head and lying at his side. Turning one of the three-inch-long ingots in his gloved hand, he said, "This gold is stolen from a mine shipment. The old Blooming Mine."

Mike looked impressed. His eyes widened. "How'd you know that, Ranger?"

"It's stamped right here," Sam said, holding up the ingot. "I heard they lost a large shipment last year, right before they went out of business."

"Oh," Mike said, less impressed now that Sam explained it. "Well, I wouldn't know anything about that," he said with a shrug. "We bought the gold in a legitimate exchange with some miners farther up. They told us that they melted and poured their own ingots! Those damned liars!" Mike exclaimed.

"Without looking close enough to see the stamping?" Sam knew better. "Blooming Mine is the only mining company who refined their own gold on site," Sam said. "No small operation could have afforded to do it."

"I stand corrected," Mike said. Then, to change the subject, he said, "It was an awful shame about the teamster. He sailed out off the edge like a damned bird! We already told him we wasn't going to harm him. I expect he didn't believe us."

"I expect not," Sam said. "Are you sure he was dead?"

"If he ain't, he never will be, jumping off the mountain like that."

"He might have weighed his odds and saw he had a better chance at staying alive if he jumped. He could've grabbed onto a tree while he was sliding down and saved himself," Sam commented. "It's happened more then once."

"You really think a man can jump off a mountain and live?" Mike asked, less skeptical than he had been.

"It all depends on how his luck was running," Sam replied, thinking of him and Summers falling with the large boulder. "I won't say he *did.* But I will say *he could have.*"

"What the hell kind of answer is that?" Mike asked.

"The only kind you'll get this time of a night," said Sam. "Why don't you get some sleep? We're heading into Cold Devil first thing come morning."

"All right," Mike said, "but I hope you won't tell Raymond I said anything — especially nothing about how I had a big fire going?"

"I won't if you won't," the ranger said. He watched the cuffed outlaw rustle with a blanket until he settled on the ground beside the fire. Knowing he could only doze lightly throughout the night, Sam sipped another strong cup of black coffee and huddled down in his coat and wool muffler with a blanket thrown around himself. During the night the snowfall came and went once again, dusting the land with a fresh white coat.

As first light appeared dully on the grainy gray horizon, Sam stepped over and nudged the sleeping outlaw with his boot toe. "Wake up, Flutes. Let's get going," he said.

"Aw, damn it," One-eyed Mike said in a sleepy voice. He looked up at the ranger with his good eye. "Why are we in such a hurry? I'm not an early riser by nature."

"You are today," Sam said. "This snow will start again anytime. We don't want to get stuck out here." He stepped away from Mike to the horses, keeping watch on him as he cradled his rifle and carried Black Pot's saddle and blanket over to where the horses stood huddled together beneath a waft of steam from their backs and their breath.

"Says you," Mike replied, standing up on wobbly legs for a moment as if having to steady himself to get a start on the day. "I come to a conclusion last night, lawdog."

Sam stared at him. "Oh, what's that?" he asked, not liking either the tone of voice or the look on Mike's face. He started walking slowly back toward him, dropping Black Pot's saddle to free up his gun hand, in case Mike had somehow managed to slip a gun past his search.

Mike gave the ranger a cold, belligerent look above a strange grin and said as he started running, "My luck's as good as the next fellow's!"

Seeing him head straight for the edge of the cliff, Sam shouted, "No! Mike! Wait!" as he raced to stop him. But the outlaw was fast and determined. Try as the ranger might, he reached the edge only in time to see Mike lunge out, his legs still running for a ways before he let out a scream and plunged straight down, his cuffed hands clawing the air as if seeking purchase. His eye patch flew from his face and fluttered away on its own like some long-legged black insect.

"Aw, Flutes . . ." Sam watched him drop belly first more than four hundred feet, an unimpeded fall that offered not so much as one rough plush bed of snow-covered pine limbs to break his fall. Looking down Sam noted there were no slopes on the mountainside where the outlaw might have slid long enough to grab on to protruding tree roots or slow his fall in any way.

Instead Flutes rode the full force of gravity through the cold air and came to a splattering halt atop the only large boulder lying beside the trail below, bald of even a cushion of snow. Sam winced as the sound of bone and flesh on rock echoed along the frozen mountainside.

Sam shook his head and stepped back from the edge, wondering as he turned back toward the horses what must've been going through Flutes' mind. "Easy, boys," he said, raising a soothing gloved hand toward the team horses, who had been spooked by all the commotion. Flutes' horse stood watching unaffected as Sam saddled Black Pot and prepared the team horses for the ride down to Cold Devil.

He wasn't sure how much of One-eyed Mike's story about Spain having lost a large amount of gold he'd been holding for Raymond Curly was true. But he kept the details of it in mind while he harnessed and readied the wagon horses for the ride down the mountain.

Before starting the slippery descent, he took the gold from the wagon and placed it behind a tall rock that leaned against the steep mountainside. He brushed snow up around the rock for good measure, then rubbed his hands together and climbed into the wagon, allowing both Black Pot and Flutes' horse to follow without tying their reins to the wagon bed, lest something go wrong and the wagon take a sudden plunge off the edge of the trail.

It was midmorning by the time Sam reached the snow-covered switchback four hundred feet below. Stopping the wagon for a moment at the base of the large boulder upon which lay the dead outlaw, Sam looked down and saw the black eye patch lying twisted in the fresh snow. Flutes' horse walked over and lowered his muzzle to it as if the strip of cheap linen offered some sort of answer.

Seeing the horse take a standing position, as if it might wait for its owner's return, Sam set the wagon brake and stepped down into the snow. "You best stick with us for a while," he said, walking over to the confused animal. He stooped, picked up the eye patch and shook specks of snow from it before he shoved it down in his coat pocket. Sam took the animal by its bridle and led it back over beside Black Pot in the middle of the trail.

In their sleeping room above the Gay Lady, Trixie arose before dawn at the sound of Margo rapping softly three times on the door. "I'm coming," Trixie whispered. Keeping a lamp trimmed low, she moved quietly to the door, opened it and looked cautiously along the dark hallway as Margo slipped inside. "Is everything okay?" Trixie asked anxiously, shutting the door and locking it.

"Everything is going as well as can be expected," Margo said, pushing back her disheveled hair. "Do you have us some winter clothes packed and ready?"

"Yes, but it's getting worse and worse out there," said Trixie. "It's starting to snow again." She gestured toward the window.

"I know," Margo said. "But if things get too bad for us here, we'll have to take our chances on the trails."

"I understand," Trixie said. "Our bags are under the bed for when we need them."

Changing the subject, Margo said, "Morgan Waite is the randiest bastard I've ever seen." She flopped down on the side of the bed, pulled a short cigar from behind her ear, lit it and blew out a long stream of smoke. "He finally fell asleep a few minutes ago." She sighed and said, "Poor bastard, he's one of those Southern boys who's got a pecker like a jersey bull . . . but he doesn't have the slightest idea how to make it count." She sighed again and asked, "How was your night?"

"Not bad," Trixie said. "Crazy John can't hold his load for a full minute. Then he shakes like he's having a fit and spends the next half hour asking if he done it good. I lie to him, tell him yes. Then he begs me to marry him." She shrugged. "I always say, 'Sure,' but he forgets it as soon as he's sober."

"They must all be kin somehow," Margo said with a tight yawn.

"You're wore out," Trixie said, stepping up onto the bed behind her on her knees. "Here, let me work you over." She loosened Margo's dress, pulled it down past her breasts and began kneading her soft, smooth shoulders.

"Oh, God, thank you, sweetheart," Margo said, slumping and relaxing beneath Trixie's fingers. She closed her eyes and smoked, the bed creaking softly beneath them.

"Don't start moaning like you do," Trixie said. "These fools already think we're lovers."

"It's a good thing we let them think it." Margo smiled dreamily. "It's the only thing that has kept all these jacks from trying to own us outright, like livestock."

"Speaking of these jacks, do you think any of them is starting to figure out what we done?" Trixie asked, working harder on the shoulders, causing Margo to moan quietly in spite of herself.

"I expect someone to figure it out any minute," Margo replied, catching herself and quieting down. "We're overdue to get out of here, but we'll be lucky if we make it down the mountainside now before spring."

"I don't know if I can take it if they start getting rough. I'm sick of getting knocked around," Trixie said.

"We've both got to stay tough for the time being," Margo replied. She reached up and placed her hand over Trixie's, stopping the kneading for a moment. "I've got to count on you being strong along with me. We're going to have to play all sides against the other, wait it out and see who's left standing."

"It's only you and me and Herns," Trixie said. "I'd feel better if Coots were here with that shotgun he carries."

"So would I," Margo said. She smiled, thinking of Coots. "He's about the only man I would have trusted in all this. But it was important for him to get out of here" — her voice lowered — "and get the gold down the mountainside." She released Trixie's hand after a short squeeze and let her go back to gripping and caressing her warm, smooth flesh. Margo closed her eyes again and continued smoking.

"I know," Trixie said. "I'm just scared, is all. I'm afraid any minute we're going to hear that Herns broke down under pressure and told Spain everything."

"I doubt it," Margo said. "Herns is good at only telling white folks what he wants them to hear."

"But if Spain goes nuts and starts hurting him," Trixie said, "he could lead him right to us." She stopped rubbing Margo's shoulders as if giving the matter fearful contemplation. "Herns didn't get rid of that hook as quick as he should have."

"Yeah, but he thought fast and handled it well when Rose asked him what it was." Margo smiled. "And he swore to me that Rose is the only other person who saw it."

"I know, but still . . ." Trixie let her words trail and began massaging again, reaching her hands over Margo's shoulders and down onto her breasts.

Margo moaned softly, taking pleasure in the warmth of Trixie's hands. "Besides, if it hadn't been for Herns making that hook, we could never have reached beneath the floor of the stock room over into Spain's office and snagged the bags of gold. Herns has earned his share. He's okay."

"Of course, he is," Trixie said. "I've just got to get a grip on myself. I'm wondering if maybe we didn't act too fast. Maybe we should've waited like we planned to."

"No, we had to get it done as soon as we heard Spain was in jail," Margo said, finishing her cigar. "You saw how quick Rose went after the safe. What do you suppose he'd have done if he'd found the trap door under the dresser? Think he would have left it there, *kept an eye on it,* the way he said he would? Ha. We're lucky he didn't beat us to it . . . after all our weeks of planning and getting ready."

"You're right. I know you're right," said Trixie. "I'm just too nervous and upset."

"Yes, I see you are," Margo said. "Maybe you're the one who needs some soothing." She reached forward and laid the cigar in an ashtray, then half turned and gave Trixie a gentle shove.

Trixie fell backward onto the feather mattress, opened her robe and cupped her firm round breasts. "Start with my peaches?" she asked coyly.

"I'd love to," Margo said. Straddling Trixie on her knees, she rubbed her hands together firmly to warm them. Then she reached down gently to Trixie's breasts.

On the boardwalk across the street, Rose, Woods and Carney Blake stood in the dark morning shadows, having watched Margo go up the stairs inside the nearly empty saloon only moments earlier. "It sickens me, thinking what they do to one another up there," Rose said, nodding through the falling snow toward the dimly lit upstairs window.

"Who cares?" Blake said. "Are we going to talk to the negro or not? Spain will be expecting us in his office before long."

"Yeah, let's do it," Rose said. "I keep thinking about that hay hook he was breaking up. There was something going on there, and I know these whores are in on it."

"So is that teamster Coots, I have a hunch," Woods said.

"Coots is long gone with the gold," Rose said. "Our only hope is to find out where he took it and how to find him. Herns or one of the whores will tell us if we lean hard enough." He gave a flat, mirthless grin. "Then we're out of here and after it."

"Weather permitting," said Woods.

"That's you, Woods," Rose said. "I'll be going weather permitting or not."

Chapter 23

Inside Bracket's Restaurant, Morgan Waite sat at a table, sipping a cup of hot coffee. Across from him, he'd had Claire Bracket set an extra cup and saucer for Raymond Curly for when he arrived, which was less than five minutes later. But Curly didn't have a coffee. Instead, when he'd given the place a quick once-over, he walked to the table, sat down, took off his hat and dropped it over the empty cup. "I never drink coffee when there's good whiskey to be had."

Waite nodded. Beyond the doorway to the kitchen stood Riley Padgett, Stanton Clark, and Eddie Mosley, rifles in hand should they need them.

"Let me make this short and to the point, then," Waite said. "We've both got a piece of Spain coming. I've thought about what you said. Taking over the Gay Lady and selling her might be the only way we come out with something at this point."

Raymond gave a thin sympathetic smile. "I feel bad that the first mine job you and me ever pulled turned out this way. But I reckon we're both big boys — we'll manage to get over it."

Waite stared at him for a moment, then said, "Ever since you rode into Cold Devil, I can't help but think you've got something you're not telling. This whole thing doesn't have you nearly as upset as you're letting on, does it?"

"Oh, hell, yes, it does," Raymond said. "I could lift Spain's chin and cut his damn throat. But I've been trying hard lately not to give in right away to my more coarse and violent instincts. If I can say so, I believe you're more upset because you've also lost a cousin."

"I'll find out who killed Clement," Waite said, "and when I do, I'll show that same person *coarse and violent instincts.*" He caught himself gripping the coffee cup handle too tightly and settled down with a deep sigh. "Meanwhile, what would we do with the Gay Lady? Do you know anything about running saloons, about whores and pimps and whatnot? Because I don't."

Raymond shrugged. "Neither do I. But I know how to stick my hand out to Spain and say, *'Hand us over the money,'* every

314

day." His smile widened a little.

"I see," Waite said. "We keep Spain and make him run the place for us?" He sipped his coffee, then said, "What if he refuses?"

"Refuses?" Raymond gave a bemused look. "Then *I'll* show him some coarse and violent instincts."

Outside, Rose, Woods and Blake walked past the restaurant on their way to the blacksmith shop. But Raymond and Waite didn't see their dark morning shadows whisk along through the falling snow.

Waite said, "What about the women? I don't want nothing happening to Margo — no rough stuff of any sort."

"Hell, no, we agree on that. Those whores are like pure gold to us," Raymond said. "I wouldn't hurt them even if I knew they *might have* had a little something to do with all this." He studied Waite's eyes, then said, "Which we both know they could have."

"I know they *wouldn't* have had nothing to do with killing Clement," Waite said, getting uncomfortable, not allowing himself to come up with any suspicions involving Margo. "That's my main concern."

"Then we're partnered up? We take over the Gay Lady and make Spain run it for us?" Raymond asked, standing and sticking out his hand to shake.

"Why not?" Waite said, shaking his hand. "We'll break the news to him first thing after daylight."

"We'll both have our men ready in case him and his two men, Woods and Blake, back him up."

"Yes," Waite said. "Woods is not much, but Carney Blake is one fast son of a bitch with a six gun . . . used to be anyway."

"*Used to be* is right," Raymond said. He put his hat on and grinned. "I always say if you want to slow down a gun hand, soak it in rye for a year or two." He touched his hat brim and said in parting, "The fact is, I can take Blake on his *best day* or my *worst.*"

When Raymond had left the restaurant, the three men stepped in from the kitchen and drew around the table as Waite stood up and finished his coffee. "Curly is acting pretty gawddamn cocky if you ask me," Padgett offered, staring hard at the front door. "If you'd said the word, we could've cut him in half right then, slick as socks on a rooster."

"We still can," Mosley said, "far as that goes."

"Say the word, and he's a dead man. So's his pards, *Idiot* John Beck and Fletcher Mays," Stanton Clark said, not wanting to be left out of the conversation.

"It's *Crazy* John Beck," Padgett corrected him, "not *Idiot*."

"I say it's *Idiot*," Clark replied sharply. Turning to Waite, he said, "If you want the Gay Lady, you can take it without Raymond's help."

"I know that, men," Waite said. He picked up his hat from the chair back and held it in his hand. He laid a gold coin on the table and walked to the door. "But that being the case, I'm going to let him and his men help take care of Spain and his two gunmen." He gave them a wise look and said, "Why dirty our hands more than we have to?" On the boardwalk, he put on his hat.

"And the Gay Lady?" Padgett asked. "Are you going to partner with him?"

"For starters, yes," Waite said. "If I don't like the way it's going, we know what to do." Looking over at the Gay Lady in the growing morning sunlight, he said, "I expect Spain and his men might be up in his office right now, armed to the teeth, just waiting for Raymond to try to take her over."

"Well, I guess we'll all find out come daylight," said Mosley, adjusting his Colt in his holster. "That won't be long."

Two blocks away, inside the empty blacksmith shop, Rose picked up Herns' stained leather apron with his thumb and fingertip.

"He's around here somewhere," he said. "He never gets too far from *this*." He gave the apron a look of disdain and dropped it on the dirt floor. On a wall peg hung a heavy woollen navy pea coat, covered with dust from lack of use. "Here's his coat," Rose said. "The fool hardly ever even wears it."

Woods nodded at a small door to the side. Walking to it, he said, "There's his living quarters. Maybe he's in bed, still recuperating from that toss out the window you gave him."

Rose said, "Naw, I've seen him since then. He's getting around all right — might be limping a little for some sympathy." But he and Blake followed Woods into the small junk-cluttered room. Lowering his voice, Rose said, "I don't see how he got so banged up on a stack of buffalo hides anyway. They should've given him a soft landing spot."

The three looked all around. "Jesus, how does he live like this?" Woods said, looking at rolls of scrap wire, chunks and plates of iron, piles of tools and open barrels of horseshoes and nails.

"Well, we know he hasn't left Cold Devil," Blake said. "There's his buggy wheels." He nodded toward four buggy wheels leaning against the side of an unmade cot with ragged blankets and loose clothing lying on it.

"Unless he left on horseback," Woods said.

Rose said, running a hand over the buggy wheels, "Herns doesn't like sitting in a saddle. Besides, I only said he's *all right*. It'll be a while longer before his ribs will let him travel by horseback." He looked all around, getting irritated and curious. "But where the hell is the little prick? I'm kind of looking forward to beating the truth out of him."

"What if he's telling the truth already?" Blake asked with only mild interest, kicking an empty tin can across the dirt floor.

"Then I suppose I'll just have to owe the little negro an apology afterward." Rose chuckled.

Listening from a hiding spot he'd created in a mound of rubble, scrap iron and wooden crates not ten feet from his blacksmith forge, Herns clenched his teeth to keep from springing out and emptying his small pocket pistol into Rose's belly. But he kept himself under control, knowing that if he did so, he would soon be headed down the mountainside to meet Coots.

"His forge is cooling on him," Woods said, holding a hand out to a bed of glowing coals. He reached up, put a hand on one of the bellows handles and pulled it down a few inches, watching the air from the end of it cause flames to rise on the glowing coals. "Herns always stokes up before daylight so he's ready for the day's work."

"He's around Cold Devil somewhere," Blake said. "We just have to keep searching."

"He likes eating at Bracket's," Rose said, turning toward the door. "He told me he likes sitting there and having food served to him." He shook his head. The three chuckled among themselves as they walked out, swinging the door shut behind them. "If we don't find him, we go to the whores next," Rose said.

In the dimly lit blacksmith shop, Herns waited a full minute before venturing out from his hiding spot carrying a battered leather travel case filled with his personal belongings. But once out he wasted no time. Grabbing the wool navy coat from its peg, he shook the dust from it and threw it on, pulling a long wool stocking cap from one of the pockets, dusting it as well. It was time to get out of here, he told himself.

Margo and Trixie had both just begun to doze when they heard two muffled knocks and the metallic sound of a key turning quietly in the lock on their door. Margo's eyes flew open first. "Relax. It's Herns," she whispered, hearing Trixie bolt upright in the bed. But even as Margo's words tried to calm Trixie, her hand slid beneath her pillow, brought out a straight razor and flicked it open in one smooth, fast motion, in case it was someone else.

"Margo . . . Trixie!" Herns whispered, stepping inside their room in the darkness of early morning. He closed the door silently behind himself. "Yas gals awake?" Then upon seeing Margo stepping toward him naked, throwing her robe on, the razor still in hand, he whispered, "Jesus Lord! Put that thing away!"

"I had to be sure it was you, Milo," Margo said.

"Who else you know that's made a key to every place in Cold Devil?" Herns asked. "I was afraid Spain would hear me coming in and *shoot* me! I should've been afraid I'd get my throat cut!"

Seeing him in his heavy coat and stocking cap, wet snow glistening on his head and shoulders, Margo said, as the razor seemed to disappear from her hand, "They came for you, didn't they?"

"Yep, not five minutes ago, Rose, Woods and Carney Blake. They're either following

Spain's orders, or else they've partnered up."

"Those three have partnered up," Margo said, shaking her head. "Coots told us gold does some strange things to people. But damn, who would have believed this?"

"Are you gals ready to get shed of this place?" Herns asked, knowing they had no time for discussion. " 'Cause I'm out of here right now, before they decide to make me into black bacon."

"What about getting down the mountain? If they follow us, we'll never get away from them."

"Yes, we will," Herns said, jutting out his chin a bit. "I've built my buggy into a sleigh. They can't touch us once we get headed down the switchbacks."

Margo just stared at him; Trixie popped over beside her and said almost gleefully, "A sleigh ride! I've heard of that! I've always wanted to go for a —"

"Trixie, keep it down," Margo said, quieting her. Then to Herns, she said, "Are you sure about this? How do you stop it once it's sliding along downhill?"

"I'm a blacksmith, woman, gawddamn it!" Herns hissed, keeping his voice down. "You think I'd make a sleigh without a brake on it? I'm no fool! Are you two going with me or not? This is just the beginning with Rose and them. The more *all* of these men think about the gold and how it had to disappear, the worse it will get here. I don't give a damn how much they *loooooves* yas. Once their nuts cool and they figure out you took all their gold . . ." He let his words trail.

"I'm sorry," Margo said. "You're right! Trixie, get dressed. We're going for a sleigh ride."

"And hurry the hell up!" Herns said. "It's coming daylight." He nodded toward the silvery dawnlight beyond the window.

As Trixie and Margo began hurrying about, grabbing coats and dragging travel bags from under the bed, a distant rifle shot split the silence of morning and caused all three to freeze for a moment.

"Uh-oh," Herns said. "This ain't nothing good!" He hurried to the window, threw it up and stared out in the direction of the shot. "Keep packing!" he said over his shoulder, seeing Rose, Woods and Blake walk out of the restaurant and look out in the same direction.

On the boardwalk of the hotel stood Waite and his men. Ten feet away stood Raymond Curly and his men. All eyes stared out through the silver morning mist toward the sound of the single rifle shot. While the many eyes of Cold Devil searched through the falling snow for the source, the silver mist drifted, seeming to part on a morning wind long enough for everybody to see a lone figure sitting aboard a Studebaker freight wagon, a rifle standing straight up from his lap.

Realizing right away that this was the wagon he'd left with One-eyed Mike Flutes, and realizing that this was not Flutes aboard it, Raymond Curly whispered under his breath, "Oh, hell!" and instinctively let his hand rest on the pistol at his hip.

Something about Raymond's demeanor caught Morgan Waite's attention. He looked at him closely and said, "Curly, any idea who that is out there?"

"Yeah," Curly lied. "It's something personal. He's here looking for me." He gave Mays and Crazy John a guarded look, saying among them, "Get your rifles and take a good firing position. Whoever that is, he knows what's going on here."

Mays and Crazy John looked puzzled by what they thought Raymond was asking them to do. "What the hell, Raymond?" Mays said. "You mean you want us to *shoot* him?"

"Gawddamn it, *no!*" Curly hissed, trying to keep his voice lowered, no longer the cool, confident person he'd presented to Cold Devil. "He's got our gold! I want you to kill any sumbitch who *does* try to shoot him!"

CHAPTER 24

The ranger watched Raymond Curly ride out to him through the falling snow, knowing that at any moment the snowfall would most likely thicken and obscure the rider from view until he drew closer. Yet Sam wasn't worried about sitting in the open. Letting Curly know that he had possession of the Studebaker wagon had ensured his safety, for the time being at least.

When Raymond got close enough to see the badge on Sam's chest, he murmured, "Aw, man . . ." His horse slowed its step, then continued and stopped ten feet away. "All right, you're a lawman, I see," Raymond said, sounding a bit crestfallen at the thought of a lawman having the gold. "Let me take a wild guess." He kept his hand away from his holstered Colt. "You're one of the lawmen those idiots Spain and Waite *think* they left dead beneath a landslide up around Thunder Pass?"

"That's good, Curly," Sam said. He sat with the muffler pulled down from his face. "You're smart enough I won't have to talk real slow or repeat a lot."

"How'd you know I'm Raymond Curly?" Curly asked.

"Don't disappoint me," Sam said. He took a breath and said patiently, "Because when you saw this wagon, you weren't about to send anybody else."

"Where's One-eyed Mike?" Curly asked.

"Dead," Sam said. As he spoke, he reached into his pocket, took out the eye patch and draped it on the brake handle. "He leaped off a cliff." He gestured toward Mike's horse hitched to the back of the wagon next to Black Pot now that they were off the treacherous mountain switchbacks.

"That figures," Curly said, disgusted. "I saw the notion cross his mind more than once after he watched the owner of this wagon do the same."

"Here's the deal," Sam said. "You and I are even up. I've got nothing on you, although if I wanted to I could come up with robbery, maybe murder. The fact is —"

"I told you he *jumped!*" Curly said, referring to the teamster.

"Did you think I was finished talking?" Sam asked in a crisp reprimanding tone.

Curly slumped in his saddle, listening, knowing this ranger had him in a tight spot.

"Thank you," Sam said, continuing. "Now pay close attention. All I want is Texas Jack Spain and Max Denton. As far as I'm concerned I'll have to take Mike Flutes' word on how you boys come onto the gold, until I get back to the lowlands and hear otherwise. By then you'll be living in a warmer climate. Follow me?"

"Like a dog on a pork chop," Curly said, sitting up straighter, hope coming back to his eyes. "You're going to give me back the gold, even trade for Spain."

"Right," Sam said. "I'm going to tell you where I took the gold and buried it. You give me Spain and Denton and follow my instructions. We'll both get what we want. Fair enough?"

"Lawman, don't move an inch," Raymond said, his voice dead serious. "I'm going to go put a bullet in Spain's and Denton's ears and bring them to you! You've got my word on it!"

"No, wait," Sam said. "That's not what I want. I don't want you to kill them. I'm taking them back *alive.* That's an important part of this deal." He raised a gloved finger for emphasis. *"Don't* kill them. Do you understand?"

"*Alive* is a little bit harder," Raymond said. But then, considering the conversation he'd had earlier with Waite, he added, "Not a *lot harder,* but some."

"I've got to ride in and arrest them," Sam said. "Is that going to be a problem?"

"Damn, why do you have to do that?" Raymond said. "That's the hardest way of all!"

"*Is* that going to be a problem?" Sam repeated.

"With Denton, no," said Raymond. "He's all alone, hasn't stuck his head out of the sheriff's office since I've been in Cold Devil. But Spain has three gunmen working for him — well, make that two gunmen and a pimp." He considered and said, "That's more like, one gunman, a pimp, and a drunk named Carney Blake."

"Carney Blake," Sam said, recognizing the name. "He's backing Spain?"

"Aha," Raymond said, "now I see you're getting a little worried, a big name like Blake comes into the picture. But like I said, he's a drunk now. Nothing to worry about."

Sam said, dismissing Carney Blake, "Where is Spain right now?"

"In his office, either still sleeping or else grieving and cussing, wondering what's happened to the gold."

"And where is Carney Blake and Spain's other two men?"

"I don't know," Raymond said, "and that's the gospel truth. But they're around somewhere. Everybody in town is sticking awfully close to their own group, just waiting for somebody to make a wrong move. Then it's going to be killing, the likes of which hell wouldn't have."

"A gunfight in Cold Devil," Sam said almost to himself, picturing it in his mind.

"I told you," Raymond said, "this is the worst way to take Spain. It's best I shoot him and drag his dead ass out here to you — Denton too."

"No," Sam said. "Ride beside me. Get me into town. Once you see me make my move, get out of my way."

"I'd feel better if you told me where the gold is before we ride," Raymond said.

"I bet you would," Sam replied. "But I'll only tell when I see that I have Spain in custody."

"But if things go bad for you," Raymond said, "I'll never know where the gold is!"

"That's the thing you'll want to keep telling yourself over and over through all of this," Sam said. He lowered his rifle across his lap and slapped the reins to the team horses, sending them forward through the snow. Raymond Curly rode alongside.

Inside the sheriff's office, upon first spotting the lone figure sitting in the wagon, Max Denton rummaged hastily through his desk and found a pair of dusty binoculars. "Oh, my God, it's you!" he gasped, focusing through the falling snow, seeing the ranger's face before the ranger reached up and pulled the muffler back over the bridge of his nose. "You son of a bitch."

Dropping the binoculars onto the windowsill, Denton raced out the back door, grabbing a coat on his way. Behind the row of stores and shops, he bounded along across the smooth white landscape toward the rear of the livery barn, kicking up powdery white rooster tails behind him. By the time he'd headed past the back of the Gay Lady, his breath wheezed shallowly in his chest and his heart pounded like a hammer on an anvil.

Hurrying from the Gay Lady, having decided to flee while Raymond and the wagon drew closer to Cold Devil, Herns and the two women stopped at the rear corner of the building and heard Denton's strange sound coming at them. "What the hell is that?" Herns said, squinting into the silver-white mist. By the time the three recognized Denton, the winded ex-sheriff was upon them, a Colt waving loosely in his gloved hand.

Coming to a halt at the sight of the travel bags in Herns' and the women's hands, Denton leveled the gun and said in a badly panting voice, "Take . . . me . . . with . . . you!"

"What?" Herns said. "Man, you're crazy! We ain't going nowhere!"

"Don't . . . screw . . . with me!" Denton gasped. He herded the three along with his pistol. "Get . . . going!"

"All right, but watch out with that gun, Sheriff!" Herns said, calling him sheriff from force of habit. "We don't want to tip nobody off that we're leaving."

Struggling through the calf-deep snow, Denton grabbed Trixie's forearm. "Help . . . me . . . out . . . Trix!" he half pleaded, half demanded.

"Do we have room for him?" Margo asked Herns, trying to hurry along beside him. She gave him a glimpse of the straight razor in her palm, giving him the message.

"Damn, woman! Put that away! We'll *make* room!" said Herns.

Across the alley from the livery barn, Herns grabbed a tarpaulin covered with snow and flipped it off his single-seated one-horse riding buggy. "Get in and get seated,"

Herns said, "whilst I go get the horses!"

"Damn! That's pretty good on short notice!" Margo said, noting he'd converted the rig to a two-horse culture. She noted the wide sleigh runners that replaced the buggy wheels, allowing the weight of the wagon to sink a couple inches, packing the snow in a smooth, slick travel surface. "I believe we're going to be all right!" She threw her bag over into the buggy and stepped back and forth in the snow, looking the buggy over as Trixie and Denton struggled to catch up to her.

"Whoever it is, he's wearing a head rag like one of the gypsies we passed on the trails," Waite said to his men, who stood strung out along the boardwalk.

Raymond spotted his men in position with their rifles and waved them toward the Gay Lady Saloon as he and the ranger rode along the snow-swollen street to the hitch rail out front. "This place is going to be mine after you take Spain away," Raymond said, keeping a close eye on Waite and his men still standing on the boardwalk out front of the hotel. "Any objections?"

"It's not my business," Sam said, stopping the wagon. He wrapped the reins around the brake handle.

"His room is first on the left at the top of the stairs," Raymond said, staring down the boardwalk toward Waite and his men while Crazy John and Mays stepped up out of the snow with their rifles. "Hurry up, lawman. Here comes Waite," Raymond said.

"Did you say, *lawman?*" Mays asked, bristling instinctively. He watched Sam walk quickly through the unlocked door into the Gay Lady.

"He's got our gold hidden," Raymond said to Mays and Crazy John. "We've got to keep him alive till he tells us where it's at!"

"Gawddamn!" Crazy John said. "Defend a lawman? What if word gets around that we did this?"

"Shut up, John, and back my play once Waite gets here, else we'll be dead and it won't matter anyway."

"What the hell is going on there, Raymond?" Waite called out as he and his men drew closer along the boardwalk. "Who is that? It looks like one of the Roma gypsies!"

"Here we go," Raymond whispered sidelong to Mays and Crazy John. "Waite, I promised this man he can talk to Spain in private." He held his left hand up toward Waite, stopping him, his right hand wrapped around the handle of his Colt.

"Talk to him?" Waite gave a suspicious

look at the open door of the Gay Lady. "Talk to him about what? You and I are supposed to be partners. Why didn't you tell me about this?"

"I am telling you, Waite, gawddamn it! And we are partners, you and me. Just stand back and give me some room here. This is some personal business between him and Texas Jack!"

On his way to the stairs inside the Gay Lady, Sam picked up a long push broom leaning against the wall. He walked silently up the stairs, keeping to one side rather than walking in the middle, where the creaking of the planks would announce his arrival. For all he knew, Spain could have been watching him ride in. He wasn't going to take a chance.

At the top of the stairs, Sam slipped along the hall until he'd arrived within a few feet of Spain's private office. There he stooped down, reached out with the long broom handle and knocked against Spain's door.

Three sudden blasts of shotgun fire exploded in a spray of shattered wood and buckshot. The first took off the door, the second hit just to the right and the third to the left, should someone have stood on either side for safety. The ranger had been right. Spain had been waiting for him.

No sooner had the third shot exploded than Sam sprang into the doorway and saw Spain behind a desk, trying to reload one of his two shotguns with trembling hands. The saloon owner shrieked with rage, threw the shotgun at Sam and reached for a Colt lying on his desk as the ranger darted forward across the office floor.

Spain swung the Colt toward him, but the ranger dived over the desk and knocked it away from his chest just as it exploded and sailed away. "You're going with me, Spain," he growled, the two of them slamming against the wall behind the desk.

"No*ooo!*" Spain screamed. In desperation he grabbed a thick wooden picture frame off the wall on his way down and broke it on Sam's back. Shattered glass flew.

Out front, at the sound of the gun shots and the following sound of breaking glass and furniture, Waite turned his gaze upward along the side of the building. Unable to see anything he looked at Raymond and said, *"Personal business?* I hope to God you know what you're doing here, Raymond!"

Mays and Crazy John stood with their rifles cocked and aimed at Waite and his men. Morgan Waite didn't want a shootout, not yet — not until he knew what was going on. He stood with his fists clenched at his side, staring upward through the falling snow at the big clapboard saloon building, seeing the noise of battle cause fingers of snow to break loose and fall along the roof line.

In a moment, silence fell suddenly from inside the Gay Lady. Waite turned his eyes to Raymond. "They've killed one another?"

Raymond only stared.

In Spain's office, Sam crouched astraddle Spain, with one hand gripping him by his shirtfront, the other drawn back with the big Colt in his fist, ready to crack the barrel across the man's forehead. But Spain gasped in a defeated voice, "No . . . enough. I'm finished. . . ."

Knowing it would be easier handling Spain on his feet than it would with him draped over his shoulder, Sam let the Colt slump in his hand. "On your feet," he said. He stepped from over Spain, still holding his shirt and dragged him upward.

While the ranger cuffed him, Spain said over his shoulder, out of breath, "I don't know how you lived through the landslide . . . but you should've gone home. Now you're dead sure enough."

Sam gave him a shove. "Start walking."

In the hallway, Spain looked at the door next to his office and stopped suddenly as if stricken by a bolt of realization. "I'll be gawddamn!" he said to no one in particular. "Ranger, do me a favor! Please! Open that door!"

"Not a chance, Spain," the ranger said, giving him a slight shove toward the stairs. "Besides, I can see it's nailed shut." He looked at the visible nail heads all around the door's edge.

"No. No, it's not!" Spain said, hesitating, leaning back and looking back as he went down the stairs. "It's supposed to be! But it's not! I bet a million dollars it's not!"

"A *million*, eh?" Sam said. "You sure throw some big numbers around, Spain."

Giving up on looking at the door, Spain shook his head and said, "Those gawddamn dirty whores! They're the ones! They stole the gold! They killed Clement too! The dirty lousy gawddamn *cunts!*"

"Watch your language, Spain," Sam said. He pushed Spain onward.

CHAPTER 25

Out front of the Gay Lady, Sam stopped with his Colt drawn and held on to Spain. In the fight with Spain, his long muffler had come unwound and lay loosely across his shoulders. He held the short links between Spain's handcuffs in his left hand.

Upon recognizing the ranger, Waite stiffened. He gave Raymond a killing cold stare, his clenched fists opening and closing tightly. "You double-crossing —"

"Morgan Waite," Sam called out boldy, cutting him off as he pointed his Colt toward the regulator's chest, "you are under arrest for assaulting a federal marshal in the pursuit of his duty."

Waite's raging glare turned sharply from Raymond to the ranger. "What the hell are you talking about?"

"You shot Marshal Summers," Sam said flatly. He didn't know for sure who'd pulled the trigger, but he wanted to single out the leader to see what he'd say. "Luckily, he's still alive. That might be all that keeps you from hanging."

Waite, sensing his men's tension, put a hand to the side, saying, "Everybody stand down." Then, to Sam, he said warily, "There's no way that lawman is still alive. You're just saying that thinking it might make me go along peacefully."

"How you go is up to you," Sam said, his Colt steady in his hand. "But you're going, peaceful or otherwise."

"Lawman, he wasn't part of the deal," Raymond said, seeing the rage in Waite's eyes as Waite gave him another hard look. "It was supposed to be Denton and Spain!"

"My deal with you was only for Denton and Spain," said Sam. "We're even. Waite is just part of my job."

"*We're even?* Jesus, lawman!" Raymond said. He knew that, *even* or not, he'd have to keep the ranger alive to learn where the gold was hidden.

"You sold me over, you Judas son of a bitch," Spain cursed at Raymond.

"The *deal?*" Waite said, everybody ignoring Spain now that he was in handcuffs. "You handed Spain to this lawman? You let this lawman ride right in here on me, knowing I'd hang for murder?" Waite raged as if

340

in disbelief.

"On the walk, Spain, quick!" the ranger said, seeing a bloodbath in the making. He shoved Spain down to the plank boardwalk by his handcuffs and squatted over him, knowing there was no time to get him into the wagon. It was time to take Waite, just the way he'd said, either dead or alive.

From the rough plank boardwalk, Spain saw Woods, Rose and Blake appear at the corner of the alley leading back to the livery barn. Even in the falling snow, they had followed Denton's tracks behind the buildings; but they had walked back to the street at the sound of the gunshot in the Gay Lady. As Crazy John Beck, unable to hold himself back any longer, let go of the first shot, Spain cried out loudly, "Rose! Don't let him take me!"

"Damn! Now *there's* a gunfight!" Rose said, seeing the fight commence as Crazy John's shot lifted PK Barnes backward and dropped him in a spray of blood on the snow.

"Yeah!" Woods shouted. "And there goes Herns and the whores! They've got the gold! I know they do!" He pointed through the falling snow. The sleigh appeared, then disappeared silently, ghostlike into the silver-white mist, as if it had come to reveal itself briefly and tempt anyone willing to give it chase.

"Gawddamn it!" Rose said, his fingers tapping rapidly on the Remington in his newly donned waist sash. Shots exploded back and forth at close quarters among the ranger, Waite and his men and Raymond and his two riflemen. Rose started to take a step, but Blake stopped him, clasping a firm hand on his forearm. "Don't do it, Rose!" he said. "Leave them to their own fight!"

"Like hell," Rose said. "Let go of my arm." He rounded his arm away from Blake and stepped forward through the snow.

"This one isn't yours! It's not worth it to you!" Blake called out above the racket of gunfire.

"Easy for you to say," Rose said. "You got yours. I'm getting mine!"

Blake shook his head and turned to Woods. But before he could say anything, he saw Woods kicking up snow as he ran back toward the livery barn. "Come on, Carney!" the pimp shouted above the melee. "Let's get after the whores!"

Blake stood cold and alone in the calf-deep snow for a moment, looking back and forth between Rose with his gunfight and Woods with his chase for the gold. He licked his dry lips, then looked at the Gay Lady sitting in the snow, men bleeding and dying on her cold white bosom, bullets flying back and forth across her brightly painted facade.

"God Almighty!" Blake gasped, somehow profoundly moved by the sight and sound of dying. His stomach twisted and cramped behind his gun belt; he clutched his belly. "I've never needed a drink so bad in my whole gawddamned miserable life!" A warm tear spilled down his cheek, brought on perhaps by the chilling cold. He waited for the cramp to pass the way it always had these past few days. But after a moment, he looked down and saw the bloody streak on his palm, and on his belt and shirt. *Hit by a stray . . .* He looked toward the raging gunfight with a sad smile. "Couldn't leave me out of it, could you?" he said as if speaking to the gunfight itself.

On the boardwalk, having dropped to his knees, Sam's fifth shot had sent George Trubough spinning in the snow, a stream of blood drawing a jagged bull's-eye around the spot where he fell. But even as his shot took Trubough out of the fight, Sam felt a bullet tug at the loose muffler around his neck; another nipped at his coat sleeve. He needed his rifle — needed it bad.

Spain lay trembling, his face flat on the cold boardwalk planks and his hand cuffed behind him. Crazy John Beck lay dead atop Mays, who had killed Ben Hevlon outright and left Lode Stewart mortally wounded, facedown in the snow, a spreading circle of red surrounding him. Now Mays seemed to relax, as if going off to sleep.

Advancing and firing on Raymond Curly, who stood leaning back against the front of the Gay Lady, Waite shouted, "Die, you backstabbing son of a bitch!"

Wounded but still fighting, Raymond took another bullet with a grunt, yet managed to fire a round high into Waite's chest. The shot didn't kill Waite, but he staggered sideways and lost direction for a moment.

Sam fired his sixth shot at Waite and saw the bullet hit him low in his side. Sam had no time to reload the big Colt. Waite turned from Raymond Curly and toward Sam with a crazed look of determination in his eyes. Spread out on the street beside him, Riley Padgett, Stanton Clark and Eddie Mosley stalked forward, wounded, bloody, but firing at the ranger as they drew closer, taking their time, as if knowing they were firing at an unarmed man.

Sam looked all around wildly for a dropped weapon, anything; but none were in sight. His hand went to the handle of a knife in his boot, his weapon of last, desperate resort, as Stanton Clark stopped four feet away and leveled his gun down at Sam's forehead. "Adios, lawdog!" he said.

But before he could fire and before the ranger could lunge forward and put the knife up into play, a shot from behind Sam nailed Clark in the center of his forehead, splattering blood on Sam in front of him and the other gunmen advancing closely behind. Clark flew backward; Sam had no time to waste. He rolled away off the board-walk, dragging Spain with him toward the wagon. As he rolled, he caught sight of the gunman standing straight and tall on the boardwalk, a big Colt bucking in his right hand, his shirt bloodstained at belt level. "Carney Blake!" Sam said, startled by the sight of him and by the fact that Blake had taken his side.

But the ranger had to turn away quickly as the gunfight continued with fury. "In the wagon, Spain," he shouted above the ex-ploding shots and whistling bullets. He dragged the cuffed prisoner upward at the hitch rail.

Noting that Spain was still miraculously unharmed, Sam shoved him up over into the wagon bed and dived in behind him as bullets pounded the wagon's side rails. Sam reached over, jerked the Winchester from beside the seat and stood up into a crouch, giving Blake help with shot after shot from the repeating rifle.

In the snow-filled street, Riley Padgett fell dead as a shot from Sam's rifle hit him squarely in his chest. Carney Blake dropped Eddie Mosley and turned to Waite. But Waite clearly had the edge. He was already aiming as Blake turned his gun toward him. "Waite!" Sam shouted, hoping to get his attention away from Blake. It worked. Morgan Waite swung toward Sam in time to catch a rifle bullet in his chest. At the same time, Blake sent a pistol shot into the big man's side, causing a puff of dust to flare up from the thick bearskin coat. "It's . . . not fair . . ." Waite said in a trailing voice as he sank to his knees and swiped a hand through the air like a wounded grizzly. He fell forward onto his face on the cold boardwalk planks.

Sam looked around quickly and saw no one left standing but himself and Carney Blake, who staggered inside the Gay Lady through the wide-open door. Looking out along the street through the falling snow, Sam saw the long line of prints left by Ned Rose. His eyes followed them from where they started, seeing them coming straight toward the gunfight. But then they veered away twenty yards up the middle of the street and headed out at a longer stride until they disappeared into an alleyway.

"Damn you, lawman," Raymond Curly said, half sobbing as Sam jumped down and trudged over to him through the deep snow. "I had . . . this thing . . . set up so sweet." He leaned back against the wall of the Gay Lady, as if the saloon had him cradled in her arms. "Here you came."

"I had to do it, Raymond," Sam said. "The fight was coming, anyway. You knew that, didn't you?"

"Now look at me . . . dying bigger than hell," he said, not even understanding what Sam had asked. He held up a bloody hand from his chest. "I started all this. Should have . . . let well enough . . . alone."

Sam untied the bandanna from around Raymond's neck and pressed it against his chest wound. "Hold it there, Raymond. I'll get you some help." He stood up and looked back and forth along the street, where townsmen had begun to venture forth through the silver-white mist, like spirits come to claim the newly dead. "We've got some wounded who need attending to," he called out. "It's over. You can all come out."

Django and one of his caravan members by

the name of Venca had ridden with Marshal
Summers aboard one of their wagons until
they reached the high point along the
southeastern side of the mountain. When
they'd stopped, said their goodbyes and
watched Summers climb stiffly into his
saddle and ride away on his roan, Venca said
to Django in their native tongue, "Some of
the men think we are crazy to go out of our
way to accommodate these lawmen."

"But not Trina and her grandpapa,"
Django said. "I do not believe they think
so."

"All right," Venca gave in. "It's true these
men saved the lives of our people. Still, this
is a long trip we made to get him over the
mountain." He stared out across the lower
valleys and slopes. "We could have made it
no farther."

"Then this was far enough," Django said.
He tapped his forehead. "When we listen,
the land tells us what is the right thing to
do."

Venca only nodded. "Right now I am told
I must relieve myself before we turn and
start back." He walked to the trunk of a tall
pine and watched a squirrel race away
across the snow. "What are you doing out
here this time of year?" he called after the
frightened animal. Then he looked down at

where the animal had scratched its way out from behind a tall leaning rock and saw the glittery grains of dust it left in its tracks. "Oh, my!" he murmured, forgetting for the moment why he'd gone to the tree in the first place.

After a few minutes had passed, Django grew restless and called out, "Venca, what are you doing? Let's go."

"Django," Venca called out in a breathless, awe-stricken tone, "did you once say you are able to smell gold?"

"Of course, I can smell gold," Django replied, sounding a bit testy and put out that Venca would even ask such a question. "Every man in my family can smell gold. Why do you ask?"

"Come here quickly, Django," said Venca, "and smell all of this!"

Django stepped away from the wagon and trudged through the snow to the tall pine. He stopped and staggered a little at the sight of the bags of gold dust, nuggets and ingots Venca had unearthed by pulling away the rock. He collected himself, squatted and picked up an ingot. He ran his fingertips along it, examining it closely.

"Well, smell it and tell me if it is gold," Venca said.

"Oh, it *is gold,* Venca," Django said. "And

this is why we went out of our way to bring the lawman here and show our gratitude for them helping Trina and her grandpapa — don't you see? This is our way of purchasing land on which we can all live in California! These things that happen are all a part of something larger, something that is planned for us if we only do what is right and humane among our fellow travelers on the road of life —"

"Yes, yes, I know all of that," Venca said impatiently. "But smell the gold! How can you be sure it is gold if you do not smell it?"

Django held the ingot and pointed a finger to the center of its glittering belly. "Because the stamping says so, right here," he said, grinning. "See?"

CHAPTER 26

Pete Summers followed the switchback trail downward to the long, rolling flatlands. During a lull in the snowfall, he stopped in the cover of a sparse, snow-covered stretch of pine and raised his field lens to his eye, seeing the women and men traveling across the flatlands in the sleigh. Recognizing Herns first, then the women, and finally Max Denton, who sat huddled in his coat with his collar turned up blocking his face, Summers collapsed the field lens and nudged the roan along the tree line.

On the other side of the sleigh, more than a hundred yards across the snowy tundra, James Earl Coots also spotted the sleigh gliding across the snow. He smiled to himself, standing beside the worn-out horse. "Come on, fellow," he said to the exhausted animal, "just a little farther. We get to the trail, I'll let you rest." He led the horse in a direction that would cross the trail ahead of the sleigh. Coots couldn't imagine what Max Denton was doing traveling with Herns and the women, but he was certain he'd find out.

In the sleigh, for the past mile, Denton had been ordering Herns to hurry the animals, wanting to get as far from Cold Devil as he could before the ranger got on his trail. But having had no success at getting Herns to push the animals any faster, Denton finally resorted to poking the wiry little blacksmith in the ribs with his pistol barrel. That did it for Herns. To Margo's and Trixie's surprise, he brought the sleigh to a halt and jumped from the driver's seat. "Get your worthless white ass out, Denton!"

"What are you doing, Herns? Have you lost your mind? Get in here and let's go!" Denton shouted, waving the pistol back and forth as he also jumped from the sleigh. The two women stared in disbelief, both of them bundled in coats and blankets.

"For God sakes, both of yas get in!" Margo said. "We can't sit out here arguing all day!"

"Huh-uh! No, siree!" Herns said. "I ain't getting!" Shaking his head vigorously, he continued. "I didn't build this fine sleigh so's some turd like him can stick a gun in my ribs!" He pointed at Denton. "You want to shoot me, go on and shoot! But you ain't poking me with that gawddamn pistol!"

"Why, you little black cricket-legged bastard!" Denton snared, leveling the gun at arm's length. "You'll get in, or I'll splatter your empty head all over this —"

"Come on, Milo!" Trixie coaxed. "Can't you see he'll do it! He's on the run. He's got nothing to lose."

"Nope, I ain't doing it," Herns said. "No more rib poking for me. I'm a skilled tradesman, an emancipated freeman and a descendant of African royalty." He stared defiantly at Denton and said in a lowered, growling tone, *"So fire away!"*

"My pleasure, you uppity little prick!" Denton said. He cocked his gun.

"Don't pull that trigger, Sheriff," Coots said, stepping onto the trail, his sawed-off shotgun in hand.

"Who's — who's there?" Denton asked, without lowering his gun or daring to turn and see for himself.

"James Earl Coots and *company*," the teamster said. *"Company* is pointed at the back of your head."

"Coots, this has nothing to do with you!" Denton said, not giving in easily. "You're meddling where you don't belong! I'm a desperate man! I'll kill him!"

Coots gave Margo a look; she shrugged. "The lawman who busted Spain's head and jailed him is back in Cold Devil. Denton's on the run all over again." She rolled her eyes slightly as if she'd had it with Denton.

"There's the whole of it," Denton said, stepping sideways with his gun still pointed at Herns. When he'd turned enough to look at Coots, he saw Coots' horse standing down off the trail fifty feet away. His eyes lit up. Coots saw what had just run through the ex-sheriff's mind at the sight of the horse. He decided to let him play it out.

"Besides, Coots, you're a teamster, not a gunman," said Denton, taking on his sheriff's authoritarian tone of voice. "You carry a shotgun for protection, but come on now." He smiled wisely. "Do you really want to look a man in the eyes and shoot him down this way? Few men have the stomach for this sort of thing." As he spoke, he walked sidelong in a wide circle, every step taking him closer to the horse that stood watching, its reins hanging in the snow, its breath steaming.

Coots kept his finger on the shotgun's trigger, but he let the barrel slump an inch, knowing how risky it could be to fire a gun out here, calling in any lawman or thief who might be close enough to hear it. He wanted a clear, empty trail to where he'd buried half the gold. "Damn it, Sheriff," he said, "looks like you win."

"Coots!" Margo said in stunned surprise.

"That's what I thought," Denton said, moving farther out of shotgun range and closer to the horse. "So I'm just going to take this horse and bid you folks adiee." He grinned.

"Coots, don't let him take your horse!" Margo said, feeling the humiliation she imagined the teamster to be feeling as Denton reached out and picked up the reins.

"There's nothing I can do about it, Margo," Coots said in defeat. "Milo, get in the sleigh. Let's get out of here."

"That's right, teamster. Tuck your tail and get the hell out of my sight!" Denton said. He stood for a moment, chuckling, watching Coots and the little blacksmith jump aboard the sleigh and put the horses forward along the snowy trail. "Suckers!" he murmured to himself.

Turning, he put his boot in the stirrup and stepped up. But instead of him going up into the saddle, the worn-out horse lay straight down in the snow. "What the . . . ?" Denton looked dumbfounded for a moment, seated astraddle the lying horse. His boots were on the ground on either side of the animal, his elbows on his knees, the reins in his hands.

"Drop the gun, Max Denton," Pete Summers said, appearing up the long slope leading up from the tree line. "You're under arrest."

Looking back in time to see Denton seated on the lying horse before the sleigh slipped down over a snowy rise, Margo and Trixie laughed in surprise. "Coots, I should have known you had something up your sleeve!" Margo said snuggling close to him.

Herns looked back, then shook his head. "Man, I can't wait to get away from here. I'm going south, back to my family. I've seen enough *white* to last me a lifetime!" He gestured a hand all around the snow-covered land. "I just wish you had made it out of here with the gold, Coots, so's I could return home and put a smile on the little woman's face."

"Oh, I think you'll do that sure enough." Coots smiled, remembering the gold he had hidden before Raymond Curly and his men had showed up.

Margo's voice turned somber and sad as she said, "We saw the lawman drive your wagon into Cold Devil, so we knew the gold is gone. But if it's all right, I want to go away with you, anyway."

"The lawman has my wagon?" Coots said, sounding surprised, handling the reins as he spoke.

"Yes," Margo said. She gave Coots a look that said she wondered why he sounded surprised.

Coots grinned to himself, staring ahead into the silvery-white mist as the snowfall started again. "But you'd like to stick with me, anyway, even if I had no money?"

"I'd like to," Margo said. "That is, if you'll have me and Trixie."

"You and Trixie?" Coots asked, watching the trail ahead.

"We come as sort of a team, you know," Margo said. "But she and I would want the three of us to be one happy family. If you get my meaning," she said, "and if it's all right with you."

Coots couldn't believe it. His grin widened. It was all still going his way. "Sure, why not?" he said. He nodded at the trail ahead and said, "You're not going to believe what I've got waiting for us halfway down the trail."

"Oh, what?" Margo beamed.

"It's a surprise," Coots said. "I think everybody will like it." He turned his smile to Margo. "Do you believe that half a loaf is better than none?"

"It all depends on the size of the loaf," Margo replied.

The ranger had handcuffed Spain to the hitch rail and stepped inside the door of the Gay Lady after the shooting. He found Carney Blake standing bowed over behind the bar, a hand clutching a towel to his wounded side. Blake raised a beer mug filled with water to his lips and threw back a drink, watching Sam walk cautiously to the bar.

"Blake, I'm obliged for what you done out there," Sam said in a gentle tone. "I have to admit, though, I was surprised you did that for me."

"You never wronged me, Ranger," said Blake. "I wronged myself *back then.*" He gestured a nod toward some distant place past the far horizon.

"I never saw you again after Cottonwood. I wanted to tell you I was sorry for what happened to the woman."

"Yeah, the woman," Blake said in reflection. After a moment, he said, "What's done is done, Ranger. I'd rather not talk about it." He stiffened in pain, then let out a sigh of relief. "Anything I can get for you, Ranger?" he asked, as if he were tending bar.

"Blake, one of the miners went to get the doctor. He's on his way."

"Obliged, Ranger," Blake said somberly. "I'm just going to stand here quiet like for a minute, see if I live or die."

Noting the water in the beer mug in Blake's hand, Sam said in a soft tone, "You're off the whiskey?"

"Yeah, I thought I'd give it a try," Blake said. Then, even though he'd said he didn't want to talk about the past, he continued. "I left Cottonwood drunk after that, and I stayed drunk — drank my way all the way here." He offered a thin, tired smile. "Don't know what brought me here. But this is where I finally ended up. I'm shaky but sober. Never thought I'd die sober."

"Is that what you decided, that you're dying?" Sam asked.

Before Blake answered, Scratch Ebbons slipped inside and eased up to the bar. "Carney, the doc is on his way," he said. "Are you going to be all right?"

"That's what we're standing here talking about, Scratch," Blake replied. "What can I get you?"

The old miner looked at Sam as if asking permission. Unable to read the ranger's expression, he shrugged slightly and said, "Whiskey, I reckon," with a puzzled look on his face.

Behind them two other old miners stepped inside, shaking snow from their coats, followed by the doctor, who rushed past them and behind the bar to Carney Blake. "It's colder than the devil here in Cold Devil," one man remarked with a nervous half laugh.

Seeing the doctor begin to treat Blake while the sober gunman stood leaning against the back of the bar, his hands spread out along the rail, Sam left the Gay Lady, pulling his collar up against the falling snow.

After Sam had deposited Texas Jack Spain in a warm jail cell and locked the iron door, he sat back in a chair and allowed himself to drift for the next two hours, letting the heat from the stove seep deep into his chilled bones. When he came to, he trudged back to the Gay Lady to see about Carney Blake. To his surprise, he saw well over a dozen customers lined along the bar, drinking and watching Blake's every move, as if he were someone of great renown.

The doctor, standing at the far end of the bar, returned Sam's questioning gaze with a raised brow and spread his hands. "Have a drink, Ranger?" he asked.

Sam didn't reply. Instead, he stood beside the doctor and asked, "Is he all right?"

"His gun belt saved his life," the doctor said, taking a deep draw on a black cigar and blowing out smoke. Raising a shot glass full of rye, he said, "Here's to living dangerously," and threw the liquor back in a single gulp. With a whiskey wheeze, he touched his own belt in two places, six inches apart. "The belt slowed the bullet. It went in here, grazed under the skin and came out over here. Talk about *lucky!*"

Sam looked at Blake while the wounded gunman poured whiskey into three miners' glasses. Blake looked pale, his shirt open, his lower belly wearing a bloodstained bandage. "Why's he tending bar?" Sam asked the doctor quietly.

The doctor let a out a lungful of smoke and coughed. "He told me he was going to run this place until somebody told him otherwise. Said who knows more about drinking and this kind of life than he."

Sam started to comment, but his attention and everyone else's turned to the front door when Ned Rose walked in, hatless and wet, his shoulders covered with snow. He walked straight toward the bar, where Blake stood with his hands along the rail, watching calmly.

Staring at Blake through hollow, black-rimmed eyes as he came across the floor,

Rose threw open his coat and clasped his hand around the handle of the big Remington in his waist sash. Sam poised, ready to snatch his Colt, but the calm look on Blake's face told him to wait.

"I've been expecting you, Rose," Blake said. As he spoke, his hand went down beneath the bar top. "Not as easy as it looked was it?" He gestured a nod toward the street and the boardwalk, where the gunfight had raged only hours earlier.

Rose did not answer, but he nodded his head in agreement, then lowered it a bit. Sam tensed again; the whole saloon gasped as Rose raised the big Remington and laid it on the bar top.

"Have you got it out of your system?" Blake asked him quietly. He brought his hand from under the bar and laid a clean white linen apron on top. He slid it over to Rose.

"Yeah, it's done," Rose said. He picked up the apron, unfolded it and draped it around his waist.

Moments later, Sam stepped out on the boardwalk and started to trudge back to the sheriff's office through the fresh snow. But in the darkening evening light, he saw Pete Summers atop his roan riding toward the Gay Lady. In front of Summers, Denton walked along, leading the horse. Beside him, Stanley Woods walked, leading his horse, as well. "Well, I'll be," Sam said, watching Summers direct the party to the hitch rail.

"I hear I missed a gunfight here," Summers said. He stopped and pushed up his hat brim, letting a mantle of snow fall from its brim.

"It could have been worse," Sam said, looking down at Denton. "I see you haven't slacked off on the job on your way here."

Summers stepped down from his roan. "Woods, you're free to go."

Woods hitched his horse and hurried inside the Gay Lady, saying, as he passed the ranger, "I'm freezing!"

"I bet you are," Sam said. He turned back to Summers, then looked down at Denton. "You and Spain have gone in one big, long circle just to end up back where you started. Will this do it for you? Are you ready to go along peaceable now?"

"Spain is alive?" Denton said. "I never figured you'd take him a second time without a fight."

The ranger and Summers both ignored him. "Any trouble getting up to the high trails, your wound and all?" Sam asked.

"No," Summers said. "Django and Venca brought me by wagon as far as the fork in the last high trail."

"Oh?" Sam said. "Where a big pine stands there on the edge with a tall rock leaning against it?"

"That's the place," Summers said. "We split up there. They said they might spend the night there and head out the next morning."

Sam pondered things for a moment, something telling him that the gold would be gone when they stopped there on the way back. But that wasn't anything to concern himself with now, he thought, gazing off across the endless purple-white land in the rising moonlight. If it was there when they arrived, they would take it along and turn it in to the trustees of the failed mining company, whoever that might be. If it wasn't there . . . well, he would just figure things were meant to be that way.

As Sam gestured toward the sheriff's office and headed Denton in that direction, more customers appeared as if up out of the snowy streets of Cold Devil. They traipsed along toward the Gay Lady like pilgrims come to pay homage to something of great and holy significance. Inside the saloon, Blake cradled his wounded side and walked out from behind the bar.

He stopped on his way to the stairs and

said across the bar to Stanley Woods, as Woods tied an apron around his waist, "You help Ned tend bar until we get some doves for you to manage." He walked away, all the customers' eyes on him. He knew he'd earned himself a second chance out there in the bloody snow today. *Some of us get that,* he told himself. *Hell, a few of us deserve it. . . .*

ABOUT THE AUTHOR

Ralph Cotton is a former ironworker, second mate on a commercial barge, teamster, horse trainer, and lay minister with the Lutheran church. Visit his Web site at www.RalphCotton.com.

The employees of Thorndike Press hope you have enjoyed this Large Print book. All our Thorndike and Wheeler Large Print titles are designed for easy reading, and all our books are made to last. Other Thorndike Press Large Print books are available at your library, through selected bookstores, or directly from us.

For information about titles, please call:
   (800) 223-1244

or visit our Web site at:
   www.gale.com/thorndike
   www.gale.com/wheeler

To share your comments, please write:
   Publisher
   Thorndike Press
   295 Kennedy Memorial Drive
   Waterville, ME 04901